praise for

ACHILLES

"A fantastic ending to the Discarded Heroes: Scions series! This was hands down my favorite adventure of the series!"

—LARAMEE, GOODREADS

"Want fast paced excitement? Check! A hero and heroine that are both strong? Yep! International travel and high stake romance? Done! This is a fast paced read that is true to a Ronie Kendig paramilitary book and I absolutely enjoyed it! The author has a way of giving such depth to her characters and that draws me in and hooks me into the story. I fully enjoyed this book and highly recommend it."

—AMY, GOODREADS

"Such a fantastic read. *Achilles* follows Dillion and Cove as they first met in Paris before their paths cross in Italy. They are both driven as they partner together to find their fathers for different reasons. Achilles is a fast-paced, end-of-your-seat romantic suspense with action, danger, and twists and turns. I enjoyed watching Dillion's search for his father unfold throughout this series."

—ALLYSON, GOODREADS

ACHILLES
DISCARDED HEROES: SCIONS

DISCARDED HEROES: SCIONS

ATLAS
APOLLO
ACHILLES

DISCARDED HEROES

NIGHTSHADE
DIGITALIS
WOLFSBANE
FIRETHORN
LYGOS

ACHILLES

DISCARDED HEROES: SCIONS

RONIE KENDIG

SUNRISE PUBLISHING

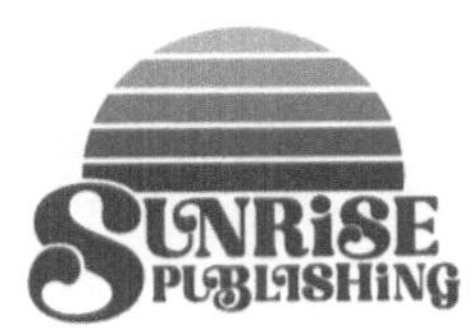

Achilles
Discarded Heroes: Scions, Book 3

Published by Sunrise Media Group LLC
Copyright © 2026 Ronie Kendig

Print ISBN: 978-1-966463-55-9

For more information about the author please access her website at roniekendig.com. Published in the United States of America.

Cover Design: Sunrise Media Group LLC

"I hate like the gates of Hades
the man who says one thing and hides another inside him.
So, when I speak, I will say what is on my mind."

THE ILIAD, HOMER

ONE

Six Months Ago
Paris, France

"A RRÊTEZ, POLICE!"

That was his cue *not* to stop as the officer demanded but to break into a sprint across Vendôme Square. Only a fool thought they could get into the Ritz Paris hotel, sneak up to a luxury suite, slip inside said suite, and scour it for a laptop, forgotten phone—a ludicrous hope but one harbored all the same—and exfil without being seen. Or caught.

Maybe the police were pursuing a petty criminal.

Well. Some petty criminal other than Dillon Jacobs.

He checked his six using the sleek black hood of a Bentley Bentayga unloading passengers in front of the hotel. Time to run. Muttering an oath, he monitored for moving vehicles. That split-second recon warned this would be close.

Dillon too late saw the door of the Bentley flinging open into his escape route. Rolling around the obstacle, he noted a beautiful brunette emerging with a handful of shopping bags. A man reached toward her, his hands jabbing into Dillon's corrected trajectory.

Like lightning, he careened between the two. Accidentally clipped the bags from the woman's hands.

Startled at his sudden intrusion into her path, she pitched backward to avoid colliding with him. Staggered.

Dillon caught her shoulders even as she bumped against the tail of the luxury car with a yelp. Was she hurt? "You good?"

Molten, hazel eyes—no, they were more than that, much more—slammed into his. Her perfect pink lips parted. Holy wow, she was beautiful! This had to be fate.

The thought rattled him as a flurry of French erupted from the man. The beauty scowled at Dillon and jerked from his grip. Her gaze struck something behind him—the way things were going, probably the police—and she pushed him away.

Already off-kilter, Dillon stumbled away from her, feeling like destiny was being ripped out of his hands. *Hey, idiot—cops, remember?* He glanced back and found them surging in his direction.

Exfil now!

"*Arrêtez*! Police!" they shouted again.

Calm, cool, collected façade abandoned, Dillon winked at the woman and muttered an apology, then bolted across Vendôme Square. A horn blared. Brakes squealed. He thudded against the vehicle, rolled over its hood, and kept moving on the other side. Cursed himself for being sloppy as he whipped around the bronze central column—which looked more green than bronze, even at this late hour and lit by floodlights. Had to respect that Napoleon replaced the statue of himself with a monument made of 1,200 enemy canons—a powerful statement—but the iconic sight stood in the gaping middle of a large square that left Dillon wide open.

"*Arrêtez*!"

Sorry, dude. Not happening. Heart pounding in cadence with his shoes, he pushed himself hard. Could not afford to get strung up *this* close to answers. The thudding of pursuit was slower but not slow enough.

Get moving!

He cleared the square, banked right onto the side street, and sprinted for all he was worth, knowing every second mattered if he wanted to escape. Once past the first building, he plastered himself into the slightly recessed area of the second structure. Effectively hidden from the corner view of the street, he had seconds before being discovered. Shadows concealed him as he seized advantage of the classic architectural style to scale the walls. The limestone ledges were perfectly spaced to create handholds.

Parkour skills had served him well on this mission to find his dad. Hearing the clap of the officers' boots on the street below, he didn't look down but instead focused on a cat-to-cat move, hiking up onto the ledge of the second story. Climbed on the balcony's iron rail and leapt up, grabbing the third-story overhang. He repeated the move to gain the rooftop. Caught it and hauled himself onto the roof.

Pulse jagged, he wanted to lie there, catch his breath, but the beam of the cop's torch traced the edge. They weren't going to give up easily. While the distinctive architecture of the Haussmann-style homes benefited his ability to reach a high vantage, the roofs were another matter. Between skylights, dormers, vents, and chimneys, he had his work cut out for him. Navigating the tricky surfaces, he trained his ear on the street. Heard shouts moving down the street on a parallel course with him.

Anger simmered. Every building and rooftop he cleared meant more distance between him and his target. Gritting his teeth, he paused on one of the rare flat roofs and looked toward the green column of Vendôme Square, still visible in the night sky. He itched to go back, but if he did and got caught . . .

Get him tomorrow.

Right. Couldn't do that if he was locked up.

Sighting the parking garage he'd scouted previously, Dillon slipped and slid toward it. At the overhang, he hopped out into thin air, rotated his body, and as he plummeted, snagged the ledge, breaking his descent. Gently landed on a balcony rail. Released himself. Caught the next one, the impact vibrating the wrought-iron rail against his palms. Once more. Then, with a check down the length of his body, released the first-story residence's rail. Dropped to the street and pitched himself in the direction of the parking structure. Pulling into the shadows, he sprinted down the street. Aimed right just as headlamps and swirling lights swung onto the narrow road, cluttered on the left with café tables.

Dillon bolted down the cobbled street, banked left, and found a duck-through alley. *C'mon, c'mon*, he mentally prodded the police, *just give up. Nothing to see here.*

The high-pitched *nee-ner nee-ner* of the siren proved relentless.

But Dillon hadn't come this far, spent the last fifteen months chasing down leads, finally ended up in the same city as Massimo Galtieri to end up in cuffs. Pushing himself, he drove his body as hard as he could, working to increase the distance between him and the authorities. Stayed in the shadows. Headed toward the Seine.

By the time he reached the park stretching out before the Louvre, he appreciated the burn in his lungs. This years-long endeavor had built him into the best shape of his life. Even if food was scarce and the nights long, he'd find Dad. Prove wrong every single government entity that had declared Max Jacobs dead. No way a Jacobs died like that, without a fight. Without a body to bury.

Calves tight and side cramping, he slowed to a walk. As he wove beneath some trees, he shrugged out of his black jacket, moving deliberately toward the next road that crossed the famous river. He turned it inside out and threaded his arms back through it. The green wouldn't be too noticeable in the night light, but at least it wasn't black, which authorities were no doubt looking for now.

From the pocket, he pulled out a black ball cap and tugged it on. It was a simple but hopefully effective way to deter first glances.

The faint *nee-ner* swelled for a second—along with his heart rate—then faded again. He nailed the next right and crossed the Seine.

Blue lights swirled.

Jaw tight, he tugged the cap down, glanced over his shoulder before changing to the other side of the road, and spotted a police car emerging from a side street.

Good night, they were relentless.

Head down, Dillon debated running. That would def draw attention. Every step felt leaden as he homed in on the densely packed residential buildings, certain he could lose them there if—

Tires pealed. Blue lights swam toward him.

"For the love of . . ." With a grunt, he threw himself down a side street with little light and worse line of sight. He broke into a sprint again, anxious to increase the distance. Darted around a corner, effectively plunging into darkness on the narrow alley-like road with no streetlamps. Perfect for concealment. Not so much for navigating. As he jogged, he eyed rooftops, searching for a quick place to hide. Moving, he clung to the buildings and shadows, working in his favor. Right turn.

This time of night, most people were in their homes. Which meant he wouldn't have many witnesses, but it also meant he would be the standout lone wolf prowling the streets.

A baby's wail jerked his attention to a woman pulling a writhing, howling child from the car. Bags of groceries hooked over her arms, she lost hold of what looked like a diaper bag. Stared at it for a long second but then hurried up the steps, aiming for the door.

Swirling blue lights crawled the buildings, tracing them, as if searching for the bug-bitten superhero. The police car glided onto the narrow street.

I must be cursed.

To change up his appearance, Dillon shrugged out of his jacket and folded it under his arm as he reached the woman, still wrangling the screaming child as she stabbed a key at the lock. Her flat door finally swung open.

Dillon snagged the diaper bag from the sidewalk, hustled the five steps up to her stoop, watching as she set down the groceries inside the door and flicked on the foyer light. Not wanting to alarm her, he pushed pleasantry into his voice. "*Voilà, madame.*"

She turned and, finding him on the step, started. Almost simultaneously came the anticipated explosion of light from the police car that blinded her. Shrinking, the thirtysomething woman shielded her eyes.

Dillon did the same, holding his hand up—an effective way to protect not only his eyes but his identity—as he looked toward the car. Y'know, as if he were any other Joe. Because what criminal would just stand on a doorstep and look at the very authorities he was trying to evade?

He checked the woman, realizing she hadn't taken the bag yet.

In her eyes radiated concern and uncertainty that had paralyzed her. Still proffering the diaper pack, he silently begged her not to shout or scream. That look on her face said she had connected the dots and guessed the police were patrolling her street, so he touched the babe's head. Hoped it didn't make him seem like a creeper.

"*Merci,*" she finally murmured, the thanks lost amid the baby's wails. Her gaze bounced between him and the police.

"*Voilà,*" Dillon said as he casually reached around her, depositing the bag inside the foyer. Stepping back, he hated the way she'd tensed and glanced askance at him, as if he were the criminal the authorities thought.

She wasn't wrong, but he didn't have to like it. In fact, he hated it. But this mission was necessary. When he noticed the wash of blue vanish from the walls, he retreated to the narrow sidewalk. "*Bonne nuit.*"

Her reciprocal "good night"—which sounded uncertain but relieved—scampered after him as he headed in the direction the cops had taken, wagering they wouldn't backtrack. At least this way, he'd be behind them, able to eyeball and anticipate their movement. But when he hit the main road, the blue lights were gone. Donning his jacket again, he switched the baseball cap for the warm beanie, hunched into the jacket, and continued down the street.

After another twenty minutes passed without incident, he spotted a flat-topped roof and scaled up to it, the surface still warm from the long-gone sun. He lowered himself against a chimney, folded his arms over his chest, and burrowed into the corner. Tilting his head back, he grunted at the smudge of black overhead, wishing for the canvas of stars. But in even that he was defeated, thanks to the City of Light's ever-present illumination.

Elbows on his knees, he hooked his hands over his head and scratched his shorn hair. Man, he'd screwed up tonight. He'd been so close to Galtieri. Took a risk he shouldn't have. While he'd gotten away, it'd been close. Too close. Cost him time. Maybe got his face on some feeds. Now the Ritz would be on alert tomorrow night for Galtieri's dinner party.

Gut rumbling with hunger, he felt his ribs poking out. Being on the lam didn't make for fattened calves or a full stomach. Clenching his jaw, he pinched the bridge of his nose. His gut grumbled again, hunger gnawing at his insides. In the morning, he'd grab something to tide him over. How much did he have left? He reached in his pocket for his money . . . and faltered when he felt only the fabric lining. His heart skipped a beat, but maybe he'd put it in the other pocket. He checked. Nothing. Empty.

No no no.

It wasn't just the money that had taken a week of tourist trolling to accrue. It was the device. The one Helios had sent so Dillon could pair with Galtieri's phone.

"Augh!" Dillon smacked his head back against the chimney. Again. Again. He jabbed the heels of his hands into his eyes as he growled. Without the device, being here in Paris—which had taken him weeks to effect—was pointless. A waste of time and resources.

But Galtieri was here. If he didn't figure something out, the billionaire connected to—*responsible for*—Dad's disappearance would leave the city. No guaranteeing he'd go back to his Italian villa, but even if he did, it'd take weeks or months before another opportunity presented itself.

Frustration soaked his muscles, making them heavy, aching. Like his soul. Now he had to find more money. Republic Square was the place to do that. If he could get money, maybe he'd be able to reach Helios in time. But the chances he could get another device before tomorrow night were pretty much nil.

God, I need a break. With the way things were going, he should add a qualifier. *And just so we're crystal, not a limb.*

TWO

Paris, France

NEVER AGAIN WOULD HE COMPLAIN ABOUT a lumpy mattress. Or about Waldo, the family dog, climbing into bed with him back home. He'd take the lumps and the wet-dog smell over dirty concrete rooftops or slimy alleys, where he'd been forced to sleep over the last year.

But for Dad . . .

An hour ago as dawn cracked the horizon, he'd climbed off the roof and made his way to Republic Square. The police interest in him seemed to have died down. He'd hustled into the subway, watching carefully for dropped money. While he wasn't intimately familiar with French currency, he had a pretty decent understanding of its values. This venture to find Dad came with a set of demands that challenged his moral code in more ways than one. He hated breaking laws—there was just no way around that, since he'd had to cross borders without valid identification. If he'd entered lawfully, he could be traced. If he could be traced, he could be stopped.

That wasn't an option. Guilt clobbered him over those broken

"

laws. Didn't make him proud. Which was why he kept everything else he did aboveboard. Staying off-grid had been whack at first, but he'd learned, compensated. Entered buildings via unlocked or opened doors. It'd shocked him the amount of untouched food tourists left on tables. He wasn't nasty—didn't touch half-eaten stuff. But no problem downing the leftover slice of pizza because a tourist gorged themselves on bread or ate dessert. Money got dropped. He wasn't a punk—if he saw a large bill fall out, he returned it to the careless tourist. That's where his rules came into play—the likeability factor, the authority rule. People were predictable and he capitalized on that. Some offered him something in return for their gratitude.

Around noon, he entered the internet café with enough money to pay for a couple puffy pastry pizza-like things and an hour of internet. Used his pseudonym—River Styx, which only those versed in Greek mythology might get—to log in at a terminal in a booth near the back door. He devoured the pastries and gulped the first cup of unlimited black coffee refills. Amazing what a guy could get used to when money was scarce. He navigated to the secure site Helios had set up and logged in. Sent his first chat message.

Bad night. Device lost. Send another. Need cash for event.

Scanning the loud American couple and their two kids who entered, Dillon slurped the coffee as he waited for a response. When the screen remained blank, he slipped over to the carafe and refilled his cup. Toyed with buying another pastry pizza, but decided to save what little money he'd foraged. Besides, he guessed the dinner party would have food. He'd stuff his face there. Assuming he still went. Assuming Helios came through.

"You know what they say about assuming," Dad had always said.

Yeah, well, Dillon had to live that right now.

The screen shifted, snagging his attention. A response awaited him.

DO YOU KNOW WHAT TIME IT IS? AND HOW MUCH THAT THING COST ME? YOU AIN'T JAMES BOND. GO NATURAL.

Tightening his jaw at the chastisement, Dillon eyed the clock on the wall. Helios was six hours behind him—wasn't even dawn there. Probably explained the snark. He set the coffee down and typed. While he understood neither of them were loaded, Helios was far better off right now than Vagrant Dillon. And the dude was fire when it came to white-hat hacking and digital spy-craft.

WHEN WILL THE FUNDS BE READY?

YOU ARE GOING TO LEGIT OWE ME.

Sure. Whatever. It wasn't like there was anything but the skin on his back left for someone to take. But if it saved his dad, he'd pay anything—*everything*. Whatever it took. Even his own life.

He waited, still ticked with himself for losing the first one. But he could not go to the dinner party without the device, and he couldn't get into the event looking and smelling like an overripe avocado—and foraging in the garbage of a restaurant told him what that reek was like. This was his one chance to get Galtieri to give up answers about Dad.

And man, he hated that he was the only one out here trying to find his dad. That there were others with endless funding and resources, all sitting on their laurels.

The screen again shifted with the newest message from Helios:

FINE. FINE. XFER READY AT 1PM.

EXCELLENT. THX. L8R.

Dillon logged out—no need to stay on longer than absolutely necessary—and left the café. He had enough money for a shower at the hostel where he had a locker. In there, he'd stuffed a suit someone had left on a park bench. There was no identification, so Dillon adopted the suit that was too wide and an inch too short, but it had served him well. And would again tonight. No tie, so he just wore it loose. Made use of the laundry place, then stored his clothes, and headed out, ready for the gala. First, hit the electronics store to pick up the replacement device. He waited at the crosswalk, ready for answers. Ready to go on with this thing. He'd been in limbo too long.

Shouts echoed up and down the street, sending his heart into overdrive. Had they found him? He glanced toward the commotion, half expecting to see authorities rushing him.

"Let her go, man!" a guy shouted at a thug who held a woman in a reverse choke hold.

Even as he watched, Dillon noticed another, more distant confrontation between a sleek black SUV and a box truck a couple blocks down.

"Easy, easy!" the first man was warning.

Dillon felt his life power down to an infinitesimal rate as recognition struck him at that blond head . . . the voice . . . That looked and sounded like—

Holy fire, what was Owen Metcalfe doing here?

Can't be.

Gut tight, Dillon moved in that direction, feeling as if he'd transported through some time bubble as he watched Apollo barrel into the man holding the woman. The two went to ground.

Tires pealed as a black SUV careened around a corner.

This . . . this wasn't just about Apollo saving some random woman on the streets of Paris. This reeked of a setup. An ambush? But . . . how? Who? Why?

Though he considered lending Apollo a hand, he could not get involved. Tonight was the dinner party. He had to get close to Galtieri. Pair the phone. Still, Dillon found himself aiming that way. Pacing his Scion brother.

Owen broke loose, shoved up and hurried the girl who'd been

accosted into the black SUV that lurched to the curb with a screech. Door closed, he sprinted off down an alley, apparently in pursuit of the attacker. Apollo reappeared on the other side, seconds behind the big guy who slipped away via a panel door. As Apollo watched.

Do what?

Owen bypassed the door. Popped out on the street again.

Peripheral awareness had Dillon locking onto men loitering on the square. Talking to no one in particular. He skated his gaze back to Owen, who returned to the café as if this were any other day in Paris.

But it wasn't. Something was happening . . . And he wasn't working alone—that middle-aged guy . . .

Understanding dawned. Balled his fists. That guy looked a lot like Pike Auberon, CEO of Omen Tactical Group. The team Dad had been partnering with when he vanished. The guy who'd straight-up lied to Dillon's face in Virginia, said Dad was dead.

What was Owen doing with that piece of dung? They'd talked about this—about *not* working with Omen. Dillon trailed the younger Scion member back to the hotel, watched him enter. About to go inside, he pulled up sharp when he spotted the Omen operators loitering in the lobby and out front. Where was Atlas? Why was the team here?

Because Owen's bait.

Diverting quickly, he overheard the barrel-chested oaf who'd played attacker earlier muttering the room number to the chief.

Dillon could only smirk, because it made this easier on him, but he also cursed them for being so careless with operational security, which could compromise his Scion brother. He made his way around the back and found a delivery truck parked at the bay door. While the driver chatted with a worker, Dillon slipped around the other side and snuck into the hotel. Headed up to the third floor. A staff member held a food tray and positioned himself in front of the door to Owen's room.

"*Ah bien*," Dillon said. "*C'est pour ici?*" He pointed to the door as if that were his room.

The man hesitated, but nodded.

Dillon took the tray before the guy could refuse. "*Je le prends*." He patted his chest to make the guy believe the food was for him. "*Merci*." He waited as the employee faltered, then shrugged and left, before Dillon used the tray to shield his face. He rapped twice. "Room service."

It took forever, doubts breeding in the back of his head that maybe he had the wrong room. What if an Omen team member was in there with him? But bait wouldn't have company. Lone fish.

The door opened and Apollo's bleached head was there again.

Dillon plowed forward. "Inside, inside," he rasped, forcing Owen backward. Clear of the door, he kicked it shut.

"What is—"

He powered into the guy, whose blue eyes went wild.

"*Dillon?*"

Man, it felt good to hear someone say his real name. To see someone he knew. He gave a chagrined nod. "Hey."

"What are you doing here?"

He checked the bathroom near the main door, then set the food tray on the desk across from a bed that was definitely more comfortable than the dirty roof. Had to admit he hated that Owen was up here sitting in luxury while he was hoofing it around the world, begging and trolling tourists to keep from starving.

"You have to get out," Owen snapped. "Leave! You could blow everything."

That pulled him around and made him scowl. "Blow what?"

Owen seemed to struggle to put steel in his spine as he jutted his jaw. "I'm on an op."

A dark anger flashed through Dillon as he scanned the room.

"Omen." He could not hide the acid in his tone as he faced his Scion brother. "You're here with Omen? Are you freaking kidding me? You know they're connected to what happened to my dad!"

Owen faltered, his mouth gaping but no sound coming from him.

That was all Dillon needed to know. Unbelievable.

Owen followed. "I'm—"

"Forget it!" Dillon headed deeper into the room. Eyed the window—good escape route. But he angled for the thick backpack on the chair at the desk. Ripped open the zipper. Rifled through it, the smell of a burger permeating his senses. Made his stomach growl.

"What're you doing?" Owen rushed him. "Aren't you listening? You can't be here. You have to—"

"You have a phone on you? Credit card?"

Owen stilled. "No. I—"

"Bullspit," Dillon growled, growing more annoyed that Owen was living high off the hog here. "They wouldn't put you on an op—"

"I *don't*," Owen ground out. "I'm here, waiting for Saudis to come kidnap me."

Dillon slowed, lifting his gaze to him. He eyed the door with more than a little anger. "You serious?—No, you're flippin' stupid! *Saudis*?" Had the kid not studied World History? Middle Eastern history? He knew he had—they'd had the class together! "They'll gut you, Apollo. They aren't anything to play around with. What's the op?"

"I'm not telling you anything until I know what *you* are doing here."

He sure had grown a pair since they'd last talked. "Chasing leads. This guy I'm tracking, who was the last person to see my dad alive, is here." He gave Owen a look. "You seriously working for Omen? Thought you hated contract—"

"Dillon. Get out of here. You cannot screw this up."

Two raps stilled them both and yanked their gazes to the door. "Room service for Mr. Apollo."

"Food's already here," Dillon said, indicating to the tray in front of him, then he darted to the door.

"What are—"

"It's one guy," Dillon said. "We can take him."

"No!" Owen hissed. "If that's the Saudis, you cannot intervene." He gripped his head. "You can't be here. You're going to screw everything up. Whatever you need, take it and go—out the window!"

"Nice to see you too."

"Says the guy foraging for a credit card."

Dillon smirked. "Fair." He ducked into the bathroom and cocked his head toward the door, telling Owen to answer it.

More knocks. "Mr. Apollo, forgot your drink. Leaving it by the door."

Even as Owen moved to the door, Dillon darted to the desk, snagged the burger, and stuffed it in his mouth.

Amid Owen's apology for taking so long and the worker saying they'd forgotten the drink, Dillon made quick work of exiting the room via the window. He climbed out onto the iron rail of the balcony and hiked up and away. Hoped his Scion brother survived the dumpster fire that was Omen. As for himself…he had a dinner party to attend.

THREE

Paris, France

WITH ONE MORE PERUSAL OF HER ATTIRE, Cove Galtieri smoothed the bow at her waist and eyed herself in the floor-to-ceiling mirror. She loved the flouncy asymmetrical hemline of the stormy gray cocktail dress. Appreciated the swath of material that arched up over one shoulder—leaving the other bare—then draped down her back, tucking beneath the faux belt, and hung almost to the floor as if a train. The sequined bodice would be too much if the designer hadn't used a dreamily soft gauzy material as a calming complement.

She might not be walking the catwalk these days, but she had left that world with powerful connections. Hugo Cadieux was more than happy to send her some pieces to wear in public. "Free advertising" he called it.

Fashion was in her blood, her mamma having modeled as well. Fine clothes and shoes were an indulgence that left Cove conflicted, feeling guilty for the extravagance, knowing so many had nothing. Lived on the streets.

The thought brought to mind the man with the intense dark

eyes who had collided with her in the square. His offensive smell and wild look warned her that he was likely a street urchin. And yet, he had steadied her, been concerned after her safety. Even though the authorities were chasing him, he wanted to make sure *she* was okay. And ensnared her with his deep, dark eyes. Who was he? What had he done to have the authorities chasing him?

"You always look fresh off the runway." Izetta Costa glided into the bathroom and gave her an appraising look.

Startled back to the present, Cove eyed her dearest friend in the mirror. "That was long ago, *carissima*." And yet, it felt like yesterday. The loss of Mamma in that terrible accident had festered into a wound that incited her to leave the fashion world behind. Devastated at losing the love of his life, Papà had floundered after the funeral, so Cove returned home to help. A year later, they were both caught up in the rumors of corruption lodged against Papà.

Eyeing Cove's dress, Izetta clucked her tongue and coiled a tendril of hair around her finger. "I see you managed to find something with a bow . . ."

Arching an eyebrow, Cove padded barefoot to the closet. "No dress is complete without a bow." She sat on the tufted bench and slid her feet into the silver strappy heels.

"Do you mean *beau*?"

Cove groaned at the pun. "You are a hopeless romantic, Izzy. I, on the other hand, am a bit more—"

"Do not act like you aren't. Especially if it is Mr. Getaway," Izzy teased as she joined her. "You've mentioned his dark eyes more than once since you woke up."

"Dark eyes, dark heart," Cove said ruefully. "More trouble than I am interested in, especially considering that man was being pursued by the police."

"Maybe they saw his eyes too." Izzy giggled. "Who knew dark eyes were criminal?" Her laugh echoed off the marble floors and vanity.

"Santo cielo," Cove muttered with a groan. On her feet, she smoothed her dress once more, pleased with the bow, and she would not let anyone make her feel bad about it. Hugo had said it was practically her trademark. Who was she to argue with an expert like him?

She moved deeper into the dressing room and withdrew her clutch from the cabinet, then headed back to her bed, where she sat and switched out her wallet, lipstick, phone . . . and the one the man had dropped in the square earlier. Catching her lower lip between her teeth as she secured the tiny buckle, she could not help but wonder if he might return, looking for this. It was not like any she had seen before, and while the screen worked, she could not figure out how to unlock it.

"Still can't get into it?" Izzy asked.

Cove shook her head and stuffed it in her clutch. A tight fit, but she somehow felt better taking it with her than leaving it here in the suite.

Izetta eyed the clutch and Cove. "So, you think he'll come tonight?"

One can hope. "If you lost your phone, would you not retrace your steps looking for it? Especially an American in Paris . . ." She hated admitting she had noticed his lack of Parisian accent and the distinctly American tinge to his question. She glanced at the clock and gasped. "Why did you not tell me the time? Papà will be furious if we are late! *Andiamo!*"

They hurried into the living room, and she smiled to find Flavio Moretti unfolding from the sofa in the front parlor.

"Ah, at last." He strode toward her with all the possessiveness of a cat who'd cornered a mouse.

"What are you doing here?" She knew the answer but enjoyed making him second-guess his assumption that she belonged on his arm.

"I am your date for the evening."

Cove nudged him back and gave him a severe look. "You mean your papà said to wait and escort us down."

He lifted a shoulder in a lazy shrug. "It is the same, no?"

"Not even close," Cove countered, knowing better than to give Flavio an inch, especially in the dating sense. He had never been quiet about his attraction to her, nor had his dad, Enzo Moretti, her papà's right-hand man. Both father and son wanted their families united.

That would never happen. Especially if her suspicions about his father were right. So for now, she would trust neither father nor son—one of them was corrupt and had gravely tarnished the Galtieri name, reputation, and businesses around the world.

Music drifted out into the hotel from the Grand Jardin, where there were already a good number of guests mingling. Clusters of white flowers accented the trellis walls that sectioned off tables and cream-cushioned benches. A *grande allée* with hedges, a luxurious carpet of grass, and boxed trees split the path down the middle. Even the fading light of day could not diminish the lavish gardens, since tree trunks were wrapped in net lights and clever, recessed lights lent to the ambience. Fragrant magnolias huddled around a circular fountain, whose mist threw into the air the sweet, floral aroma that had a hint of citrus and musk. Musicians sat in the far corner, adding to the ethereal night.

"It is romantic," Izetta said with a giddy laugh as she snagged a champagne flute from a waiter making his rounds.

"Elegant," Cove corrected, knowing that was her intention with all the details she had poured into this little tête-à-tête. Tonight was about business, a trap she had laid for Papà's business partners. Get them all in one place, keep the wine flowing, and surely tongues would wag and secrets would slip free. Someone here had sparked rumors that Massimo Galtieri was corrupt. That he dealt in nefarious practices. And she would uncover them.

Having lost Mamma, Cove refused to lose Papà as well. Not to rumors. Not to some purported corruption.

"Look, it is Henri!" Izetta said with a gasp. "Let's say hello."

"Go ahead," Cove said, excusing her friends. "I would say hello to Papà."

He stood near the fountain with a low-ball glass filled with amber liquid. The drink was only for appearance and he would never take a sip. He looked stylish in his brown tweed jacket and rich brown sweater. The scarf tied and tucked into his brown sweater gave him a debonair presence. One that—since Mamma's death, and admittedly, before it—had drawn every woman seeking an easy life with a billionaire nobleman. Her family may have distant royal ancestry, but it had been a long time since Galtieris had worn crowns or Italians had recognized a monarchy. His dark hair was swept through with touches of gray at the sides, which only made him appear more distinguished. Not only was he a handsome man, her papà was a good man. A very good one. He laughed alongside his longtime investing partner, Claude Didier.

She strode over to the fountain, nodding to guests, greeting aristocrats and royalty alike.

"Ilaria!" Paris It-girl Adelaide de Damas swooped into her path. "Glorious to see you, darling."

Ilaria. Cove's middle name and the one she had used for the catwalk. The same name she had shed along with that career. "Adelaide." She gave the customary double-air-kiss greeting. "You are stunning as always."

"And you," Ady drolled, motioning to Cove's dress with a flourish, her brown eyes alive with admiration. "Fire, *carissima*!" She flashed both hands as if there were an explosion.

Smile in place, Cove accepted the compliment though she knew having Adelaide call her "dearest friend" was hollow. The woman would drive over Cove's corpse with her latest import and arm candy in the passenger seat, laughing all the way back to her French château.

Adelaide ducked closer. "I see you brought Flavio, hm?" She purred. Literally *purred.* About Flavio. "Can I have him yet? Are you done toying with his fragile little ego, dear?"

Bristling at the cruel accusation, Cove knew relations were key in this world, especially here while Papà courted business partners. "You know Flavio has one loyalty—to himself."

When Adelaide let out a trilling laugh, Cove used it to excuse herself. Saw a Monégasque royal heading her way and diverted sharply, not up to any more pandering.

Papà started at having someone suddenly appear at his side but gave a broad smile when their eyes met. "Ah, *amore.*" His tenor radiated warmth as he hooked an arm around her shoulder while motioning with his drink to the man before him. "Claude, you remember my daughter, Cove."

"Of course, mademoiselle." Claude, ever smooth and classy, took her hand and kissed it. "You are as beautiful as ever."

Then Papà pointed to another man with a severe countenance she hadn't noticed before. "And this is Crown Prince Maaz."

"Saudi Arabia?" She noted the prince wasn't wearing a shemagh, so maybe she had that wrong.

"Central Kingdom," Maaz confirmed with a curt nod of greeting, which she returned, wondering when Papà had become friends with a Saudi crown prince.

Through the years, Galtieri money had forged connections with many important friends and business partners. The Saudis were powerful and influential. The two kingdoms had made nice with the American president in the last year, which altered some of the tension emanating throughout the Middle East. It made sense that Papà would recruit a country known for having trillions and a love of technology.

"Will we see you on the runway again soon?" Claude asked.

"No, I . . ." Saying she quit because her grief over Mamma's death felt smothering was probably too much information. "I decided I liked food too much to continue starving myself."

Claude and Papà laughed, but the prince eyed her warily. There was something quite unnerving about him. Had Papà invited him? She certainly had not, and she controlled the attendee list. Maybe she could work her way around the party, see if she could overhear his conversations.

"Enjoy yourself, gentlemen." Cove gave Papà a kiss on the cheek and left to wander and greet the other guests. Mingle and hopefully pick up tidbits. Eavesdropping was not something she was proud of, but she was adept at absorbing what others were careless with. The skills were a bit mercenary, but necessary. She must prove Papà's innocence before his trial in a few months.

"What of Yemen?" a man asked, his low, brusque voice drifting from where two men stood all but hidden in shadow.

Cove deliberately slowed, nodding to guests, while training her ears on the men.

"Volatile."

"I meant triggers," the first hissed.

"That is what I meant as well."

She slid her gaze toward the well-dressed men talking by a boxed tree. One had a head of near-white, a thick black unibrow, and a salt-and-pepper beard. She did not recognize him, but the man with him—the one with balding hair, a white beard, gray mustache, and *two* brows—she did know. And he'd noticed that they'd drawn her attention.

Not wanting to appear caught at listening in, Cove smiled and moved toward him. Besides, she needed to ingratiate herself and learn the man's identity. "Minister Abashidze," she said and inclined her head. Papà had spoken fondly of him, despite their political differences. "Glad you were able to make it."

The Georgian political adviser had his work cut out for him

back home since his country had entered a constitutional crisis. But the man held more power and influence in his little finger than most had in a lifetime.

"It is truly my pleasure, Miss Galtieri," the white-bearded minister said. "As always, your father has outdone himself."

It did not bother her that Papà received compliments for her work, because she had done this to honor him, to support him. What better compliment could there be? "You know him—he will go to great lengths to ensure his allies know they are appreciated." She considered the other man as she replied. Since neither had introduced him, she must insist by extending her hand. "I do not believe we have met, Mr. . . . ."

"Ah," Zviad Abashidze said, touching the man's shoulder. "This is Yusif Rasulov."

The unibrow man gave her a gap-toothed smile but said nothing as they shook hands.

"He does not speak English well."

And yet, Rasulov had spoken English quite smoothly when they were not aware of her presence. Mentally logging the name, Cove wondered at his tight grip. It might be acceptable in patriarchally dominated cultures, but in her circle . . . a man kissed a woman's hand or shook it lightly, not *crushed* it—especially with a look that made her feel like he wished it had been her neck.

"Welcome to the GIS Meeting of Minds, Mr. Rasulov." Something about this man urged her to move on. She offered Abashidze another smile. "Please, be sure to say hello to my father, Minister. I know he would be pleased to talk with you tonight."

Abashidze looked in Papà's direction, his smile wavering. "Of course."

Why was he nervous?

Even as she walked away with their well-wishes, she drew over to the side and opened her clutch to make a note of Rasulov's name. When she tugged out her phone, she accidentally flipped

Mr. Dark Eyes' device out. It clattered to the walkway. She quickly retrieved it, checked for damage, then returned it to her clutch, which she tucked under her arm. In her phone, she typed "Yusif Rasulov" into her Notes folder, then into her browser.

Huh. There was a Yusif Rasulov serving as Chairman of the National Assembly in— "Azerbaijan."

Santo cielo. A Georgian minister bringing an Azerbaijani . . . That could be a really interesting conversation.

Did Papà know Abashidze had brought this man? Looking up, she sought Papà, wanting to be there when the three of them talked. Or at least closer to listen in. But her heart fell when she spotted Papà motioning the four men—Claude, the prince, the minister, and Rasulov—through a side door that led to a bar. Likely to talk.

Hm, I am suddenly thirsty . . . Even as she took the first step in that direction, a vise clamped onto her arm. Startled, she glowered at the person who'd waylaid her.

"*S'il te plaît, s'il te plaît,*" hissed Adelaide, begging as she touched their cheeks and dug her sharp fingernails into Cove's bicep.

"*Ow!*"

"Who is he?" rasped Adelaide hungrily. "You must tell me who he is, *s'il te plaît.*"

Cove scowled at the socialite and tugged free, no idea who she meant. "Who?" she balked, rubbing her aching arm.

"*That.*" Adelaide pointed between two magnolia trees near the fountain. "That delicious piece of art."

Cove spotted Flavio and Izetta chatting with a couple. "I don't—"

But then she did—past the foursome. In a dark gray coat that looked too big, black shirt, and slacks, he held a glass of champagne as he scanned the party. Those brooding eyes swung around to her, stealing the breath from her lungs. It was him—*Dark Eyes.*

FOUR

Paris, France

H E WAS BEING FOLLOWED. THAT PRICKLY sensation at the back of his neck sharpened his awareness and said, "heads-up." Getting back into the hotel had been easier than expected, which made up for the total loss at the tech store. Yes, Helios had placed the order for a replacement device. Yes, it had been paid for. But no, the shop did not have any in stock. And no, the shop would not refund cash for a credit card purchase. Which left Dillon with no device and no cash to pick one up on his own.

He was batting zero. So, slipping into Galtieri's private dinner party, grabbing some food and a drink, shifted his mood from *Foul* to *Irritable*. Moderate improvement.

But this tail he had—the one who'd followed him from the fountain, into the hotel, and around to the bar where Galtieri sequestered himself with the four assets Dillon hoped to identify— had that meter shifting back to *Foul*. If he didn't lose the tail, he couldn't eavesdrop. Wouldn't get what he needed—proof the filthy rich spent lives as easily as they spent Gs. That this billionaire was the Al Capone of Europe. That this guy not only had something to do with Dad's disappearance but was directly responsible.

Yeah, Dillon wasn't bitter—or unfocused. His real purpose here was to nab Galtieri's phone. The rest was just frosting on the cake.

He moved swiftly past the concierge desks, earning more than one speculative glance from the staff, but he'd learned that if you acted like you belonged somewhere, everyone else believed it. He hustled down the steps and banked left. Spotted tall glass doors leading to a quieter hall with a grand piano on the right and a restaurant up three steps on the left.

Tail was still on him.

Before the doors, he ducked down the side hall at the last minute, taking shelter behind a massive wardrobe cabinet thing. Narnia would be proud of the scale.

Listening to the quickening steps of the tail, he slowed his breathing and pressed his spine to the wall. The pursuing steps were light, fast—not just because the person had sped up but because it was a woman.

Interesting.

Movement blurred into view. He reached out. Hooked the woman by the waist. Spun both of them deeper into the small alcove. Whipped his pursuer back against the wall. Heard a gust of air as she thumped against the stone even as he aimed his forearm at her long, bare neck. As he did, their gazes connected. Hazel-bright eyes registered. In a lightning move, he narrowly shifted his forearm in time to avoid crushing her throat. Planted it against her clavicle to avoid harm but also keep her in place. Under his control.

She flinched and shrank, eyes squeezing shut in expectation of violence.

"Why are you following me?" he demanded in a low voice.

Like some wicked vortex, her eyes opened and pulled him in. Mesmerizing. "I . . ."

It'd be a nice ego stroke that his good looks had robbed her of words. But this chick had been working that crowd for the last hour. "No lies," he warned, flexing his forearm so she felt the pressure at the base of her throat. One hand over her head, he had her pinned in the corner and pressed into her personal space, using his intrusion against her desire to be free. Most people didn't like others in their space and would cooperate to free themselves.

"You do not have an invitation," she ground out from between tight lips.

His pulse skipped a beat—this was the same woman he'd bumped into outside. That's right . . . her eyes . . . same eyes. Only this time, they weren't filled with surprise. There was a focused determination. The same kind that said she had a lot of brass to follow him.

Situational awareness told him the doors behind him were clear but anyone who came up that hall would see them. He hoped they'd assume lovers stealing a moment. He detected her hand moving at waist level. Recalled the small purse she carried. In a flash, he caught her wrist. Jerked it up above her head, eyes flashing with anger. "What're you doing?"

She winced. "You dropped this . . ."

Only then did he see the device in her hand. "And what, you were just going to give it back?"

She blinked. "Yes."

This chick did not make sense. How did she know he didn't have an invite? "Who are you?"

Her head wobbled beneath an indignant, fiery streak that all but made her eyes glow and warned she was mustering courage. Growing angry at being restrained. "You first."

Had to hand it to her—she had guts, beauty, yet she was some kind of dumb to face off with him. But man—he'd been right when he'd crashed into her yesterday—she was beautiful. And those eyes . . . what color was that? Not merely hazel. These were practically gold with flecks of green and streaks of brown beneath the chandelier that seemed to caress her bare left shoulder. Ironically, despite the bare shoulder, she was modestly dressed. Not hanging out like a lot of the women in that dinner party. Unlike them, she had "sexy" down to the nuance. And the smattering of freckles lent her a down-to-earth feel that made her seem like a girl he could bring home to Mom. Not some heiress who spent more on her shoes than he'd paid for his Hayabusa.

In the square, he'd thought it fate that they'd met. Maybe he wasn't wrong—she was, after all, handing the device back.

"See something you like?"

Flirting, huh? Regardless of the very real, primal draw to her, Dillon knew her words weren't meant as an invitation but as bait. To ensnare and distract.

She was playing a dangerous game.

But so was he. Since she worked for Galtieri, Dillon would play her like a drum. Not gonna lie—he liked that flush rising through her cheeks. She might be trying to take back the control he'd yanked from her hands, but he . . . What would she do if he played into this? He lowered his face to hers. "You like danger?" Deliberately focused on her very nice, very full lips, he felt an ache somewhere deep within roaring to life. It was called vengeance.

"N-no." That was the first time she'd faltered.

Lying did that to a person. He angled his head closer. "You sure . . . ?"

Her lips parted, gaze darting to his mouth and back to his eyes. And though it was just a fraction, her chin angled toward his. Subconsciously, she wanted the kiss he teased her with.

Should he?

Man, why not? He'd never see her again. And he was digging how she looked at him. He caught the blonde money pieces framing her face. Traced their silkiness. Slipped his fingers to her cheek. Appreciated the way she reflexively parted her lips more. Drew in a breath.

Dillon bent to catch her mouth with his.

"Cove?" someone called from around the corner.

Slack jerked out of him, Dillon focused on her eyes.

She refocused too. Wet her lips, coming back to herself. That lost-in-the-wilderness-of-attraction expression fell away as she took in a ragged breath.

Dillon eased off with a smirk. "Maybe next time . . ."

"Cove!" Concern thickened the man's authoritative voice.

Backing up, Dillon guessed they saw him. He aimed toward the glass doors at the same time none other than Massimo Galtieri stalked into view with two guards.

Cursing his distraction and subsequent delay, Dillon palmed the door as one of the men produced a gun and held it low, down.

"Who are you?" Galtieri demanded. "Stop him!"

"No, wait!" The beauty—Cove?—surged between them, holding a staying hand to Galtieri and his thugs. "H-he lost his phone. I found it." She pointed to the device Dillon held.

Thoughts ricocheting through his thick skull, he couldn't fathom why she would defend him. Protect him. He glanced at the device. Held it up. "Thanks."

"Get him." Galtieri ordered the men into motion.

"No, Papà! *Please.*"

Papà? Are you freaking kidding me?

FIVE

Six months later
Orvieto, Italy

YOU'RE SURE?" DREAD SPLASHED HER BELLY, nauseating Cove as she stood at the floor-to-ceiling window of her bedchamber overlooking the gardens and pool of *Vigneto Corallo*, the Galtieri vineyard, villa, and estate that had been in the family for generations.

"I heard it from the bank manager myself," Zio Santi said gravely. "I would not burden you with this, but Massimo is not taking my calls. I cannot stand to watch this happen. Your papà is a *good* man. This makes no sense for him to give that monster Moretti signatory authority over the entirety of the Galtieri fortune and GIS."

Chest and jaw tight, Cove fixed her gaze on the man down by the pool, who had upended their lives. Felt the bitter roots of anger and resentment. "No, it does not."

More than once she had begun to wonder if he was the rot eating their lives from within. The trial was in a few months and she had . . . nothing. Enzo, however, had taken more and more control, nudging her out of GIS business. Ever since Yemen almost three years ago, he had pushed Papà to seek "better qualified" heads for business, not his fashion-model daughter. She had thought she'd proven herself, but that incident in Paris, when she'd defended and protected a man she did not even know, had been unwitting ammo in Enzo's campaign to remove her.

On the lawn, Enzo barked orders to the staff who were preparing the dinner party for Papà's sixtieth birthday. *She* had been planning this for Papà since Mamma died. Wanted it to be special, honoring, intimate—with family and close friends. Now, she was relegated to an adornment. Told to dress nice. Smile prettily.

Flavio sauntered behind his dad and stopped to flirt with one of the waitstaff they'd hired in for the celebration.

"*Per favore, Lupina.*" Zio Santi really knew how to tug on her heartstrings with the "little wolf" nickname he and Mamma had always called her. "Talk to Massimo," he urged. "I fear something is amiss. This cannot be right."

"It is not," she agreed. "I have suspected Enzo for a while, but there has been no proof. Papà defends him." She sighed, heart heavy and feeling as if her entire world was crumbling. "I wish you were here to talk sense into him."

"*D'accordo.*" He agreed—they were often of the same mind. "But this trip to the States has me tied up. I am sorry, *Lupina*. You know your mamma would be furious about all this."

"*I* am furious." And powerless. How could she get Papà to listen? "Enzo has been taking over little by little here. I have been all but shut out of business decisions. Papà even let him move into the main house." Which only served to deepen her fear that Enzo was involved in something corrupt. "It's maddening—why is he letting him take over? It makes no sense."

"One would almost think . . ."

Her breath caught at the heaviness in his words, in what he didn't say. "What?"

"I wonder if Massimo is being blackmailed. It is a dreadful thing to accuse a man who has worked at your father's side for a decade," Zio Santi said somberly, "but that is the only way I believe he would do such a thing. Never would Massimo surrender control. Not like this. Never!"

Heart stuttering, Cove covered her mouth with one hand and wrapped the other around her midsection, the earbud tucked in neatly. Visually followed the snake Enzo from poolside back through the large glass-and-steel doors into the enclosed terrace. The twenty-foot table had been festooned with flowers, candelabras, silverware, and crystal for the forty-two arriving in the next hour. All business partners.

If Papà was being blackmailed . . . then did Enzo have proof that Papà had done something illegal? "I cannot believe there would be anything to—"

"Tread carefully, *Lupina*," Zio Santi warned. "Your papà is a proud man. If there is trouble, he will not easily admit to it."

Especially if he was being blackmailed over some transgression, indiscretion, or mistake! And this explained so much how Enzo Moretti had all but taken over. *Santo cielo*, she detested the Morettis.

"I will talk with him—I promise." Oh that she had an ally here. Someone to help her, protect her. Two loud raps at the door startled her. She whirled and lifted her phone. "Someone is knocking. I should go," she said, crossing the room.

"*Ti voglio bene.*"

"Same, Zio. *Arrivederci.*" Ending the call, she drew in a breath for courage and opened the door.

Flavio grinned as he pushed his way in, but then a scowl stole beneath his thick mop of curly hair. He assessed her gravely. "*What are you wearing?*"

She had tolerated his intrusions and assumptions long enough. "Get out, Flavio," she said, motioning him back out to the hall. "I am in no mood—"

"You can't wear that tonight. You're supposed to wear the pink dress—"

"I will never take fashion advice from you." Besides, there was nothing wrong with her button-front gauzy black blouse whose neckline boasted a casual, drapey bow and diamonds. In fact, it was a favorite. The gray slacks and black wedges were a perfect complement. It kept her presentation comfortable, sensible, and elegant. "This celebration is for Papà, not me."

"No, you have to wear the pink—"

"Enough." Irritation flaring, she planted her hands on her hips, phone gripped tight, in no mood to deal with him. "I have much—"

"You realize my papà is handling things," he said, sauntering toward her with a sleazy grin. "No need for you to worry your pretty little head about it."

Heart thundering at his patronizing tone, she worked to temper her anger. "*Scusi*," she said, pointing to the door again. "I must get ready for the party."

Glee hit his muddy brown eyes. "*Assolutamente sì*! Pink dress."

Resenting his giddy agreement made it next to impossible not to let the door hit him on the way out. Once she heard his leather shoes on the stairs, she let out a frustrated growl. She really must talk to Papà. Now. A moment later, she peeked out. Verifying it was clear, she strode down the hall of the upper level. While Papà did have an office downstairs, she knew that he preferred his desk and library adjoining his bedroom for this work. She'd hoped to find him there because it was less likely that Enzo would be around.

She knocked on the door and waited. When no invitation came, she let herself in. "Papà?" Making sure to close the door, she did not want to be interrupted as Enzo had been wont to do every time she tried to talk business with her papà. In the library suite, she found him on the small balcony, palming the ancient stones as he peered out over the lush estate and vineyards. She joined him.

"Your mamma loved this view," he said solemnly. "This . . . this was the one thing I had that seemed worthy of her." He sighed and shook his head. "And it was not even I who did it but my ancestors."

Cove touched his back. "Mamma loved you very much—and first. This beautiful villa was just *la ciliegina sulla torta*."

He sniffed. "I did not deserve her, and now . . . she would be ashamed of me."

"I disagree. Mamma was always understanding and patient when I made mistakes. Her love never changed."

Looking so dignified in his suit and cravat, Papà touched her cheek. "You were always her fiercest champion."

Swallowing hard, Cove had to broach the topic. "And yours," she added. "But, Papà, I fear I must ask . . ."

He grunted. "Later, *amore*. Later." With another heavy exhale, he turned back inside.

But Cove could not let it alone. "Zio Santi said the bank called him."

Papà stopped short, a dark cloud moving over his olive complexion as he faced her. "He has no business putting his nose in my affairs! What I do does not involve him! I needed the help and . . ."

Shock ricocheted through her. "So, it is true?"

He looked tortured. "It is a good thing . . . I had to . . ."

"Papà—"

"It is not for you to question me, Ilaria!" He only resorted to her Italian name when angry.

It struck her to the core. "How can you trust Enzo over me? He has cut me out, pushed me aside. The transfers—"

"*Basta*!" he hissed. "I will not—"

"Papà," she balked, taken aback by his temper. "I do not mean to—"

"Is something wrong?" The calm, cool voice of Enzo Moretti sliced into the heated conversation.

Papà jerked to him, his eyes ablaze.

The man had enough sense to don a modicum of contrition. "Forgive me, Massimo. The door was open . . ."

It was most certainly not open. She had closed it. Very conscientiously to avoid this exact situation.

"I was concerned when I heard Cove yelling."

Yelling? She had not yet begun yelling!

"She was just leaving," Papà said, turning to his dressing room.

Crushed at his dismissal, Cove struggled to contain the hurt and the desperate need to throat-punch a gloating Enzo as she walked out of the room.

"Ilaria."

Heat shot down her spine at Enzo's call. She faltered on the threshold, thinking she did not answer to him, but common decency slowed her.

"Your father is under a lot of stress," Enzo crooned. "Do not add to it by behaving like a child."

God, help me. Curling her hands into fists, she did not reply. Just pushed herself out the door.

The fight with Papà hung over her as guests arrived. As they mingled. She watched in silence, aching for what had been lost already. They sat poised on the brink of disaster. What would happen to GIS, to *Vigneto Corallo,* with Enzo at the helm of all financial and business matters?

Mamma . . . What would Mamma do?

As the courses were served, she took just enough to not draw attention to her extreme lack of appetite. She could not bring herself to eat, even if it was Papà's birthday celebration.

Only it wasn't a celebration. It was business. In fact . . . Her gaze swept the length of the table, taking in the guests. She felt a creeping dread, realizing she did not know a single person in attendance, save Enzo and Flavio. Even their normal staff had been replaced by temporaries. Which made no sense.

Everything in her wanted to get up and leave. Hide in her room rather than participate in this farce.

A laugh bellowed from the head of the table where Papà smiled at Enzo and another person. But she recognized that smile was not a true smile. This was a practiced one. The same one he'd fastened on daily following Mamma's wake and funeral when friends offered their condolences and shared fond anecdotes.

He's grieving.

Throat tight, she glanced at her plate. Tears pricked her eyes. No way she could leave Papà alone with these . . . *vultures*. That's what this was, wasn't it? A feasting on Galtieri and GIS profits.

What could she do? Desperation coiled through her with an oppressive smothering.

"You didn't wear the pink dress," Flavio said, his breath hot and reeking of wine against her cheek as he pressed in closer.

Disgust roiled through her as she slid him a cold glare. "Wow, so observant." Why did he sound so panicked? Disappointed with herself for such an obvious display of vitriol, she pushed her gaze away. Saw a shadow flicker at the corner of the main house's upper terrace. What . . . ?

"You do not understand—"

"And never will." God forgive her, but she hated him. Hated his father. She eyed him, and past him, she saw a light go on in the house, glaringly obvious in the darkening night.

Her heart jumped into her throat. Wait—that was Papà's office! She skipped her gaze to the men now gathered poolside. Papà was there, talking with Enzo and a few other men. So . . . *who* was in his office? Did not matter—nobody should be in there without him.

"*Scusi.*" She set aside her drink, stood, and strode toward the house.

"Where are you going?" Flavio demanded as he caught her arm. "You—"

"*Vado al bagno*," she hissed at him. "And I don't need your help." Though she felt bad for lying about needing to avail herself of the bathroom, she felt no remorse for his mortified expression. Grateful she hadn't worn that dress he'd been so adamant about— and its heels—she was able to hurry into the house in her wedges much quicker. And quieter.

Moving swiftly through the semidarkened hall, she eyed the threshold where light scampered out beneath the heavy door, anxious to rout the intruder. Easing up to the side, she strained to listen. Heard drawers opening. Doors closing. *Clicks* and *clinks*. Enough noise that the man, who had his back to her as he dug through Papà's desk, did not hear her enter. He bent toward the laptop and touched something. Palming the desk, he squinted, the blue glow of the screen washing his black hair in a halo. "Yeah, it's in . . . No idea why not, but it's in."

Was he trying to hack it? "*What* are you doing and who—"

He whipped around.

Breath snatched, Cove gaped. "*You!*"

SIX

Orvieto, Italy

SWEEPING AROUND THE CHAIR, DILLON TOED the corner of the desk. Leapt toward the door. Slid into it, slamming it shut, then flipped the lock. "Took you long enough."

"*Scusi?*" she balked at him.

He moved past her with a look. "Not you." He returned to the desk and eyed the laptop. "I already said it's in."

"What are you doing here?" she demanded. "How dare you—"

"Quiet, Gelato. I can't hear." He touched the earbud. "Repeat, Helios."

"Make sure the stick is in all the way."

"I *did*!" Dillon again nudged the small stick that would give Helios control of the Galtieri laptop.

"Ah, that did it."

He felt more than saw the object flying at him. With a flick of his wrist, he deflected it. Glanced at the thing that struck the lamp and sent it toppling. "A tennis racket?" He glowered at the woman who'd just tried to decapitate him. "Are you crazy?"

"*Me?*" she railed, her voice low and controlled as she stomped toward him. "I catch you breaking into my father's office and you—"

"You didn't catch me," he countered calmly as he lifted a stack of bills, thumbed through them, then tossed them back down. "I baited you in here."

Mouth open, she stared incredulously.

Palming the laptop on either side, he pushed his gaze to her over the screen. "You didn't think I was a complete backbirther who accidentally turns on a light in a darkened house, making it apparent to any of the fifty or so people on the lower terrace that there's an intruder, did you?"

Her gaze swung to the window, and a noise escaped her still-gaping mouth.

"Okay, I've got it," Helios said. "Rootkit planted. Pull the stick and get out of there."

Dillon snagged the piece and tucked it in his pocket.

"Why?" Gelato asked, her expression knotted in confusion.

He smirked and slid around the desk. Moving into her personal space just as he had at that hotel, plotting another distraction. "Still hoping for that kiss I didn't give you?"

Before he could anticipate it, she punched his gut. "I do not want anything from you except your absence."

Dillon lifted an eyebrow. "You sure about that?" He cocked his head to the window. "Notice anything about the guests out there?"

Uncertainty scampered through her pretty features. Yeah, she'd noticed—it was written all over her face. "Tell me," she said quietly.

Huh. Hadn't expected that. Easing back against the desk, he took a load off his feet and crossed his ankles. "Those guests"—he stabbed a finger toward the east lawn—"are not your friends."

Gold eyes held him fast. "How do you know that?"

"Because of you."

She drew up, her lips parting. "What do you mean?"

"For the last hour, you never once spoke to a single person. Unlike Paris, where you worked that event like a pro. With ease, aplomb. Smiling, making people feel welcome and comfortable."

Those mesmerizing eyes widened slightly.

"Here? Nothing. You . . ." He shook his head, knew he probably shouldn't say she wasn't the same girl he'd wanted to kiss at the Ritz. "You're easy to read. And you did not like what was happening out there. That's why I called you in here. Because those men, every one of them . . . I can point you to some very shady dealings."

Understanding—no, it was more than that—swept through her expression. "Who are you?"

He wanted to tease her. Make some joke about that kiss—*why are you so obsessed with a kiss?*—but time was short. "I wish I had time to lay it out, but—"

A worming vibration drilled into his awareness.

"Your name," she said. "I want your name."

Dillon straightened to his full height as he realized what that noise was. What it meant. He snapped his gaze to hers. "You know someone who'd use a bird?"

"Bird?"

"Helo." Still no recognition. "Chopper, helicopter." Frustration spiked because that chopper, if not expected, meant trouble.

"Sure—most of my dad's partners have one." But clearly his meaning was still lost on her as her gaze lifted to the ceiling.

Dillon whipped around her and cut the light, then hurried to the window. Peeked through a slit in the curtain as the enormous black chopper descended. "Were any of them arriving late by one?"

"No," she said, coming to his side.

Half expecting her to tug the curtain aside, he was relieved when she merely shifted around him to peer through the same opening. "Then that's trouble."

"This reeks of Enzo . . ."

Dillon glanced down at her, liking that she wasn't afraid to be near him. That her hair brushed his arm. "Your father's right-hand man, the one who shot me in Paris?"

She started, looking up at him with surprise. "I thought you got away."

"I did—with a souvenir." The thunder of the helo again drew his attention to where the wheels of a sleek black helicopter touched down. "It's a Sikorsky."

"What does that mean?" she asked over the droning rotors and engines.

"A Sikorsky can carry—" Dillon swallowed his words as the bird's door opened and armed men emerged. AK-47s. They were moving with lethal intent and determination, rifles coming to bear "*That.*"

Cove pressed forward, her shoulder bumping his arm. When she saw what was happening, she jerked to him, face awash in panic. "What do—"

The hollow, mechanical repetitive thumping of shooting silenced her. In a heartbeat, she whirled toward the door, stricken.

Guessing she intended to rush out and help her father, Dillon lunged. "No!" He caught her hand, stopping her from exposing their location and putting them in danger.

"Hey!" Cove jerked away. "Let go!" she shouted, expression wrought as she strained for the door. "*Mio papà—*"

"You can't help him," Dillon warned, tightening his hold on her wrist. "Going out there is suicide. They didn't bring AK-47s to *talk.*"

"I can't just stay here and let them—"

"That's exactly what you have to do," Dillon countered.

She let out a strangled cry. "I can't—"

"Quiet!" The sound of rotors seemed to deepen, and he scowled, looking toward the window. "Wait. Something's not..." He wasn't into manhandling, so he released her, and when she didn't bolt away, he hurried back to check the situation outside. Another bird was lowering. Why two?

"What's happening?" she asked, her words nearly lost to the roar of the helos as curiosity forced her back to his side, then she shifted in front of him.

Watching over her head, he monitored the chaos where two thugs were hauling someone up the lawn to the new bird. A handful of additional firepower trailed the trio. The man being dragged writhed and fought, making the thugs lose their grip. He dropped to the ground, but they jerked him back up.

"Who do they have?"

The captive's head lifted.

Cove gasped and jerked back—straight into Dillon's chest. "Papà!"

Bracing her, he prayed she didn't do something stupid.

"*Papà*!" she screamed.

Like that.

From behind, he clamped a hand over her mouth as the assault team forced her dad into a chopper. But then two men swarmed in front of the window, six feet distant.

Cursing his position, Dillon hauled her back against his chest. "Shh," he breathed against her ear.

She railed for a second—till she registered the incoming threat—and froze.

There were two logical reasons for those thugs to come to the upper terrace and enter the house: They were looking for something. Or someone, like Cove.

"We have to get out of here," Dillon rasped.

"The woman," came the dull shout of the thug beyond the window. "Pink dress, where is she?"

Cove went rigid.

Dillon released her and kept his voice low. "Who was wearing a pink dress?"

Her wide gold eyes met his. "Me."

He frowned. She was definitely not wearing pink.

"I-I mean, he wanted me to. But I refused."

Well, that was a confirmation on what the men were searching for. "If they find us, they'll kill me and take you. Maybe kill you too. Understand?"

Gaze rife with fear, she swallowed and gave a clipped nod.

"I need you to trust me, because we have to find a way to get out of here without being seen or shot."

"The kitchen." Angling in his direction, she said, "If we can get down there, I know a way out."

He indicated to the door and met her there. When she reached for the latch, he touched her shoulder. "Cove."

She swung back to him.

"No matter what happens once we leave this office, you get to the kitchens."

Uncertainty wavered in those gold depths, then understanding. Fear took over. She wet her lips, composure fracturing. Crumbling. "I can't—"

"You can. Will. Just keep moving. I'll be right behind you." As quiet as possible, he unlocked the door. Gently, slowly, he eased down the handle until he felt it disengage. "Which way?"

"Right," she said, her focus rock-solid and intense. "Down the hall, a left, then a right."

Dillon gave a nod. He lifted a finger for her to wait as he opened the door a crack and checked both directions of the hall. Slipping aside, he cocked his head to the rear, telling her to move.

Cove slid out, then darted away.

Dillon trailed her, walking backward to protect their six. They made the first turn without complication and continued. She raced ahead to the next juncture, but he caught the telltale sound of thudding.

Perceiving a threat, he surged in front of her and backed up, forcing her back a step even as a radio squawked in the next passage. The crackle acted as a homing beacon. He waited . . . three . . . two . . .

As the steel muzzle of an AK-47 slid into view, Dillon grabbed the wood stock with his left hand and yanked hard to the side, effectively pulling the thug straight into his fist. The guy stumbled back, the weapon ripping from his grip. Dillon shoved in and drove the butt at the man's face. Following a resounding crack, the guy dropped like a boulder, head bouncing off the stone floor.

Cove gaped at him.

"Go!" Dillon said, drawing her from the shadows as he slid the rifle to the low-ready and trailed her into the darkened passages.

They worked in tandem, her running to every corner and waiting. Giving him time to clear it before they moved on. Banked left. At the end of the hall, he spotted the kitchen. Inside, he was not surprised to find trays of food abandoned. The place empty. He wouldn't have stuck around either with gunmen shooting up the place.

"Where?" he asked, searching for a door in the industrial-style kitchen that belied the much older architecture found in most of the villa.

"Back here," she said, rushing to a stone wall.

The *thump-thump-thump* of an AK-47 narrowly preceded searing heat in his shoulder. "Augh!" He pivoted and fired at the gunman advancing on them. The guy went down, but so had their chance at stealth. "Go!"

Cove palmed the wall.

Dillon hesitated, trusting her but not seeing any sort of an exit. "You sure—"

Click!

A panel popped, eliciting a grin from her. She quickly dug her fingers in the crevice and tugged it open, revealing a set of very old stone steps leading down into darkness.

She coiled around it and vanished into the shadowy depths.

Had to be a tunnel. Heart in his throat, he faltered. For a half second, considered going back and trying to shoot his way out. Anything was better than claustrophobic suffocation. Not happening . . .

"C'mon," she hissed. "It's the only way."

He wasn't one to chicken out but—

Bok-bok.

Shouts from the hall made him bite back a curse and get moving. Catching the iron ring on the back side of the door, he pushed himself down the steps, shutting himself into the void. No sooner had he heard it click than the blackness was complete.

Terror seized him. Forbade him from moving. Frozen on the steps, he again considered going back—there had to be another way, right?—when voices carried through the thick barrier from the kitchen. Bullets from an AK-47 or the smothering darkness?

Equal odds . . .

He closed his eyes. Opened them. Zero difference.

Cold, tentative fingers touched his arm, making him flinch. "This way," she whispered—much closer than expected—and slid her hand down his arm, threading their fingers. "Come."

He felt her tug him onward . . . Could not make his feet move. "Where does this lead?" At least his voice hadn't cracked.

"Shh," she hissed, and the warmth of her body pushed the chill from his. "The walls are thin here."

Gut seizing at the way her words skated along his neck, he fought that reaction and the fear immobilizing him. *Move, idiot. She's going to think you're weak.*

He'd done a lot of things, stolen into several countries. Escaped more. Avoided thugs and bullets—caught a couple. Nearly frozen to death. Swam till his lungs seared . . . But this—*too much like the dryer* . . . "If they find us down here—"

"They won't. Besides Papà, I'm the only one who knows of this passage." She squeezed his hand. "I know it by heart," she said. "Trust me."

Did he have a choice? He was being stupid. Foolish. Letting fear control him.

"Look, you broke into my papà's office, and this is the punishment."

Valid.

When she tugged again, somehow, his feet came unrooted.

"Thirty paces straight, then a left. Watch the—"

His head cracked against something, making his teeth clack. He groaned, hand lifting. Found cold, hard stone at his temple.

"Oh. Um, the ceiling is low." He heard the smile in her words. "Be careful."

"Little late with that warning."

Coffin. This is a freakin' coffin.

SEVEN

Orvieto, Italy

ANGER AT THIS MAN WARRED WITH HER ANGER at whoever had attacked her home. She was not sure which she despised more, now that she found herself trapped in the tunnels with the one man who had the ability to steal her breath and infuriate her at the same time.

His crushing grip defied her will not to cry out. Her mind wrestled with the fact this handsome, capable man, whose death grip was clammy, was the same man who'd pinned her to the wall at the Ritz and had her fantasizing for the last six months about the kiss he'd withheld. He had infected her dreams and distracted her from finding out who set up Papà.

They'd moved but fifteen feet from the door, his every step stiff and halting. How could this man be *scared*? It seemed such a small thing for this larger-than-life man. "Just a little farther . . ." It plucked at something deep in her, this visceral fear of his. Made her wonder if there was a story behind his claustrophobia when he had seemed so utterly fearless.

That wondering distraction made her lose count of her paces.

Had to be close . . . She crouched as she advanced, arm extended, tracing the volcanic stone wall at thigh level. Somewhere around here . . . When he resisted moving again, she reminded herself to keep talking. Hoped she hadn't forgotten the way. "I left a . . ." It was here somewhere. Finally, she found the lip of the natural ledge. Oh good. She'd started worrying her mental map had been skewed by time. "Now, where . . ." Her fingers tipped the cold metal. "Aha."

She lifted the torch. Now, the real miracle would be if the battery still worked. She slid her finger along its length. Light flared through the tunnel like a flaming beacon. Oh, thank heaven!

He groaned and she glanced back, realizing once more that she had failed to warn him—this time about the light. Which was only fair since he'd broken into Papà's office, into their home . . .

After looking in both directions, he grimaced. "Maybe it was better *without* the flashlight."

"Remember," she bit out, "you would not be stuck down here if you hadn't—"

"Yeah, yeah. I got the point."

Irked at his gruff words, she clenched her jaw. She'd given the guy the benefit of the doubt, despite not knowing a thing about him. "I cannot believe you are afraid of the dark."

"I'm not."

She scoffed. "If you are going to break into people's homes and want to get away unscathed, you have to toughen up." And yet, she was not untouched by his very real panic over the claustrophobic conditions. "It's safe down here. I played in these tunnels as a kid. Clearly, I made it out alive." She might not be callous, but she couldn't resist taunting him. "Want to pinch me to be sure?"

Those brown eyes darted to her and away, his jaw muscle jouncing beneath stubble that seemed more pronounced in the scampering shadows.

Wow, he was acting just like Vicenzo when they'd gotten

trapped in the well as children. It pulled on her heartstrings. She angled toward him and reached out. "Look, I—"

"Where does this lead?" The barked manner of his question startled her, and his gaze skipped around, as if not knowing where to look. No, not wanting to meet her gaze. To look at her and own his fear. "How far?"

Fighting the urge to snap at him, she noticed something shift in his gaze. A type of . . . regret. Over his harsh words? Had he realized his fear was warping his mood? Well, then. Maybe she would let it go, especially considering the tremor in his words.

As for his question about how far, she worried he would not like the answer. Worried what it might do to this already-tense guy. Because they would be down here for a while . . . a *long* while.

"That question too hard for you? Thought you knew these tunnels."

Surprised at his sharp tone again, she had to remind herself this was likely nerves talking. Barking. Whatever. "I will pretend you did not just bite the hand that's leading you, the hand whose home you invaded."

His expression tightened.

"And before I answer, how about you tell me your name?"

His brow furrowed. "Why?"

Santo cielo, he was hard work. "Because when I lead you out of here, I want to be sure I have the name of the man who broke into my papà's office to give the authorities." Her heart thundered a little at the threat. Or maybe because he was being so difficult.

He cocked his head, brow diving to that broken nose. "Are you—"

"Serious?" She nodded with a sigh. "I am. However"—she extended her hand—"I'm Cove Galtieri."

"I know who you are," he grumbled.

"Missed the point, Dark Eyes." She nodded to him. "Your name is . . . ?"

He seemed to consider her, and in a way, the guy looked as if she were asking him to sacrifice his life. "Achilles."

She laughed. "There is no way that is your name." But when he just kept scowling at her, the amusement fell away. "Seriously?"

"How far?" he bit out.

Who named their kid Achilles? "The tunnels are long," she finally conceded. "Quite long. They lead to the underground beneath the old city, which—while old—is still very much active and populated. Once there, we will have options."

Achilles looked down the direction they would head, where light succumbed once more to the pitch black. "How far?"

"Several kilometers."

He muttered something. "How long will it take to reach it?"

The popping of those rifles peppered the night again.

Cove froze, peering up. "*What* are they doing?"

"You don't want to know," Achilles said, then nodded down the passage, away from the house. "And we don't want them to find us down here. So, how long till the end?"

Catching her lower lip between her teeth, she hated the only answer she had. "I do not know," she conceded. "I have never gone all the way to the end."

"You don't know?" His eyes widened as he craned his neck toward her. "Wait, that means you don't even know if it's intact!"

"What I do know is that the underground city is not only intact but it's a tourist attraction." Even though parts were crumbling and unstable, but no need to mention that. "Then however long it takes us to work through the maze of partially lit passages to the surface."

He slumped back against the wall and pinched the bridge of his nose. "So that's what, an hour? Two?"

"Guessing somewhere in between. Hard to judge. Orvieto was built on a large tufa plateau—a stone plateau formed from volcanic rock, separated from the surrounding area, so there will be a fair amount of climbing to reach it."

"If you've never gotten that far, how do you know the tunnel leads there?"

"*Vigneto Corallo* was built hundreds of years ago on the site where some people escaped the city when the French laid siege to it." She shrugged. "It's all legend. I can't prove it." When he didn't answer, but stayed there, looking at the ground, her own uncertainties screamed louder. "I know—"

"Fine." He straightened and exhaled heavily. "Let's do this."

Cove didn't miss that he balled his fist as he shifted in front of her. Had to admire the guy for facing his fear head-on. When he started moving, she hustled behind him, aiming the flashlight on the path. "D-do you want—" She crashed into him like the brick wall he was. "What's wrong?"

Looking down, he said nothing. His breathing seemed shallow. "I . . . I can't."

Claustrophobia again.

It tugged at her heart. "So we go back."

"No," he ground out. Flexing his fists.

"Okay." Cove eased around him, caught his hand, and placed it on her shoulder. "Keep your eyes on the path at your feet. Not focusing on the walls will help your mind shift around the fear."

"I'm not a child."

Giving him a sidelong look, she let him try to save his pride. "You helped me get out of the house. I help you get out of the tunnels. Deal?"

Shots echoed aboveground, muted by volcanic rock ensconcing them.

"Yeah. Keep moving." That sounded pretty forced.

But she complied. Faced front and started walking, slow and steady, his hand never leaving her shoulder as they walked in silence for a good ten minutes before a distant noise scampered from behind. Pulling in a breath, she stopped and glanced back.

Head down, he slammed those dark eyes into her. "Keep going."

"Is that . . . ?" Her mouth went dry, wondering what had happened to the guests, what would happen if the shooters came in the tunnels.

Achilles gave a slow nod. "I know it's normal to be buried underground, but it's usually *after* you die. I'd rather not do it in reverse." A half smirk. "Please."

"Right." When she turned back to the darkness, Cove felt her own courage falter. What if she was wrong? What if—

"Hey." His deep voice was husky. "You're doing good. Just keep moving, right?"

"How could you possibly know I—"

"Tension in your shoulder."

Disbelieving the marvel that he was, Cove resumed walking. With a sniff of laughter, she shook her head as her shoes crunched rocks. "You don't miss anything, do you?"

"I miss the light."

She breathed a laugh.

"And air. Air's good. And not having to duck my head to walk."

"Complain much?" she retorted, then rolled her eyes. "I'm surprised those shoulders of yours are clearing with the huge ego."

"Only because I'm walking cockeyed."

She laughed, but then sobered. Reminded herself he'd broken into Papà's office. And he'd been in Paris . . . Not just Paris but at the dinner party. "Why are you chasing my papà?"

A dozen or more steps echoed with nothing more than a grunt, his steps clumsy as he tripped or hit something.

"You were in Paris and now our home. Why?"

More silence from him.

Cove stopped. "I am not moving any farther until you tell me—"

Thud.

The skitter of voices behind them silenced Cove. Made her again peer back in that direction.

"We can stand here," he said, "have it out, let them catch up and kill us . . . or we can table this until we're safe."

His offer seemed entirely too convenient, especially considering how easily and quickly he'd suggested it. "I have a feeling *safe* is a very relative word for you, *Achilles*."

"Isn't it for all of us?"

Santo cielo, she resented his *laissez-faire* attitude. "More for some than others, I believe." Resisting the urge to continue bickering, she decided to put more distance between them and the house. "You should know that I have a long memory. Like these tunnels." That was probably ill-humored of her, considering his claustrophobia.

He didn't respond.

Trekking in silence, she got lost in the doubts plaguing her. About being here with him, about the possibility that there was no way out of this tunnel system. *Cielo*, what if she had it wrong? What if this led . . . nowhere?

The tunnel started narrowing, making even her chest constrict. Was the air thinner or was it her imagination? When Achilles muttered something indecipherable, she knew it wasn't just her. The passage funneled to the right and then made a hard turn that was a tight fit, even for her. She shimmied through. "Thank goodness," she laughed as she turned in the wider, taller tunnel.

But he wasn't there.

Her heart jarred. "Achilles."

Through the opening that was not even a foot wide, she saw him on the other side, not moving. Head down, pinching the bridge of his nose, he had a hand on his belt.

"Hey." She reached through and touched his shoulder. "It's just—"

"Yeah. Yeah. I got it." He straightened and turned sideways. Wedged in.

Holy sky, that was a tight fit. *Could* he make it through?

Shimmying, he looked up at the ceiling—which probably wasn't much help since it was practically in his face—and huffed a breath. Grimaced. Shook his head. He tightened his mouth. Tried again.

"Good. That—"

He shoved himself backward out of the tight space and clenched. "Freak." He bent and gripped his knees, growling. "Augh." He rotated and ran a hand over his head. "Son of a . . ."

"Hey-hey." Worried he'd have a panic attack, maybe pass out like Vicenzo had, she hurried back through and caught that well-muscled bicep. "Hey."

"Get off." He jerked away and paced from her, raw tension roiling through him. "We have to turn around." He hoisted up the rifle as if he'd use it to fight their way free.

"You're not thinking clearly. You know we can't—*they're* there."

"What I know is that I *can't* make it through that pigeon hole!"

Heart tugging at the panic in his dark eyes and voice, she kept her voice and expression calm. "You can—just draw in a breath and let it out, then push through."

"Not everyone's the size of a mouse!"

Fear—this was fear again. Amused that he likened her to a mouse, Cove told herself not to react at his strident voice bouncing off the volcanic rock walls. He was panicking. When he slumped against the tunnel wall, she eased closer, wary of setting him off. "Achilles . . ."

Jaw tight, he glared at the narrow gap. "Yeah. I know." He stretched his neck, avoiding her gaze. "I suck. Quit being a baby."

"You only suck if you give up." Well, not really, but he apparently operated on tough talk. "Look, I see you battling this, and that's the attitude of a warrior—to *battle* it. Fight it."

He sniffed. Shook out his hands. Again stretched his neck. "Okay."

She edged toward the point of compression. "Ready?"

He nodded. Bounced on his toes.

Wedging into the opening, Cove pushed herself through, but

instead of looking toward the opening, she faced him and went slower. Which even for her felt suffocating. "Come on, Dark Eyes."

He smirked and shifted sideways.

"Take a deep breath, hold it, then step in."

Locked onto her, he nodded. Took that breath and entered the gap.

Seeing his expression flicker, Cove caught his hand as she shimmied toward the opening on the other side. "Now, slowly let out that breath and keep moving."

He nodded, air expelling from his lungs, shrinking his chest cavity.

Again she saw alarm spirit through those dark orbs. "Look at me."

He complied as they shuffled sideways. "You have beautiful eyes."

Having him staring at her had a side effect she hadn't anticipated—the swirling jellies in her belly. She told herself to focus on helping him. Breaking free of the constriction, she felt her own breath explode in relief. But in that same instant, she felt resistance in his grip. Knew the fear was swarming him again. "Breathe, Achilles. Shallow breaths." Without any hesitation, she yanked him toward her.

"No!" Panic lit his eyes.

But she already had in him motion.

Achilles stumbled out. Surprise streaked through his expression when he realized he was free. He barked a laugh. Then shouted and pumped a fist in the air—which struck the ceiling. "Yeah!"

Laughing, Cove caught his arm. "Shh," she said around a laugh.

But he was unrepentant. Hauled her into his arms and hugged her. "Thank you," he breathed against her neck. "Thank you. That was muffed up."

Shocked to be crushed against him, she stiffened, acutely aware of every place their bodies touched. Electricity shot down her neck and zapped her belly with giddiness. And a heaping measure of attraction. She stepped out of his hold, blushing. "We should get going. Especially after that shout."

EIGHT

Orvieto, Italy

THERE WAS ONLY ONE WAY TO SPELL COWARD: D-I-L-L-O-N.

Legit thought he was going to die, trapped in that crevice. Might as well die of humiliation, because he'd sure never live it down that she'd saved his bacon. Which had technically been the second time. In Paris, she'd stopped her dad from having him arrested. And while he'd taken some lead escaping, it would've been worse if she hadn't intervened.

This girl . . . They might be heading to a fortress, but she had one within her.

Confined spaces were not his specialty. He'd conquered some tight spaces before, but this . . . this tunnel was eating his breakfast, lunch, *and* dinner. Now that they'd passed through that gap, at least he could walk with his head up.

A stiff compulsion to explain his claustrophobia to Cove wrestled to vomit itself into the cool, damp tunnel. Let her know he wasn't the coward that was written all over his actions. That he just . . . Had no excuse. What must she think of him?

Why did he care?

No idea. But he did. He eyed her, remembering their banter. The way she'd talked him down, walked him through that suffocating experience. Good night, had he really told her she had beautiful eyes? He recalled that slate-gray number she'd worn at the Ritz with the bare shoulder. The kiss he'd nearly taken from her. Found himself wanting it all over again.

She stopped and turned to him.

Head in the clouds, Dillon nearly collided with her. Swung the rifle away to avoid cracking it against the wall or her.

She smiled and cocked a nod toward the path ahead. "Look."

He did, but wasn't—

"It's lightening," she said softly. "We're getting close to the underground city."

"The sooner, the better." A weight lifted from his chest, knowing they were nearly done with this nightmare. "I almost died when I was a kid—got stuck in an old dryer."

Cove drew in a breath and stopped to peer up at him with a wad of sympathy.

"Just didn't want you thinking I was a chicken."

Her wide gold eyes took him in. "I never thought that. I can't imagine the terror you felt, being trapped inside."

"Freaked out pretty bad when I realized I couldn't get out. Then I fell asleep . . ." He shuddered a breath, not sure it was smart to talk about this while they were still stuck down here, but it kept his nerves at bay. "I was unconscious when the paramedics came."

"What a terrible memory, and it explains your reaction to the confined space." She smiled at him. "But I see no chicken down here."

The thudding that sounded like ground-penetrating sonar was actually his heart beneath her gaze. He wanted to say something profound. But his brain was still lost in her gold orbs. He cursed himself when she started walking again.

Another twenty minutes delivered them to the first juncture with spotlights spaced sporadically along the path. They slipped past more than one rope barrier. And for another half hour, they climbed a winding circuit up . . . up . . .

"My calves are burning," she complained. "Why aren't you tired?"

He huffed a laugh and managed to shift ahead of her. "Life on the lam and a violent need to be out of these tunnels," he muttered as they passed another cordon. "Plus parkour."

"Park-what?"

He leapt at the wall, toed it, then did a backflip off it. Landed, facing her, hands out in demonstration. "Parkour."

"We call that acrobatics here."

"Dude. Not even close." Dillon frowned. "Parkour is . . . cooler." *What are you, twelve?* He had to get his head in the game now. Once they got out of this insufferable underground city, what would he do? Couldn't stay with her. That wouldn't work.

Down one passage, up a flight of stairs, down a narrow corridor—that felt a mile wide compared to the tunnels—and the lights grew brighter.

"Just a little farther now," she said as they entered a central area with arches and doors up a solid six or seven levels. They passed a large circular piece. "Almost there."

"You've been saying that for over an hour." Even though he challenged her, he could feel the air taking on a more normal quality. "You have family in the area?"

She gave him a look.

"Other than your father?" By the time they reached the top, Dillon noted a slight burn in his muscles.

"No, my uncles moved away. No aunts or cousins." Cove huffed, lagging farther and farther behind. "There," she said around a panting breath as she took a breather and indicated to a gate with a sign attached with O-rings. "That's the main gate. At this hour, it might be locked."

"I can remedy that," he promised, unwilling to be trapped underground any longer than necessary. "Got any cash on you?"

She frowned up at him. "What is this interrogation? My family, money . . . ?"

He made quick work of freeing the gate and pushed it open, then climbed steep steps up out of the cave system. Night proved as smothering and potent an adversary in blocking his ability to see. A stone wall ran fifty or sixty meters straight up on the left side. A worn path led to an arch.

"You didn't answer my question," she pressed.

Cove was bright—should've known she'd pick up on the questions. "Trying to get the logistics sorted." He chided himself for the half-truth. "You know the way from here?"

She stopped and eyed him, then chewed her lower lip, her flashlight flickering. "I think before we go another step, you need to make good on your promise for answers."

"Never promised." Man, what was it about this chick that made him feel like a heel for protecting his interests and freedom? It was those eyes. The hurt that splashed across her gold irises. "Fine." He flashed his palms. "What do you want to know?"

"Why were you in my papà's office?"

"Looking for a trail."

Tilting her head, she considered him. "A trail to what?"

"Not what, *who*."

She lifted her eyebrows and wagged her head, as if telling him to expound.

"My dad. And no matter how you bat those pretty eyes at me, I'm not telling you more." Because he had a feeling he'd spill his guts if she kept prodding and looking at him like that. He hiked up the steep path, itching to get to open ground. "Now, do you have somewhere you can go or someone to stay with?"

Cove shot him a quizzical look. "Are we not going back to the house? And why are the questions only about me? What about you?"

Holy fire, she didn't miss a thing, did she?

Her expression fell. "You're planning to leave me."

Ignoring the plaintive sound of those words, he had to help her see the logic. "The house will be dangerous. They brought in guns and helos to get your dad, then asked about you—expecting you to be in a pink dress." He gave a cockeyed nod. "Which means you were part of their plan. That suggests they'd leave a scout or two—or ten—to wait for your return."

"That's crazy. I'm nothing."

Dillon arched his eyebrow, appreciating how the moonlight glinted off her hazel eyes. "Beg to differ—you're the lone heir to a billion-dollar fortune." He stepped out, the cool of the night swirling around him as he considered the route back up to the city. If he could get up there, maybe he—

She grabbed his arm and pulled him around. "You're *not* leaving me."

Surprised at her vehemence and warning tone, he tried to sort what brought out that venom. But one fact remained. "I can't take you—"

"What does finding your father have to do with mine?"

Dillon started at the direct and sharp shift in conversation.

"Come on—you were in my papà's office," she persisted, her words terse. "You said that you were looking for your dad. Why were you looking for your dad in my papà's office?"

He had nothing to lose at this point. And maybe this revelation would set her back a step. "Your dad was the last one to see mine alive."

Surprise spiraled through her expression, her full lips parting. "My papà knows yours?"

"Apparently."

Narrowing her eyes, she studied him. "What is your dad's name?"

Dillon smirked. "Nice try." When he'd offered the name Achilles and she'd questioned if that was truly his name, he'd expected her to ask for his real name.

"I wasn't trying to trick you," she growled, then sighed. "Before Enzo took everything over, I was my father's admin and communications director—I handled appointments, communications, and events."

He sniffed. "Yeah, pretty sure whatever they were doing wouldn't be on a planner."

She drew back, her reaction screaming offense. "What does that mean?"

"Nothing." Grinding his teeth, he glanced around, searching for an exit so he could be done with this fiasco. "Look, we're losing time. Do you have somewhere to go?"

"Yes," she asserted, staying in step with him. "Wherever you are going."

"Not happening." He pivoted and started up into the old city that was jam-packed with buildings, one on top of another.

"You cannot just abandon me," she argued, hustling after him, her words cracking on raw emotion. "I have no one here. No money—I do not even have a phone to call someone."

"Welcome to my life," he muttered and aimed in a southerly direction, hoping this elevated city could give him a decent vantage to see the Galtieri villa. "And you're seriously going to tell me you've lived here your whole life and don't have friends in this village?"

"You don't have to make it sound so absurd," she hissed. "Why do you think I traveled with my papà so much? We lived too far from the city, and when you have money, people assume things about you."

At the clear insinuation that he'd assumed something, he cast her a sidelong glance as they wound along the cobbled streets.

"You should conceal that rifle," she said, "before someone in the village looks out their window and sees an armed gunman prowling the streets."

"It's not like I can tuck it at the small of my back." But her point was fair, so he held the weapon along the length of his arm and pressed to his side to conceal its shape as much as possible.

Shops and houses lined the tightly packed streets, locked up and lights off. This place was oppressively cramped.

"I went to boarding school and came home on holiday," she volunteered, picking back up that conversation about friends in the city. "Orvieto is built like a fortress."

"No kidding."

"It's separated from the surrounding lands, so it was not easy for me to reach. The shopkeepers know me, but I'm not *friends* with them. Izetta was my dearest friend, but she was from school. Came home with me so I would have company, since her life was anything but nice. But we often spent holidays in Greece with my uncle."

"A real hardship, I'm sure." Rubbing the back of his neck, he didn't really care. He stopped short, knowing the longer she stuck around, the harder it'd be to ditch her. Granted, she was really easy on the eyes and sharp as a tack, but it was hard enough taking care of himself without money or promise of tomorrow. He didn't want the responsibility on his shoulders for her too. "I can't take you."

"I'm not asking you to," she countered sharply. "But maybe . . . maybe you need an admin."

"I don't—"

"Someone to watch your back."

"You?" he challenged, stopping to stare down at her. "You're going to watch my back?"

Chin lifting, she drew up. "I've been watching it for the last hour."

He bit back a laugh and resumed course, peering down each tight alley, checking if he could see the land beyond the fortress-like village.

"Someone who has connections would be useful to this mission of yours, right?"

Dillon clenched his teeth. Wouldn't answer that. It wasn't happening. He didn't want her getting hurt, and there was a lot of hurt where he was going.

"Someone who could provide a couple thousand euros."

He stopped cold, half ticked that she was trying to buy her way. "So you think I can be bribed? Bought?"

Brown hair in disarray, she shrugged casually. "It is only fair I pay my way."

He considered her, noting even shadows couldn't hide her beauty. "Pay how? You just told me you didn't have money."

Cove wet her lips. Pointed up the ever-sloping cobblestone road. "You're climbing up instead of going down. I assume that means you're trying to get somewhere high." She brushed the hair from her face. "To see *Vigneto Corallo*, yes? You are planning to go back to the villa." With a staggering breath, she offered, "I can access my papà's safe. Get money, clothes, and a phone."

"No phone. They're homing beacons."

She gave a ghost of a smile and drew in a steadying breath. "*D'accordo.*"

"No idea what that means."

"'Agreed,'" she translated.

He frowned. "That wasn't me agreeing."

"*Niente ripensamenti!*"

He blinked. "What?"

"No second thoughts—it, eh, means you cannot take it back."

She was adorable. He wanted to laugh at the childish challenge.

Then holy fire, if he wasn't reconsidering letting her come. He cursed himself for not being stronger. But man, the idea of having someone with him, someone who had a brain and knew how to think—that sounded nice. Real nice. Especially since it was Gelato.

What're you thinking? It's asinine! You'll have to keep her alive.

He'd have to do that anyway, since she didn't have anyone to shelter with. While he didn't like the plan, he would not abandon her.

"This way," she said, throwing him a smile that said she was relieved and pleased, before slipping down a darkened alley that wasn't any wider than their shoulders.

"You have got to be kidding me," he muttered, eyeing the tight space.

This was when he had a deep appreciation for the wide-open spaces of America. Drawing a breath for courage—and to shrink his chest cavity like she'd taught him in the tunnels—he ducked in and followed her. Each step thickened the darkness and filled him with a heady suspicion that he'd follow her to his death, if she'd just flash that smile again.

A moment later, they were skirting a path that had stone-walled structures on the left. On the right, a rail that protected them from a deadly drop. Trees and scrub obstructed their view, but then she turned into another shadowed alcove.

Dillon tripped, not realizing there were stone steps.

"Sorry—steps."

He gritted his teeth. Really had to talk to her about those late warnings. The stairs led to a roof terrace.

"We'll have to be quiet," she said, waiting for him at the top. "There's an apartment below, but I thought . . ." She motioned toward the blackened sky.

No, not the sky . . . The terrace offered an unobstructed view of the southern valley. "Yeah . . . nice," he whispered. Light on his feet, he went to the stone half wall that served as a rail and scanned the area. Even with the moonlight, the valley and rolling hills seemed to drink in the shadows.

Cove came alongside. Indicated more to the right. "*Vigneto Corallo* is there."

Though Dillon squinted, he couldn't see the villa. But then it struck his tired, confused brain. "No lights." Dots of illumination peppered the surrounding area, but there was a literal blackout where the villa sat.

"*Sì*," she said softly. "It is very strange—it would normally be very bright. So, if the lights are still out, maybe they are no longer there?"

Dillon shifted and hiked a leg up, sitting on the wall. Took a load off his feet. "Maybe."

Copying him, Cove sat next to him and folded her arms as she considered him with a long look. "You sound doubtful."

That wasn't the first time she'd acted like she knew him well enough to call him on things. The bigger surprise was that each time she'd been right. "It's possible they left after not being able to find you."

"Or?"

He met her gaze and felt that strange feeling in his gut. "Or they're using the darkness to conceal their positions as they lay in wait for you."

"Oh." Wariness crowded her expression as she studied the void in the terrain. A certain defeat dimmed the brightness in her eyes that'd been there a second ago. Then her jaw set firmly and intensity radiated through the gold eyes that found him beneath the moonlight. "I would make a deal with you, Achilles."

Dillon mentally braced. Not because he dreaded what she'd ask but because he dreaded his ability to tell her no. He had, after all, followed her through a tunnel and back into the suffocating passages of the old city. That, and despite his determination not to get saddled with the responsibility of someone else, he knew he owed her for saving his bacon when that compression point happened. Without her, he'd still be stuck there. Or he'd have gone back and tried to fight his way out through the house, only to end up dead.

"For the last two years, I have been trying to prove my papà's innocence. Since you have been following him, it is not a surprise to you about the . . . scandal."

"That he's funding the Houthis, taking payoffs?"

"Massimo Galtier would *never* fund terrorists!" She glowered and flared her nostrils, looking once more in the direction of her family home, then back to him with a fire of determination. "I will fund your search to find your papà if you will help me find what I need to exonerate mine. You saw—they kidnapped him. Whatever is happening, he is not willing or complicit."

"I saw they took him," Dillon conceded. "I did not see anything that proves he's not complicit—he could've angered whoever wanted him taken."

Hurt splayed through her pretty eyes.

"But I'd also imagine your father's fortune is tied up in companies and stocks. The money we'd need—"

"There are tens of thousands in his vault, and I can access it. Too, I have several thousand in my safe." Defiance and tenacity looked nice on her. *Real* nice. "It should be enough for a good start, *sì?*"

"Yes," he said, surprising himself. But he had to reclaim some control here. "Two conditions."

She waited, eyes afire.

"One, this is *my* mission, so you follow my instructions—not to be patriarchal, but because I have training you do not."

She gave a reluctant nod.

"Two, no technology. At any time."

Her lips parted as if to object, but then she closed her mouth and gave another nod.

"D'accordion?" he said, deliberately butchering the word to

hide his uncertainty over how to pronounce it. When she smiled, man, the air suddenly felt hot.

"*D'accordo.*"

NINE

Orvieto, Italy

HOW HAD THIS BECOME HER LIFE? TO BE crouching at the edge of the high grass that separated the valley from the manicured property of *Vigneto Corallo* like a common criminal . . . They had taken shelter behind the last of the massive oleander bushes that flowered beautifully pink and magenta in late spring and summer. Their blooms were long gone, but the elongated, leathery leaves were thick and provided perfect cover.

From this position, she could see the three terraced levels. On the lowest, the pools—both the natural one with fish and frogs as well as the Olympic-size pool with gazebo and outdoor kitchen. The middle terrace housed the entertaining terrace—where hours earlier, she had endured Flavio's attention and the intense feeling that things were not right—the winery and storage, as well as the nearest guest house, which was home to their staff, cook, and the Morettis—at least, until more recent days. There were three other guest properties with multiple apartments, but those were farther away. The uppermost terrace boasted the main house, orangery, greenhouse, and winery shop for the locals.

Achilles lowered his shoulder toward her, bringing his face closer as he pointed in the direction of the greenhouse. "Movement," he said, his voice barely audible.

Trying to see what he meant, she quickly caught sight of a shape gliding along the side in deep shadow. "The front door is visible from there," she whispered.

He nodded. "So, how do we get in?"

Cove considered their options for a moment. "The garage," she suggested quietly, retreating a pace. All this surreptitious behavior was not easy, but neither would she let these brigands win. "It has a side door."

Dark features were deepened in the darkness, but his uncertainty bled through. "Show me."

Grateful for the oleander hedge that hid them, Cove hustled toward the end. She crouched there, feeling him do the same at her back. Together, they watched for a long time—at least ten minutes. Despite the lingering silence, she did not have an urge to break the moratorium on talking. She found it . . . somehow comforting to be here with him, to have a plan. To know she was not alone, even with Papà in trouble.

But were they safe here? What if someone saw them? "I don't see anything," she said, feeling vulnerable and exposed, despite the concealment.

Achilles didn't answer, but moonlight revealed his knotted brow and frown. The intensity and raw power roiling off him seemed to hint that he'd seen something.

"What is it?" she whispered.

"It's too easy . . ." He swiveled and lowered a knee to the ground, which brought him closer, his mouth practically against her ear. "They've had hours to scout the house and take up positions. No way they don't know that door is there."

Good thoughts. Ones she hadn't even considered. Her gaze drifted back to the sloping line of the drive that descended the kilometer-long road from the front gate, arced down and around to the six-car garage bay, where some of Papà's most prized possessions sat. Next to the bay, a farm-style door that Mamma had loved. And nobody in sight. It did seem suspicious. Yet . . . they had been here a long while and nothing. But this was his forte, not hers. So, she would trust his instincts.

Once another ten minutes had passed, she did not like wasting time. They could have been inside by now. She eyed him. "What if it is not?"

His gaze shifted to hers. *Santo cielo*, that brooding expression made her stomach do the very flips he had demonstrated in the tunnel. That raw intensity, the depth of thought, and his cunning mind left her breathless. Of course, the dark eyes, brows, and shorn hair did not hurt . . . "Not what?"

"Guarded. What if they only left one or two people . . . ?"

He pursed his lips and shook his head as those probing eyes searched the house again. "That . . . that'd be stupid."

Was he saying her idea was stupid?

He touched her arm, luring her closer as he whispered, "Tell me the route to the office from the garage door."

She eyed the house, mentally mapping it so she got this right. "Once in the door, go straight through the garage, past Papà's six cars, then through the door that will lead to the rear hall. Up the stairs to the main level. Turn left, then first right. Down the hall, second left. It's the second door on the left."

Achilles rubbed his lower lip as he stared at the house. "Left, first right, second left, second left again."

It was so incredible that he could do that. Like an American version of James Bond. That he was so focused and could recall the route. If their roles were reversed, she would still be stuck on the dark eyes and belly flips.

"Cove?"

She blinked, realizing he had said something, and gulped at being caught appreciating him. "What?"

Achilles smirked as he shifted the weapon to the front. "Will the doors be locked?"

She shook her head. "Keypads."

"There's no power."

"They operate independently."

With a nod, he looked to the house. "You lead, but let me clear every corner first. If we get separated, meet back here."

Another good thought she hadn't considered. "Right."

"When you're ready, run for all you're worth. I'll be right behind you."

Heart in her throat, Cove caught a limb of the enormous bush that towered over them and readied herself.

"Three . . . two . . . Go!"

She shoved up and sprinted across the open yard. Every step felt like a kilometer. Each thud of her shoes on the gravel drive like the clap of a weapon firing, making her anticipate a bullet searing through her. But as she hit the small stoop to the door, she couldn't believe she'd made it without injury.

Achilles barreled up and bumped into her.

Punching in the code on the keypad, she pushed even as she heard the tone that signaled a wrong code. She grunted and entered it again. The obnoxious *ergh-ergh* of a wrong code seemed to scream through the night.

His hand landed on her shoulder. "Slow is smooth, smooth is fast."

She frowned even as she tried again. "What—"

"Slow down. Nice and slow."

Buh-leep!

The latch disengaged and she thrust open the door. Hurried inside.

"Go, the other one," Achilles said as he took the door and closed it. Flipped the lock.

Cove darted past Papà's cars and raced up the two steps to the interior door.

"Holy what?" he rasped. "This is a Ferrari 250GT California!"

"Boys and their toys," she murmured as she punched in the code on the second keypad.

"No no no, this cannot be a Miura."

"It better be"—she hit the last number—"or Papà will be very upset at how much he paid for it." She turned to chastise him about not stopping, when he all but careened into her. Swung around her into the rear hall, weapon up and aiming up the stairs.

In the space of a couple minutes, they ducked into the office without crossing any gunmen. Even as Achilles locked the door, she faltered, just then seeing the chaos that had overtaken the normally pristine room.

"*Santo cielo*," she whispered, looking around at the complete disarray. The broken lamps. Shredded leather sofa. Shelves disgorged of their books.

"Someone already hit the safe," Achilles said.

Her gaze landed on the painting behind the desk that hung askew. The steel, fireproof door ajar. "That one, yes." She strode to the side, shifted the armchair away from the wall, and knelt in the corner. Popped the floorboard and smiled down at the keypad. She entered the combination and the entire panel depressed and receded.

"This house has a lot of secrets," she said as she rose and moved to the credenza. She opened it and tugged out Papà's favorite satchel, then tossed it to Achilles. "Fill it up. I'm going to get the money from my safe."

"No—"

"Two minutes." She sprinted for the foyer and took the stairs two at a time.

"Gelato!" he hissed through the darkened house.

But Cove had already reached the upper landing and bolted to the right. She flung herself through her room to the closet. Dove at her winter clothes and parted the hangers. Depressed the panel and entered her code into the keypad. From her personal safe, she grabbed the stack of bills and her passport, then retrieved a backpack purse. Stuffed the items in there. Grabbed a couple shirts and jeans. About to leave, she stopped short. Glanced back and knew better than to leave the clothes parted. She returned things to their former state, then raced out of the closet, across her room . . .

On her nightstand, something lit up. Her heart climbed into her throat. *My phone!* Indecision rooted her to the floor—Achilles had said no devices. They could be tracked. But who was calling her? That wasn't as important as realizing some of the images and evidence she had gathered was still on that. She couldn't leave it behind.

TEN

Orvieto, Italy

WHAT WAS TAKING HER SO LONG?

Dillon waited in the shadows of the juncture to the foyer, weapon at the low-ready. *C'mon, c'mon . . .* Gaze locked on the stairs, he willed her to hurry up and angled aside, catching sight of the lawn below. A serene blue hue from the moon washed over the grass and hills. The villa had everything a guy could want. Even the rare, antique cars worth between 7.5 and a cool ten mill.

Man, I do not belong in this world.

He hadn't grown up poor, but this . . . Didn't matter how beautiful Gelato was. How much he wanted to kiss her. They were not just from different worlds. Entire galaxies separated them.

And that two minutes had turned into ten. "Cove!" he whispered as loud as he dared without alerting anyone to their presence. Hoisting the strap of the satchel crossbody, he stilled at movement on the lawn.

Two men emerged from a small stone structure that was likely a shed. Gut tight, he watched them pause, the dull glow of a phone screen illuminating their faces. A third and fourth joined them. "*Cove*!" he growled, a little louder toward the stairs, still watching the men.

The guy holding the phone looked up at the house. Another pointed.

Holy fire, what had she done? "Incoming!" Dillon didn't worry about being quiet.

The *tap-tap-tap* of shoes snapped him in that direction, weapon up and trained on the noise. Relieved it was her, he then shifted to irritation at whatever had taken her so long. "Move-move! They're coming!" Even as she flung herself across the foyer, he shifted toward the side passage. "What'd you do?"

"Nothing."

"Bullspit!" He palmed her spine and felt a backpack there now. "They got a signal."

She drew in a breath and faltered, looking at him.

"Keep moving—the garage." They abandoned stealth for speed. "The cars—are the keys in the garage?"

"Yes," she said, hustling down the stairs to the rear hall. "Which one should—"

"Land Cruiser."

She nodded and kept moving. Opened the garage door. Scuttled down the steps, swung over to a panel, and grabbed keys. Threw them at him.

Dillon caught them and unlocked the vehicle. "Middle row. Get in and stay down." He climbed in and pitched Papà's satchel to the back.

"The door button—"

"No time," he said, starting the vehicle. After glancing back to be sure she was down, he pressed the brake and revved the engine. Tires squalling, he released it. They barreled through the garage door, bucking it away.

Shots pinged off the side and he ducked, whipping the wheel to the right and sending the antique Cruiser around the arcing drive. He gunned it up the hill, the bullets falling away.

"Is it—"

A man stepped into the drive, aiming an AK-47 at him.

Dillon accelerated as bullets pinged off the hood. Cracked the windshield.

Cove yelped.

"You okay?" he asked, unable to look back as he plowed toward the man, who dove away at the last minute. Dillon veered around the curve to the right.

"Go left! Go left!" she shouted from the floorboard.

"There's no—"

"*Left!*"

He whipped the wheel to the left, and only then saw a small, narrow rutted road there. Jouncing along, he didn't slow.

"It's a quick access to the main road. The other way will take you straight past the house."

In other words, the shooters. "Smart. Thanks."

"I'm just trying to stay alive," she muttered with a nervous laugh.

He careened down the dirt road, then spied the access to the road and took it. The Cruiser bounced and trounced off the rutted road onto a smooth, paved road.

"Is it safe?"

"Too soon to tell," Dillon answered, knowing full well if those shooters had a vehicle—

Lights exploded behind them.

"Stay down! They're coming!"

They barreled over the road, and he kept a sharp eye bouncing between their tails and the exit. Whoever was on them, whoever wanted Cove captured, had skills. "Got any ideas for us to ditch them?"

"After the next turn," she said, staying low, "there's a bridge. Lots of trees. If you go to the right before the bridge, there's a side road. It's often concealed by overgrown trees and shrubs, but it's there. We could trick them . . ."

"Got it," he said, pressing the accelerator even harder. The engine strained and he prayed bullets hadn't done damage that would put them at the mercy of these thugs. Gaze flipping between the front and the rearview, he took the curve.

Saw the spot she'd mentioned. Maybe if they—

Lights blinded him from behind. Which meant they'd see him take the diversionary route. "No good," he ground out, gunning it. "Stay down, but crawl up here. I have no idea which way to go. You need to guide us out."

She dragged herself between the two front bucket seats and secured herself with the belt.

They'd gone several miles on the winding road without the thugs gaining. Why . . . why weren't they gaining?

"I think we have a problem," he said, eyeing their pursuers. "They should've already overtaken us."

Cove peeked around the seat, looking back. "You sure?"

"Dead sure."

She started at his phrase.

"Modern-day SUVs have more horsepower under the hood than this antique." He indicated ahead of them. "What's up there?"

"Farms, a small village."

"Do the roads intersect?"

"No, I—" She gasped. "Wait! Yesss," she breathed. "The road from the winery leads to this one, which has a roundabout way into Orvieto."

"Then why in heaven did you tell me to go *this* way?"

"I do not usually use this road," she balked, her tone plagued with defensiveness, "but I suggested this because of the turnoff, which you passed."

"They were too close." Dillon muttered an oath, then exhaled as he tore up the road, trying to put more distance between them. But no matter how fast he went down the winding road, the vehicles stayed back a quarter klick. He huffed. "I need a way to ditch them. Any ideas?"

"A kilometer or so ahead there should be a side road. It leads to the vineyard."

Did she really think they could hide in a vineyard?

"The roads are very twisty that way," she explained. "A lot of abandoned buildings. If we can get enough of a lead, maybe we could pull into one of them and hide."

"We've already tried the 'enough of a lead' thing. Didn't work."

Hope bled through her gold eyes. "It might this time."

Dillon considered her, frustrated. Worried. He did not know what hornet's nest he'd stepped into by coming to Italy to pin down Massimo Galtieri. But it was massively blowing up in his face.

"This road with its switchbacks will also lead to the autostrada."

"Highway?" he guessed.

She nodded, then indicated to the side of the road. "That white sign—turn there."

Not sure that was the right call, he considered their tail. Wondered if things might be different this time with the "enough of a lead" for him to trust her again.

"You should slow down to make the turn," she said with a hint of nerves.

But doing that meant committing to her suggestion. He wasn't there yet.

A car erupted from a side road, fishtailed, and whipped straight—facing them. Coming head-on.

"Guess we're taking that road," Dillon said. "Hold on!" He accelerated, not wanting to slow down and give the gunmen behind them more opportunity. Waited until the last possible second, nailed the brake, and yanked the wheel. The Cruiser fishtailed. He compensated, aiming for the narrow side road.

Cove screamed as the back tires skidded off the paved road. Thudded into the ditch.

Calm, focused, Dillon pulled it out and trounced back onto the road. Gunned it, dirt and rocks spitting from beneath them.

The rear windshield exploded.

Crying out, Cove grabbed the back of her head.

Alarmed, Dillon snapped to her. "You okay?"

Still cupping her head, she nodded, but her expression was pained. That looked like blood on the seat and her hand.

"Cove—"

"Turn!" she shouted, pointing.

He faltered for a split-second, worried about her, then whipped his focus back to the road. Spotted a sharp curve. Nailed the brake and spun them around the corner, the backend fishtailing again, but not near as bad. They tore off. The road ahead was straight, giving him time to count the seconds until the first black SUV took the turn.

Freak! That'd only been five seconds—

The vehicle went airborne, having taken the turn too sharp. It spun like a top. Bounced. Flipped again.

Dillon kept driving. Saw the second vehicle even as he was taking the next turn. Ahead, a nightmare was playing out. From opposite sides of the road, a large tractor and a massive harvester advanced toward each other. If those vehicles blocked the road, they were as good as dead.

"No no no . . ." He pressed the gas, but he was already giving it all he could.

"We won't make it!" Cove quailed, drew her arms and legs to herself, anticipating a crash.

"We will!" *Have to.*

"They're too close!"

"Don't . . . don't . . ." he warned the drivers of the farm equipment as if they could hear him. Felt his breath stall as he raced closer.

"No! No!" Cove shouted, curling in on herself with a squeal.

Narrowly diving between the two scraped off a mirror. But they made it. Dillon let out a whoop!

Behind them, the two entered the road.

No. *Blocked* the road.

Cove laughed. "That was Signore Giordano in one of Papà's grape harvesters and Signore Barone, a vineyard manager!" She caught his arm. "How did they know?"

Dillon did not slow down as he raced to the next curve, took it, even then stealing a glance. Seeing the SUVs fighting to get around the large equipment.

Laughter dying, Cove drew in a breath as she watched the confrontation. "No . . ." She slapped his shoulder. "They're shooting at them!"

Tightening his jaw, Dillon knew he couldn't slow. Not yet.

"Stop! Stop, stop—they're going to kill them!"

"We can't." A breath caught in his throat. He swallowed. "If we stop, they'll kill *us*."

ELEVEN

Somewhere West of Orvieto, Italy

STUNNED, COVE STARED OUT THE CRACKED windshield at the abandoned stable they'd taken shelter in. Numbly, she watched Achilles walk to the old door and tug it closed—well, as far as the weather-beaten wood allowed. The roof of the stable was missing sections, allowing moonlight inside.

He stood there for a long time, a silent sentry, watching through the sliver caused by age and disrepair, to be sure they were safe.

She recalled the report of the rifles, the chaos of the harvester lights when they exploded. Had both of her father's workers died? Gunmen had killed people at the villa too . . . all because these people were trying to get her.

Me. Everyone's dying because of me.

When she saw Achilles turn from the door, her heart gave a little leap, wondering if there was trouble. However, he wasn't running. And that raw intensity did not seem to be in high gear as he stalked to her side of the Cruiser. Was everything okay?

He opened the door and thrust his jaw at her. "Let me see your head."

She blinked. "My head?"

"There's blood . . ." He motioned her out of the truck and stepped back to give her room.

Hand going to her head, Cove realized there was a dull ache emanating from the spot. "Was I shot?" With all the chaos and running for their lives, she had forced the pain to her periphery. Especially after having to watch Signori Giordano and Barone defend them—possibly with their very lives!

"Gelato," Achilles said, gently drawing her out.

Cove slid out and turned so he could see the back of her head. That's when she spotted the bullet hole in the panel of the Cruiser. She traced it with a finger.

"This might—"

Pain shot through her neck, yanking out a yelp.

"—hurt. Sorry."

Wincing, she tried not to move too much, but the sensation burned.

"Got it." He showed her a large piece of glass.

Gaping, she stared at the bloody sliver. "That was in my head?"

He nodded. "Hang tight. Let me grab the first aid kit." He reached around her into the Cruiser, grabbed Papà's satchel, and drew out a red hard-sided box.

"Where did you get that?"

"Spotted it in the garage. Figured it'd come in handy." He opened it, drew out a couple of tubes, and then motioned to her. "Let me apply this to stave off infection."

She let him work and felt the cool gel applied to the cut.

"Bleeding has stopped—head wounds always gush, so your shirt and hair are a mess, but nothing serious. I could put a bandage on the cut, but I'm not sure it'd stick because of your hair and the odd angle."

"That sounds like torture, trying to get a bandage out of my hair later."

He handed her some gauze pads. "Use these as needed."

She took it, wondering about her papà's workers. "What if nobody finds those men till morning . . . ?"

He started packing up the kit and satchel. "Did they have families?"

She nodded.

Angling around her, Achilles set the satchel in the Cruiser again. "Do they normally harvest before dawn?"

This time, she shook her head.

"Then I'd guess their families knew they went out, maybe even called local authorities."

"I feel so bad," she admitted, heartsick. "They were helping us, and they might have died."

"Let's remember their heroism and not presume death," he said. "We don't know the ending because we weren't there."

"True." She liked that, the idea of clinging to hope instead of darker possibilities. It made it seem . . . possible that Signori Giordano and Barone were still alive. That they would go home to their families. *Per favore, Dio . . .*

"Hey." His voice was soft, caring. "You okay?"

The deep ache in her wanted to cry but . . . "I feel numb."

"That's the shock." Achilles opened the rear passenger door. "Your body protecting itself. Probably should get some sleep."

Mutely, she climbed into the back but sat there for a long time, staring at nothing in particular. Drained of her fight. From the corner of her eye, she saw Achilles shrug out of the jacket, then haul up his shirt.

Her breath spasmed at the sight of his corded abdomen—not that it was so sculpted but at the wound and red, marred flesh. Alarmed, she pitched herself out of the Cruiser. "You got shot?"

"Some people have all the luck," he muttered, then eyed her. "Aren't you supposed to be lying down?"

"I thought I should be sure you do not die."

With a huffed laugh, he applied antiseptic and hissed. "It's a through-and-through." He shrugged, indicating over his shoulder to the exit wound. "I'll be good."

"*Ma sei matto?*" she balked, checking his back and indeed spotting another wound.

He smirked. "No idea what that means, Gelato."

"Why didn't you tell me you were shot? What if that hit an organ or there's internal bleeding?"

"Oh, I guarantee there's internal bleeding," he snickered, using a bonding gel to seal it closed, then he applied a bandage. His brown eyes lifted to her, then his brow furrowed. "Hey. I'll be okay. Not my first bullet wound."

"Well, it's my first time seeing one."

"Trust me. It's okay."

"This"—she stabbed a hand toward his bloody mess—"is *not* okay!"

"Gelato, relax. I'll be fine—I'm not going to die."

Only when he said that did she realize that had been her exact panic. That he'd die too.

Glancing over his shoulder, he tried to see the other wound. Then he angled and tried to twist to reach it.

"Here." She took the bond gel from his hand and moved around behind him. "*Cocciuto come un mulo.*" Saying he was stubborn as a mule in Italian made her feel better, since he could not understand her, and it let off some frustration. She shifted to see better. Her mouth went dry at his muscular back. This time, she let herself appreciate the view. Respect his effort to keep himself in shape. She had seen bare backs before—any pool or beach had an abundance. But they were not . . . this well-muscled or attached to the most *uomo bellissimo* she'd ever met.

Swallowing her attraction, she cleaned the wound, added the antiseptic, then the gel. *Don't think about his warm skin beneath your fingers.* She applied the bandage. "You should have told me you got shot." Her spiraling attraction to him thwarted the anger meant to be in those words she'd forced out.

"Couldn't do anything about it." He peeked over his shoulder. "You done?"

"I could have packed it or something. There." She straightened and cleaned up the supplies.

"Not while whipping around hard turns." He sniffed a laugh and turned to face her as he lowered his shirt gingerly. "That would've been about like getting stabbed. Repeatedly."

The mental note about stabbing somehow evoked stress. When he met her gaze, his brown eyes were warm and filled with more of that cavalier attitude . . . "*Cocciuto come un mulo*," she muttered at him, taking too much pleasure that he did not know what she was saying.

His left eye twitched as he considered her. "Why do I have a feeling you didn't say I was your favorite person?"

A smile threatened, but just as fast, the last vestiges of her courage crumbled. Trauma catching up with her, she fought the tears stinging her eyes. "Why is this happening? Why did they take *mio papà*?" She choked back a sob. "The reason had to be big for them to come with helicopters and rifles. He is not a bad man! What . . . is going on? Why are they trying to catch *me*? Or kill me? What did I do to them?"

He shifted closer. "Gelato."

"*Stop* calling me that!"

His expression sobered.

Hunching in on herself, she ducked her head and rubbed her temple. "Sorry. I do not know what is wrong with me."

"Nothing's wrong with you," he said calmly. "You've just been through a lot and you're injured."

"It is a cut." She wagged a hand at him. "You have two holes in your body and you are not going to pieces." No idea how it happened, but the next thing she knew, she was in his arms, crying into his shoulder.

"Hey, it's okay," he whispered, holding her. "We'll get it figured out."

"How?" she whined, ashamed of herself for doing it, so she pushed back. "Never mind. I . . . *Sto andando a pezzi*." Unable to look into those perfect eyes and see pity or disappointment, she pulled away and climbed into the Cruiser. "I should rest."

Achilles closed the door behind her, then walked around to the driver's side and sat behind the wheel.

Embarrassed at crying like a baby into his shoulder, Cove lay down on the bench seat, hands beneath her head. Exhausted, scared, and depleted, she was not sure how much more she could take. But he had taken plenty, had he not? She let her gaze drift to where he sat up front, noticed moonlight tracing the outline of his strong profile. "How do you do this? All alone."

Silence reigned for a long moment. "I remember what's at stake."

That pinched at her heart, made her think of Papà. "Your dad."

Exhaling, he leaned back against the headrest and folded his arms. "Yeah."

Hers had only been missing hours, and already she was falling apart worrying that he was dead. "How long have you been looking for him?"

"They declared him dead three years ago."

She lifted her head. "I thought he was alive."

"He *is*," he ground out, then dragged a hand over his mouth. As quiet returned in the surprisingly peaceful darkness, he huffed. "They say he's not. Gave him the full burial rights at Arlington, presented Mom with a flag, twenty-one gun salute—the works." He shook his head, staring out the windshield. "Never sat right. Small contradictions. No real answers. Facts not lining up."

"So, you do not believe them."

"No."

Her heart tugged at that, feeling a deep connection with him. "Like me with my papà. They say he did these terrible things, but I know Papà." Vehemence clenched her chest. "He would *never* do such a thing or be that monster."

"And you want my help to prove that."

She caught the hint of suspicion in the way he said that, but she would not let him off that easily. "As you want my money to find your dad."

He grunted.

Though it hurt that he did not agree or see the similarity, it was okay as long as they worked on this together. She could admit to needing the help of another, of someone capable. "So, now what?"

"We get rest."

"Is it dangerous to just . . . sit here?"

His silence proved unnerving as she lay there, staring at the back of the front passenger seat. "I wouldn't tell you to rest if it was dangerous."

Amazing the reassurance that gave Cove. But her mind was not ready to rest. "So, after sleep—what then?" Where would they go? Whose dad did they focus on first? "They took Papà, and your dad is . . ." She shifted her gaze to him. "Where would we start?"

"I know where my dad went missing, been there. No help."

She liked his definitive, determined answer. "What did you find in my papà's office?"

He peered back at her from the front. "What?"

"You broke in—"

"Technically, didn't break in," he said. "The whole house was wide open for the party."

She rolled her eyes. "Does that really appease your conscience?"

"Yes."

It amused her how casually he answered, never moving, his mouth barely shifting beneath that answer. "Did you find what you were after?"

He considered her, then looked out the windshield again. "I work with a . . . partner. With a USB I plugged in, he uploaded a root kit onto your dad's laptop so he could access everything on it. He's now trying to find out what your father knows about my dad."

"You really think he knows something?"

"Hope so."

"What was your plan after brea—doing that?"

He shrugged. "Been trying to figure that out." Again, he dragged his hand over his mouth and seemed to sag in the silence. "Honestly, the leads have been drying up . . ."

"So desperation had you enter the villain's lair."

Achilles gave her a scowl. "You call your dad a villain?"

"No," she balked with a disbelieving laugh. "But that is what *you* believe, no? That my papà is a villain?"

"I would not use that word," he said dully, "but your dad was with mine before he vanished."

Was there an accusation in those words? Or was she just feeling defensive of Papà? "How do you know he was?"

"A photo. Same location, same day as the explosion."

"What explosion?"

"The one they say evaporated my dad."

Cove fell silent, stunned at his words. "The American government has proof an explosion took your dad's life?"

"*Supposedly.*"

"And you . . ." She had to be careful—she was dependent on this man for survival and angering him would not help. His valuable skills were crucial to helping her stay alive. "You don't believe that because . . . ?"

"Just like you know your dad, I know mine." Challenge lit his words and eyes. "He's been doing ops for the better part of three decades now. Everything I know, he taught me." He stared forward, arms folded. "Besides, there was no body and no proof he was *in* the vehicle when the RPG hit. And your dad is still alive, so . . ."

She wanted to sit up, look him in the eyes, but her heart and head ached too much, thinking about her own father being dragged to that helicopter. It took a great level of audacity to go against the word of an entire government and military to find a father who could very well be dead. Their fathers had been together . . .

"What if—"

"Don't."

"But why would they say—"

"Is your dad guilty of paying the Houthis to clear out the Yemeni port to protect his interests there? Or what about—"

"Your point is taken." Annoyed he would shove that in her face, she tried to slow her racing heart. Not give in to the anger sprouting roots through her chest. But she couldn't argue it—he had a valid point. She could not prove her papà's innocence no matter how much she believed in him. "Do you think the men who took my papà killed him?"

Quiet seconds droned by without an answer, awakening a perilous alarm. He thought Papà dead? Had she lost both her parents now?

"No," finally came the deep rumble of his answer. "If they wanted him dead, they would've done it there. Not take him."

A fiery breath freed itself from her hold as relief staggered through her.

"Get some rest. I'll stand watch."

Considering him for a long second, she realized that even though he knew their fathers had met at some point, he did not argue about her defense of Papà. Even though the possibility— remote possibility—existed that Papà had been with his dad when he went missing.

But . . . what did that mean, that Papà had seen or been with this man before whatever happened? How would they find answers— or their dads? They had no clues. Only conviction. It all seemed so impossible. Weariness strangled her, sapped the strength from her limbs. She closed her eyes to prevent more tears. She had cried more today than she had in the last year.

Defeat pushed her into the greedy claws of sleep. Filled her dreams with vivid, cruel images of Papà dying, of a funeral overtaken by gunmen. Of her falling into a void where Mamma and Papà grasped to catch her but missed. And most bizarre—of her racing down a black corridor, holding hands with Achilles, then being trapped in a cistern and him kissing her with their final breaths.

Gunfire erupted.

Cove jerked upright with a shout, panic rending her sleep. Desperate for purchase on where she was, she searched the darkness. Sweating, gasping, she clutched at her chest and sat up, all the facts rushing at her like that nightmare.

Her gaze flicked to the driver's seat. "Achilles…" Her tired, bleary eyes searched the shadows… He… he wasn't there. Alarm jammed her spine straight and injected a blazing concoction of alarm and panic into her veins. "Achilles?" The plaintive desperation of how she called for him as she peered through the holes and cracks of the windshield made her pulse jump.

She shifted to the door and opened it. Eased out, listening—straining to hear him. His movement. "Achilles?" she whispered into the…

Wait. It was not dark. The realization drew her gaze up through the broken stable roof to where she saw— "Blue sky," she whispered, stunned. It was day.

How long had she slept? But more important—where was Achilles?

Why was there daylight and no Achilles?

Her heart jumped in her chest as she hurried around the truck, hand tracing its hood as she eyed the stalls and moldy, dirt-strewn watering trough at the end. "*Achilles!*" Cove crept along the stalls, peering into each one and finding nothing but mice, more dirt, and mold. She whirled around and returned to the truck. With each step as she hurried to the opposite end that had the large door that didn't quite close, she felt her control on her panic slipping.

He wasn't here. Which meant . . . "He left me." Somehow, speaking the words made them real. Ignited her fears. "He left." Why would he leave her?

Because you have nothing to offer.

That raw wound haunted her again. She had nothing to convince Brendan at uni to stick around. Nothing to recommend herself for the internship beyond good grades, which everyone had. With Papà missing, she had no access to anything that would be of benefit. No phone she could use, no money in hand—

"Money!" She pivoted and raced back to the Cruiser. Yanked open the door to grab the backpack. But . . . where was the backpack? She scoured the floorboard of both the front and middle rows. "*Santo cielo!*" Pivoting, she shoved the hair from her face. Pressed her heel to her hand. "That monster stole the money!" Looked in the back of the Cruiser, then again the front, as if another perusal would reveal some miracle she'd missed the first time.

Disbelief choked her. "You naïve, *foolish* girl!" She had trusted this man, put her life, heart, and money in his hands . . . And he'd disappeared. Left her in a stinking stable!

Though she couldn't blame him for leaving, she cursed her stupid, trusting self. With a growl, she fought tears and more panic. "*I* would not have left him behind, no matter how rude he was. Or how gorgeous." Hands on her waist, she squeezed her eyes shut to stave off the tears, and tilted her head back, looking at the sky. "I cannot believe he abandoned me!" She huffed, air struggling through her lungs. "That is what you get for trusting a gorgeous hunk."

Movement to the side startled her. Extracted a yelp when she saw someone standing just inside the stable door. "Achilles."

TWELVE

Outside Orvieto, Italy

ARMED WITH A BAG OF SCONES, WRAPPED sausage, and bacon, Dillon pushed himself toward her, not quite believing what he'd heard her say. When he reached her, he paused. Looked into her beautiful eyes. "I would never abandon you." He couldn't resist teasing her with a wink. "Even if you didn't find me gorgeous."

"I-I . . . you were gone."

Arching an eyebrow, he hoisted the bag. "Breakfast." He had to admit she was freakin' cute when riled, her mouth partially open, a pink stain in her cheeks. "Let's eat and get a game plan in place." He didn't want to exacerbate the issue by teasing her about that, even if it did irk him that she thought he'd just walk out and leave her . . . He had more character than that. And he was fed up with people discounting him.

Back in the Cruiser, he monitored her trek to the front passenger side, acknowledging the fact that despite what they'd been through—being shot at, on the run, and sleeping in a Land Cruiser, clothes smudged and bloodied—she looked great.

Once she climbed in and shut the door, he used napkins to set out a scone for each, along with bacon and sausage, then handed her a bottled water.

"Where did you get all this?" Her gaze narrowed. "Did you steal it?" she asked in her accented English.

The words hit with the force of a two-ton nuclear device. "Are you kidding me?"

"Then where did you get it?"

Yeah, not so beautiful now. "After all I've done, protected you from—can't you believe in me for longer than two seconds?"

She did not back down. "You would ask the same thing if our roles were reversed."

"No, I wouldn't." Ticked, he drew in a breath to calm down. "While you were sawing logs, I hiked out and found a farm. Offered to do some chores in exchange for food. The old lady—Signora Barbieri—appreciated it," he bit out, gauging her expression and glad when she seemed to regret her accusation. "Her husband died last month and her son bailed, so she was glad for a strong back to help with chores."

Eyeing the food, Cove swallowed. Looked chagrined. "But your wounds . . ."

"Ache a little, but I'm good." Even though it was nice to see some contrition from her, Dillon wouldn't rub it in her face. He'd heard that rant, the sheer panic and fear in her voice—legit terror.

"*Perdonami*," she said quietly. "I . . . I . . ."

He really wished he spoke Italian, but that sounded like an apology. "I get it. You thought I'd left you and it frightened you."

"No!" Her eyes widened, then she dipped her head, picking at the scone. "Yes."

Dillon paused and let his frustration settle. Stared out the front windshield, knowing they had to find common ground. Understand they were in this thing together. He'd had time to think while searching out food. He put a hand on hers, which brought those gold orbs up. "This is a team effort, Gelato. And that means we have to make a decision right now to trust each other. If we don't, neither of us will get what we want—proof about our dads." He recalled too late that she didn't like the nickname, but thankfully, she didn't object. "We'll figure it out."

A wisp of a smile ghosted her expression.

"But I have to ask you a question."

Wariness barged into that near-smile.

"I want you to answer honestly . . ."

She stilled, looking pale.

"Am I more gorgeous than Flavio?"

Cove laughed and tossed a piece of scone at him. "Maybe," she conceded and added a rueful smile, "but entirely more full of yourself."

"Fair." He liked hearing her laugh, seeing a smile brighten her eyes, and held her gaze for a long second. "Guess I'll have to work on that."

As if trying to hide her smile, she pinched off a piece of scone and put it in her mouth, then eyed him again. "I'm sorry I accused you of stealing . . ."

Dillon wanted to blow it off, but that had been a sharp blow against his honor. "I get why you might think that, but it's not who I am." He took a bite of his scone, thinking. "In the two years I've been on the lam, searching for my dad, I've only stolen once. And it"—he shook his head—"seared my conscience."

"It is incredible that you've managed this long like that. How have you . . . ?"

"Rules," he said, then guzzled water to wash down the too-dry scone. Give him a donut or biscuit any day of the year, but these in-betweens were tough to choke down.

"What rules?"

He inhaled the rest of his water and capped it back off. "There are several. One is . . . Reciprocity: Do something nice for someone, and most people will want to return the favor."

She chewed slowly, then lifted her food. "Like the chores and scones." After another bite, she nodded at him. "What is another?"

"Likeability: People want to work with people they like, so being nice, being friendly, goes a long way in convincing people to let you in."

"This feels . . . jaded. Does that not mean you're working people?"

He sniffed and stared out the cracked and hole-riddled windshield. "Everyone works someone. When you called people to set up that gala in Paris, were you nice to them? Or did you just order them around, demanding what you wanted?"

"That is . . . not fair. I was being professional."

He cracked a smile. "You were working a well-known fact that being nice gets you farther than being demanding. It's not wrong or mercenary."

She wrinkled her nose and chewed more of the scone. "I suppose . . . But it still feels wrong."

"Because you have a good heart."

At that, she eyed him speculatively. "Is this you being likeable . . . to get me to do something?"

Man, he hated that Cove felt she couldn't trust him.

She touched his bicep. "I . . . that was a bad joke."

"I know we just met, so you don't know, but—character, honor, integrity? They're my foundation stones." He tossed the scone back into the bag, no appetite for it. "Yes, I've broken some laws like entering countries illegally, but . . . it's the only way I'm finding my dad. I'll pay for this eventually, but . . . I'm not . . . corrupt."

"I know that," she said softly. "I really do. You have shown a lot of integrity and honor since our paths collided in my papà's office. I trust you, Achilles."

Yeah, so much for that trust you're touting. Should he tell her his real name?

Going soft wouldn't get his dad back.

After drinking some water, she put the lid back on and set it aside. "So . . . what is next?"

"Dillon." He tightened his jaw and slowly met her gaze. "My name's Dillon."

There was nothing like a Northern Virginia sunrise and the moment the hazy blue of dusk surrendered to the gold and pink of dawn. And that, *that* was exactly what it felt like when Cove smiled at him just then.

"Nice to meet you, Dillon."

He was stupid but he would pay her to say his name again. It felt right. Good. And it'd been ages since he'd heard his name spoken.

She held his gaze for a long second, then sighed. "Thank you. I understand the gift you handed me—not just your name, but your trust." A smile caressed her fair features and stained her cheeks. "I do not take it lightly."

Crazy, the way his gut heated at her soft words. "Neither do I." Because it was colossally dumb. Wreckless. He cleared his throat. "As for what's next . . . first thing is that Signora Barbieri said to bring her the truck and she'd let us take her sedan."

Cove faltered. "Why would we—"

"Bullet holes."

"Wait—so you told her . . . *everything*?"

"I'm American. In a remote Italian countryside. She'd already heard about the attack on the villa and the gunmen who shot up the Galtieri estate. It's a small area, smaller than I realized," Dillon explained, chagrined. "I didn't say anything, but she did. I think we should take her up on it—driving around in a vehicle full of bullet holes is only going to draw attention."

She didn't seem sure.

"Up to you, since this is your dad's," he said, not wanting her to feel like he was ordering her, "but it makes sense. Also, if she saw you, I think it would ease her mind that I wasn't lying."

"You told her about me?"

At her incredulousness, he huffed a laugh and shook his head. "I told you—the signora knew it all. That your dad was taken, that you were missing. Wanted to know what I'd done with you, threatened me with the pitchfork before letting me use it to feed the pigs."

"Oh." She scrunched up her face. "I accused you again."

Yeah . . . she had.

"You're right, Dillon. It's a good plan."

"It's the start of a plan," he amended. "The signora said there were lots of black vehicles heading toward the villa, so once we trade vehicles, I think we need to get out of the immediate area. Maybe even the country."

"I have my passport."

"For obvious reasons, I don't have one on me, so we have to take less direct, *un*official routes to wherever we're going next."

Her eyes brightened. "Mykonos!"

Dillon frowned. "Do what?"

"It's in the Greek Isles."

"I know where it is, but what does that have to do with us?"

"My uncle lives there."

Not really sure he wanted to be mixing it up with more of her family, Dillon figured they could sort that as they made their way out of the country. "Hang tight." He got out and opened the stable door, then returned. They drove up the road a good ten minutes before he turned onto a dirt road and pulled to a stop at a small stucco-and-stone home. By the time he cut the engine, he spotted the signora coming around the side of the house.

"Should I offer her money?" Cove asked. "Oh. Where is the backpack?"

"Under my seat. But she suggested the trade, so no money. We need to be smart with what little we have." He cocked his head toward the woman. "Don't tell her too much. Just enough that she won't worry. Or call the police."

When they climbed out, he received a warm, almost exuberant greeting. "Hello."

Signora Barbieri lifted both arms with a broad smile. "You come back!"

He indicated toward Cove. "This is Signorina Galtieri, as promised."

"*Salve, signora,*" Cove said as she smiled and drew closer. "*Sono Cove Galtieri.*"

"*Bene, bene. Sono Guilia Barbieri. Ho incontrato tuo padre una volta. Molti anni fa. Un bell'uomo.*"

Dillon hesitated, watching as the two women chatted quickly and completely in Italian. *Please . . . please don't tell her we're going to Greece.*

"*Hai trovato un bell'americano, vero?*"

Had the signora said American? That must be about him . . .

Cove gave him a speculative glance, a coy smile parked on her pink lips. "*Sì, abbastanza.*"

"*È uno dei bravi. Tienilo stretto.*"

"*Questo è il mio piano.*"

Okay, she said something about a piano. Which made no sense. But then the signora handed Cove some keys and pointed behind the house. They walked around there and found a one-car garage.

"She says her late husband bought the car. It is old." She indicated to the double door on the garage, and they both grabbed a handle and drew back.

"If it can last us long enough to get out of the—" Dillon stopped short as he stared at the vehicle lurking in the shadows of the small garage. He chortled a laugh, circling the car. "This is an Alfa Romeo Stelvio!" He covered his mouth. But then he felt the enormity of what the older woman offered. Knew this was wrong. "This can't . . ."

"What is wrong?"

"This can't be right. Nobody would hand strangers the key to *this*."

"She said it does not get used. That—" Her cheeks went pink.

"What?"

Clearing her throat, she drew in a breath. "She said young lovers should enjoy it."

Dillon coughed a laugh. "You corrected her, right?"

"I was so stunned I could not figure out what to say."

"You remember to tell your dad that so he does not kill me." He considered the car again and could not stop the grin. "Maybe we should go before she changes her mind."

They climbed in and Cove passed him the keys to the luxury sedan.

Dillon shook his head, still disbelieving this was happening. "My dad will be so jealous . . ."

As they pulled around the front, Signora Barbieri waved them to stop. Arms full, she sauntered over and passed them a basket of bread, fruit, and cheese.

"*Grazie, signora. Sei troppo gentile,*" Cove said, then said something else in Italian.

The woman reached into the car, and Dillon caught her hand, which she squeezed tight, then eyed Cove with a devious gleam. "*Sposa questa ragazza o te ne pentirai.*"

"Oh." Cove's eyes widened and she started. "*Grazie, signora.*" Her smile was weak, awkward.

Not sure what he'd missed, Dillon nodded. "Yes, thank you. *Grazie.*"

The woman backed away and waved as they left her property.

"What did she say? You looked alarmed."

"I . . . I, uh, nothing. It was just an Italian pleasantry."

A standard pleasantry panicked or alarmed her? Yeah, he wasn't buying that.

Cove set the basket on the back seat as they hit the main road. "So, I was thinking that we should drive down to Pescara—it's about a three-hour drive. My papà has a couple of boats docked there, and we can use one to get to Mykonos."

Was she changing the subject? "Do you know how to get to Pescara?"

"I do." She gave him instructions and they headed that way. A while later, she tugged her backpack onto her lap. "And . . . do not get angry, okay?"

Dillon gave her a sidelong look. "Don't like the sound of that. Can't put any bets on my anger until I know why you're saying that."

"When I was the house, I . . . I had to get something that I think is part of proving my papà's innocence." With that, she drew out a tall, black something . . . device? Looked like a sleeve. "It's a Faraday bag—with my phone."

THIRTEEN

ARE YOU SERIOUS RIGHT NOW?" HE FISTED his hand and banged it against the steering wheel, furious she had defied him. "I told you—two conditions—"

"My dad has several of these. They work. My phone cannot be tracked. But I also turned off the Wi-Fi, GPS, and tracking at the house."

"Holy fire. What're you thinking, Gelato?" He ran a hand over his shorn hair, panic growing thick, deep roots in his gut.

"Are you even listening? Or are you just in panic mode?"

"After all I've done to make sure we're safe . . . of all the . . . I cannot believe you'd do that." Doing his best to stifle the rage—and dig into that trust he'd been so cavalier about earlier—he eyed the protective sleeve. *Breathe. Breathe.* "You're sure that thing works?"

"Of course. My papà uses them. Has several in the house for various devices."

Dillon pulled the car over and nailed the passenger side window control. "Toss it. Do it!"

"No! You are being ridiculous!" Cove yanked the phone away from his reach. "Look, I did not have to tell you—and I am starting to wish I had not. But this is the only thing I have with any semblance of—"

"You're going to have *nothing* if they track us—and they will because this thing with your dad and mine? It's bigger than some thug with a grudge. They'll find us, kill us, then destroy that. Is that what you want?"

"Of course not. But it is safe. I promise." She set a hand on his forearm. "Trust me, Dillon."

"I wish I'd never told you my name."

"Why?" Hurt plagued her word.

"Because."

"You asked me to trust you going into the tunnel, going back to the house . . . And now I am asking for trust too."

He muttered an oath. Hated himself for cursing, but he had this jacked feeling they were about to have trouble breathing down their necks. "You broke one of the Rules, Gelato."

"Which one?"

"Unity." He thumped the steering wheel again and slumped back with a huff. "We do things together, talk about them. Agree on them. I can't protect us from what I don't know about."

"Is that the same unity that had you leaving me in the Land Cruiser while you went in search of food and found Signora Barbieri's house?"

"You were sleeping," he said miserably.

Her brow winged up as she gave him a strange look.

"You needed the rest," he defended himself and pulled back onto the road.

She touched his arm, something she seemed to do a lot—he wasn't mad—and eased closer. "Please take this as my trying to be open and honest with you. I could have hidden it, but it was eating at me. And I was afraid you would find it and think the worst of me. But . . . I cannot throw it away, Dillon. It is all I have—there is a video on here of the warehouse."

He stretched his jaw, even as she signaled him onto the access of the autostrada. Man, he could not stay mad at her, even when she seemed to deliberately lay a trap for a diversionary discussion. "What warehouse?" he made himself ask.

"I'm glad you asked," she said softly with a mischievous grin.

Rolling his eyes, he knew he was in trouble. Had to harden that protective cover around his heart because this woman could probably ask him to jump off a cliff and he'd do it.

"Two and a half years ago," she began as they merged onto A1/E35, "I was in Yemen with my papà. GIS was building warehouses down there. Even then, I did not trust Enzo. I overheard him talking on the phone, saying something about weapons."

Dillon frowned at that, recalling the Houthi rumor with getting those warehouses up a year ago.

"That was my reaction too," she said. "So that night, when I spotted him leaving the resort, I trailed him."

"You don't value your life much, do you?"

Cove gave him a disapproving glare.

"Did you miss that they were talking about weapons?"

"Did *you* miss the part where I am still alive, so I clearly survived?"

"You're trouble, Gelato."

She gave an exasperated sigh. "*Santo cielo*, would you let me tell you the story?"

Amused at how worked up she got, Dillon had to fight the smirk.

"I followed them," she ground out, "and it was . . . crazy. I took photos and a video on my phone of who went in and who came out. There was an explosion—"

That yanked his gaze to her again.

"Yes, see? Things got pretty crazy, but nothing came back on

GIS or Papà. In fact," she said, quirking her head, "nothing came of anything."

"So, you don't know why he went to the warehouse? Or what the explosion was?"

"No. It was all so terrifying—so much I did not understand. It scared me. I was too afraid of being caught, that maybe it would come back on Papà."

"So what was happening in the warehouse?"

Her gaze went distant. "I . . . do not know. But later, that's when the reports of corruption tied to Yemen started happening."

"And your dad didn't know about this meeting?" Was he supposed to believe that?

"They were not on his books—I handled those, so I know."

"Like I said, things like that wouldn't be on appointment planners."

"True, Papà did not know about the meeting. He was there later. I have it all on my phone."

Dillon couldn't believe he was going to say this . . . "If we can find a place to power up that phone securely, I'd like to see those images or video." When she didn't answer, he glanced at her. Found her smiling. "What?"

"Nothing," she said quietly. "I would like your thoughts on what I recorded. From a military, tactical standpoint. I . . . just have this feeling about them."

After a few more highway changes and another 1.5 hours, they made it to the port in Pescara, where Cove directed them to a dock. They grabbed her backpack and the remnants of the food Signora Barbieri prepared for them, and walked down the dock.

"I do not think it wise to use the yacht," Cove said, squinting back at him as she led him onward. "The *Ilaria* is probably better. It still has GPS, though."

FOURTEEN

Pescara, Italy

IT HAD BEEN A LONG TIME SINCE SHE'D BEEN on the *Ilaria*, but even seeing it listing next to the speedboats and sailboats made her heart soar, recalling happier times. When Mamma was still alive. Cove plodded down to it, feeling an excitement she'd all but forgotten. "Here we are." Stopped at the speed cruiser, she smiled back at Dillon. "Do you know how to drive a cruiser?"

Dark eyes took in the boat, then her. "Do you people know how to do anything small?"

She shrugged. "*Ad maiora.*"

He frowned. "What is—"

"Toward greater things," she explained. "It is an expression that means you wish someone bigger, greater success—always toward bigger things." She cocked her head toward the cruiser and stepped from the dock onto the transom. Passed through the kitchenette on the right and the L-shaped seating arrangement on the left— where she deposited her backpack—and headed to the safe by the cockpit. Accessed it with the code, then retrieved the key.

"And this is the *small* boat?"

She grinned at him standing just inside the saloon, gaping. "Papà bought a superyacht from a Saudi prince when I was at boarding school. But it requires a crew and staff, so I thought that might be risky."

Dillon walked closer, shaking his head in disbelief. "We are from very different worlds, Gelato."

Catching her lower lip between her teeth, she felt this tug in her chest at that comment. She did not like that he was putting a gap between them. "And yet, we fight the same battle, Dillon." She moved to the cockpit and used the key to power up. "There are two cabins below," she said, pointing to the opaque hatch to her left that led belowdecks. "And ahead—toilet and shower."

As she worked the instruments, he joined her at the helm, peering out through the windshield. "How far to your uncle's house?"

"It will take a full day, give or take . . ."

"And this thing has enough gas?"

After checking the instruments, she nodded, then cast off from the dock. "It does." Back at the helm, she eased the boat from the slip.

"Do you have to notify a dockmaster or something?"

She pursed her lips and gave a one-shouldered shrug. "It's not busy. They like you to give notice as a courtesy—mostly to be sure there are slips available upon return—but they've never hassled anyone here." It felt good to be back on the water, though it also made her miss Mamma again. She sensed his gaze on her and looked up at him. Liked the way his gaze took her in, assessing. "Surprised I know how to drive it?"

"Impressed," he admitted, lowering himself to the leather sofa curving near the captain's seating. "Did your dad teach you?"

"My uncle," she said. "Zio Santino and my mamma were practically raised on the water. We would leave the villa and holiday down in Mykonos every summer."

Dillon snorted. "And here I was impressed my uncles—who aren't even really my uncles—took me out on the Potomac for fishing on their little dinghy."

She accelerated, slowly increasing speed as they put distance between them and Pescara. "Who were they?"

"Huh?"

"You said they weren't really your uncles . . ."

"Ah." He leaned back, the water sparkling against his dark eyes. "My dad was part of a military team. Very tight. He didn't have any siblings. Mom has a brother, but our family came from the team—they were my uncles and aunts." He met her gaze for a second. "That's where Achilles came from."

"So it *was* your name."

"Callsign. The team dubbed their kids the Scions and gave each of us a name to maintain operational security. Protect their kids."

"So, the other Scions," she said, hesitating over the name, "they are like cousins?"

He bobbed his head. "I guess. To me, they're brothers and sisters."

"How many Scions were there?" She really liked that he was talking to her, sharing and opening up about his life and past. He had been so uptight, mysterious. But she supposed the way they were running for their lives created a bond, changed the dynamics.

"Ten, besides me."

"You are close?"

Nodding, he watched the coastline.

A jealous thought squirmed through her. "Girls?"

His gaze flicked to hers. He held it for a long second. "Yeah."

"And you are close . . ."

"Already answered that."

She hated herself for the jealousy that she could not overcome. The thought of him having a female friend that he was close to . . .

"That is nice." It was not—not at all. Because it did not make sense that a girl might be close to him and not have other feelings too. One only had to look at him or be around him for two seconds to know he was incredible.

They fell into silence over the next hour, ate one of the loaves and some cheese from Signora Barbieri.

"You said there's a shower . . . ?"

She pointed to the hatch. "Down and on the right. You might even see if any of Papà's shirts fit you. And there is a washing machine down there too."

He nodded but didn't move. "You good up here on your own?"

She smiled, liking that he asked. "Yes, I am fine."

Dillon vanished belowdecks and left her to her thoughts. She itched to check her phone, but she would not violate his trust. He had been so angry when he realized she'd brought it, but she could not risk losing it. If she had not locked it up during the party—a practice Papà had insisted on for many years so no one would spy on him and his guests—the men who had taken him might have found it. Taken it, too, or worse, destroyed it.

He emerged a half hour later in one of Papà's polo shirts and a pair of board shorts. Mercy, even his calves were well-muscled. "Put my clothes in the washing machine." He cocked his head to the lower deck. "You want to shower?"

"I do," she said, then glanced around the instrumentation.

He hovered, looking nervous. "I have no idea what to do . . ."

Cove stood, shifting aside to squeak past him. "It is on cruise assist, so you do not have to do anything. Speed and GPS course are set. Only trouble might be other vessels." She scanned the Adriatic Sea. "Should not be a problem."

Acutely aware of how close he stood to her, she recalled him holding her when she had fallen apart last night. It had been very nice. "Okay. I will be back."

Showering the dirt and grime off herself felt so good—save the minor pinch of pain from the glass cut at the back of her head. Cove slipped into a tank top and lounge pants. She grabbed a hoodie since the waters got cold at night, then searched for a scrunchie or hair tie but came up empty.

Back topside, she smiled at him standing by the wheel, uncertain but seemingly at home. "You survived your first turn at the helm," she said, braiding her hair so it would not get tangled in the sea air. "The Scions would be proud."

"You mocking me?"

She scrunched her nose. "Maybe a little." She plodded over to the cabinets and found protein bars and noodle packets. "Want something to eat?"

"I'm good."

Protein bar in hand, she sat on the curved sofa and drew up a leg and opened the packaging. "I was thinking, since it is a long trip and you did not sleep last night, you should go down and get some rest."

"I'm good."

She frowned at him. "Not true. You might be superhuman, but you are not immortal. Bodies require rest." She wagged her bar at him. "You have bags under your eyes."

Dillon considered her and the offer, and he seemed to need some encouragement to go ahead and rest.

"Go on. I will be okay," she said, taking a bite of the bar. "There is quite literally nothing to do for the next twenty-something hours but sit or sleep."

He indicated to the sofa in the saloon. "I can sleep there." He stretched out on the leather cushions, grabbed one of the waterproof decorative pillows, and soon snored so loud it vied for dominance with the engines.

Cove peered back over the small serving station at him and smiled. To sleep that hard told her he trusted her, let his body relax that much. As the sun went down, so did the temperatures. It was soon quite cool, so she slipped on the hoodie. When she checked on him next, he had huddled, arms crossed. Cold.

She hustled down to her cabin, snagged a blanket, and returned topside. Afraid to wake him, she gently laid the blanket on him. Stood over him, appreciating the view. Thankful that he had been there during the attack. That he had protected her, guided her . . . "Thank you," she whispered, then returned to the helm.

No matter what he said, he *had* broken into Papà's office. And she had never been so glad for a criminal act or its perpetrator.

FIFTEEN

Ionian Sea

A DISTANT SCRAPING LURED DILLON FROM A deep sleep. Vision blurry, he struggled to get his bearings. The world felt...odd. Off, like it was...moving. He jerked upright, his location coming into sharp focus. The speed cruiser. Daylight.

Holy fire, had he really slept all night?

His gaze tracked the saloon, helm—she wasn't there. A *shink* yanked his attention to the galley. Cove stood with her back to him, preparing something. "Why didn't you wake me?"

She looked over her shoulder and smiled. "*Buongiorno.*"

He pushed to his feet and crossed to join her. "Why'd you let me sleep all night?"

Cutting Signora Barbieri's bread, she kept working. Smeared jam on the bread. "You needed it. You let me sleep the night before."

"But you need rest too."

"I will—tonight when we are in Mykonos." She held up a slice of jam-slathered bread. "Here. Breakfast."

Irritated that she'd let him sleep, that he'd been a slacker and left her to stand watch all night . . . "You should've woken me."

"*Va bene*," she said, lifting a shoulder, then folded a piece of bread in her mouth.

"It's not fair." He felt wrecked, despite sleeping.

She, on the other hand, looked amazing with her tussled hair and the morning sun glowing softly against her golden skin. She chewed, wiped the corner of her mouth, then smiled mischievously at him. "I might have dozed a time or two."

"*What?*"

"For a little while," she said with a small shrug. "Not long. I was sitting there watching the moon on the water, but then I jolted awake."

"You realize—"

"Dillon." She set her hands on his chest and leaned in for emphasis. "Nothing happened. We are okay."

Heart thundering at their close proximity, the warmth of her hands seeping through the polo shirt, he faltered, mouth suddenly dry.

"You worry too much."

"And you don't worry enough." As annoyed as he was over her not waking him, over her falling asleep too, he knew they were both exhausted from the last thirty hours.

"So, we make a good pair." Her eyes widened. "I . . ."

Fire in his gut told him to kiss the dot of jelly from her lower lip. And common sense would smack him all the way back to the States.

"I did not mean . . . you know."

He needed to step off before he did something stupid.

The ship swelled upward.

They braced themselves using the counter as an anchor. The *Ilaria* canted. Pitched Cove into him. He caught her, too aware of the curve of her hip and waist as he steadied her.

She laughed when the ship rose again, pulled her away then urged her back to him.

Good night, she was amazing and beautiful. He loved when she laughed. But then . . . he sobered. And so did she. Her gaze dipped, depriving him of those gold orbs, glittering beneath the glow of the rising sun. Desperate to see her eyes again, he hooked a finger below her chin.

Those full, pink lips parted and he felt her stiffen.

Dillon decided to take the kiss, homed in. No more missed opp—

The *Ilaria* dove sharp, slamming her face toward his.

Pain exploded across his mouth. He tasted blood. Even as she yelped in pain, Dillon jerked back, holding on to the counter, heel of his hand to his busted lip, the swelling almost immediate.

Serves you right, idiot.

She cupped a hand over her forehead where it'd connected with his jaw, brows tangled in concern. "*Mi dispiace tanto!*" Looking mortified, she grabbed a napkin and thrust it at him. "Are you okay?"

He bent toward the sink and flipped it on. Ran the water and rinsed his mouth. Son of a buttered biscuit. Man, he was a piece of work. Gave her his name, let her keep the phone, slept all night while on watch, and now this.

I'm going to get us killed.

Then he'd never find his dad. He had to get his head in the game, or everyone he cared about would pay. Napkin to his lip, he turned himself back to the sofa and sat down, noting the waves had miraculously calmed down. Guess even God was trying to tell him to get in line.

"I am so sorry, Dillon," Cove said, coming over to him. She winced. "I, uh—we do not have ice or an ice pack in the kit." Worry creased those beautiful eyes. "I am sorry. Is it bad . . . ?"

Yeah. It was bad. *He* was bad. "I'm fine." He was the one who should be apologizing. But he couldn't even bring himself to admit what he'd just attempted.

Only then did he realize she'd gone quiet. Staring at the deck. She covered her mouth, and in his periphery, he saw tears slipping free.

Dillon set a hand to her leg before he could stop himself. "Hey, it's not worth the tears." *I'm not worth the tears.* "We've had a long couple days. It's okay." But it wasn't. Not if he didn't correct course fast.

Sniffling, she wiped her face and sat back against the seat. "It is all hitting me."

He nodded, understanding. "It's a lot . . ."

"I do not know how you have done this for two and a half years." She scoffed. "I would have lost my head—I *am* losing my head." She wilted and rubbed her forehead. "It has only been two days since they took Papà, and already, I fear I will be too late."

Able to appreciate that sentiment, Dillon sat back. "You can't think like that," he said, feeling the pinch of pain at his lip from speaking. The throb and thickness made him not want to talk much. "It's self-defeating."

"I just keep seeing him fall on the grass, them dragging him . . ."

"Focus on the men who dragged him away. Take that fear and funnel it into determination and a bit of anger to drive you to the end." He eased forward and swiveled to face her. "After the funeral for my dad, that's what I had to do. I was going ape, sitting around listening to Mom and my sister cry."

"You have a sister?"

He faltered, surprised at himself for giving that away. Normally didn't talk about family. But she was safe, right? "Yeah, and a brother. Anyway—you take those things that seek to paralyze you and turn them into fuel to drive you to the answers you're after. How you respond is completely in your hands. Choose to make it work for you rather than control you."

She gave him a smile, drew her feet up onto the seat, and slouched into them. "I have a lot to learn from you."

Heart thudding, Dillon realized nobody had ever said that to him. He had always been the one learning. But that . . . that's what he'd wanted from his dad. Always yearned to hear. Yet . . . it worried him, for her to learn anything from him. He hadn't found his dad, and it'd been nearly three years. "Not sure that's a good thing. I'm just winging my way through this."

She chewed her lower lip. "How did you make the connection between our fathers?"

"Dad was the leader of his team," he said quietly, remembering back to that time. "His death rocked our worlds. One of my Scion brothers, Helios, and I overheard a couple dads talking, saying it felt unrealistic. They had doubts, but there wasn't anything actionable. So Helios has a knack for white-hat hacking, and he started digging. He spent—I don't know how many hours trolling every site and social media platform for any sign of my dad."

"Social media?" she balked. "Did he think your dad would post something?"

"Nah, but everyone has a phone camera these days, and Helios knows how to exploit that. Terrorists love to tout victories. Most people have zero security on their phone and have tracking turned on. They don't even know that a photo is geotagged to the exact location it was taken. You'd be surprised how many people are completely unaware that exists. Or they think it's great to drop a friend a pin for a meet-up or if your phone gets lost. But it's a op-sec nightmare if someone wants to hunt you down. One forgotten setting leaves a wide-open door."

"And where were our dads together?"

"From what I've been able to discern from the image, Yemen."

Her lips parted. "No wonder you gave me that look when I talked about Yemen."

He had? "Shortly after Paris, a picture surfaced that showed my dad looking pretty messed up, walking into a luxury resort in Tanzania."

"What was he doing there?"

"That is the question," he said with a heaving breath. "By the time I got down there, nobody who worked back then was still on staff. They reviewed the footage with me—my dad goes down a rear hall with a manager, but he's never seen again."

"So, if he was there, then why do you say my papà was the last person to see him alive? I mean, logically, the picture of them was taken before the resort, yes?"

"Yeah, clearly—the picture was in Yemen, the resort in Tanzania. Footage shows my dad wearing the same clothes he had on in that picture with your dad."

Brow furrowed, she fell silent.

"By the time my dad made it to the resort, he also had a black eye and cuts on his face. Those clothes that were fine with your dad were then torn and dirty. He looked like he'd had a fight with a lawnmower."

She lowered her feet and shifted to the edge of the seat, hugging herself. "And this was . . . how long ago?"

"Almost three years ago."

Cove paled. She stood and paced the small saloon/galley area. "Do you think that night with Enzo . . . ?" Blinking, she shook her head. "But I . . . I was with my papà in Yemen on that trip. And I knew everyone he met."

His heart jarred. "So, you're saying I'm lying?" A trickle of anger spilled into his veins, bringing him to his feet to meet the challenge.

"No!" She sliced a hand in his direction, coming up short when she realized he stood before her. "It is only . . . I was there, Dillon. Papà and I went to every meeting together because he was teaching me the business."

Yet *she* wasn't in the photo . . . Dillon frowned, recalling something. "Didn't you mention that you left the hotel to follow this Enzo guy?"

She drew up a bit and her lips parted. "I did . . ."

"Could your dad have met with mine while you were gone?"

"I suppose . . ." Her bright eyes flicked to his. "That was clearly a busy night with all that happened."

"Wait—night?"

She faltered. "It was after a dinner."

Hope collapsed. "That photo of our dads wasn't taken at night."

"And you are sure it was Yemen."

"Wasn't until I went down to check things out. Can't tell exactly where they were, because of fencing, but I could see structures in the background."

"Okay," she said quietly, pacing and thinking. "I really wish I could see this picture."

"Once I can get on a secure computer, I'll show you."

"Good. What else was in the picture?"

He leaned back against the galley counter. "They were standing about a dozen paces from a silver SUV—I matched the model to a 2023 Lexus." Mentally, he stared at the photo. "My dad was closer to the person who took the photo—that was one Helios tracked down. Guy was a dockworker, but he's dead now, so I can't ask him about what he saw and photographed. Your dad was farther away, in profile with his head down. Took me nearly a year to identify him—and I only made the connection because I was in Armenia tailing a Russian said to be linked to that dock in Yemen."

"*Armenia*?" she balked. "*Santo cielo*, how many countries have you searched?"

"Too many."

A big yawn stole her breath, quelling the conversation for a moment. "I still think—" Another yawn interrupted her.

Why hadn't he thought to tell her to rest before now? "Hey, we have hours still—why don't you get some sleep?"

"But you do not know how to drive the cruiser."
"You said the cruiser was on assist, right?"
Cove glanced to the helm, considering the offer. "Yes . . ."
"And that's sort of like autopilot?"
She smiled. "After a fashion."
"Then go—sleep. If anything funky happens, I'll wake you."

SIXTEEN

Aegean Sea

COVE."

In the dregs of sleep, she struggled to pull her mind from the heavy sluggishness. "Mm?"

"Cove. Need you topside. There's ships . . ."

Cobwebs evaporated from her mind, pulling her upright and reminding her she was on the *Ilaria* headed to Mykonos. She hustled off the bed and climbed to the upper deck. Only as she slipped into the captain's chair did she realize it was dark. Shaking the dullness from her mind, she looked at Dillon, who was staring out the windshield. "You let me sleep too long."

"You know what they say about payback," he said with a smirk.

She checked the instruments. "We are only a few minutes from the dock," she murmured, disbelieving the coastline and the GPS. Which meant she'd slept for more than eight hours. "Disappointing—you won't see the house as well at night." She guided the boat to the dock.

"You kidding me?" Dillon said, peering up the flight of white wood steps that scaled the rocky incline of the island.

"Too small for you?" she teased as she brought it alongside. "Can you hop onto the dock and tie us off?"

"Sure." He stepped out onto the transom.

Realizing he was readying to jump, she strangled a shout. "I meant—"

He went airborne, leaping from the boat to the dock. Agile, graceful, he made the six feet seem like nothing.

The *Ilaria* tapped the edge. She cut the engine, hustled back, and tossed him a rope. As he secured it, she grabbed the backpack. They hiked up the thirty steps to the lower terrace of Zio Santi's house that had a bamboo roof and small firepit, then banked right and conquered another fifteen steps. She knew—having counted them as a little girl. She wound back along the ever-rising path.

"Holy fire," Dillon whispered, then let out a low whistle as they headed past the infinity pool up to the half-dozen stone steps to the covered patio. "This place could make me wish I was rich."

"You see why I loved spending holiday here?"

"Def." Dillon stalked up behind her, glancing around. "Interior lights are off."

"He could be asleep . . ." At the double glass doors, she rapped on them. "Zio Santi?" Using the keypad, she entered the code and heard the lock disengage. They slipped inside and she turned on the lights. Travertine flooring and the beige couches were the only touch of color in the sitting room. She moved through it to check the dining room with its bank of windows, the kitchen, the master suite. All dark and empty. "Huh." She wandered back to Dillon, who stood, hands tucked under his armpits. "I think . . ." She frowned at the way he stood there, hunched. "You okay?"

"Yeah . . . just afraid I'll break something and end up an indentured servant to pay it off."

Cove laughed. "And you weren't worried in my papà's villa?"

"Guess it had a warmer vibe."

"Well, get comfortable," she said, as the phone on the counter started ringing. A second later, an old-school recording started. "You want to come back here? I'll show you which room—"

"*Buonasera*, Ilaria."

She whipped back to the kitchen island and hovered over the machine. "It's him—my *zio*."

"Saw your access code come through on my phone," he said quietly through the machine. "I got a call about what happened at *Vigneto Corallo* and your father missing, so ironically, I'm here at the villa. I've just had a good chat with Signora Barbieri, and Signore Giordano called. Stay there, safe."

Oh mercy, had she told *zio* about loaning the car to Cove and Dillon?

"Pick it up," Dillon said, his tone urgent.

"Why?"

"He can't tell anyone where you are." He grabbed the phone and handed it to her.

Seeming to understand, she hit a button, putting it on speaker, and interrupted her uncle. "Zio?"

Her *zio*'s breath stalled.

Afraid he'd use her name in front of someone, she rushed on. "Please do not say my name."

"*Va bene*."

Relieved at his agreement, she continued. "Zio, I need you not to tell anyone where I am. They were looking for me."

A long pause gaped between them for a second. "Understood. Once I get things secured here, I'll head home. And tell the young man I can see . . . everything. *Buonasera, Lupina*."

"*Buonasera*." She eyed Dillon, feeling heat in her cheeks.

"Protective uncle," Dillon grunted.

"He is," she said with a smile.

"Guess we're on our own then."

She nodded, swallowing. Thinking of Zio Santi at the villa, what it must look like . . . "I was a witness . . . Should I have returned to tell the authorities what happened?"

"You were a *target*," Dillon corrected firmly. "Staying there was not an option. Especially if you want to find your dad."

"I suppose you are right . . ."

He bobbed his head down the hall. "Show me the room, then . . . does your uncle have a computer here?"

A smile flicked through her. "He's an investment banker. He has several, and they're all secure and in a room that is basically a giant Faraday cage."

"A SCIF. Cool."

She headed down the hall and opened a door. "This is yours."

Dillon slipped past her into the white, linen-decorated room. Two brown leather ottomans sat at the foot of the bed, and directly opposite was a credenza with a wall-mounted TV that was flanked by doors that led onto the private terrace.

Cove pointed to the door on the other wall. "Shower and toilet there."

"Unbelievable," he said, staring out the glass doors.

Watching him stand at the doors overlooking the infinity pool and a perfect view of the Aegean Sea, she considered his height and shape. "You are very close to the same size and height as my *zio*. Come, you can get some clothes."

"Where are you sleeping?" he asked as he trailed farther back down the hall.

They entered her *zio*'s room, and she turned on the light, crossed the room to the walk-in closet that was nearly as big as the room itself. "My room is on the other side of the house." Indicating to the shelves and drawers, she smiled. "Help yourself. He won't mind." She tapped a rack of clothes. "I wouldn't touch these. He pretty much lives in them, but his personal shopper stocks the closet with other styles in the hopes he will branch out. It is a lost cause."

"I should feel bad about taking his clothes..." Dillon drew jeans and a black shirt from the drawers. He picked up a pair of shoes and muttered, "Same size."

"Good." Admittedly, she couldn't help but wonder how good he would look in some stylish pieces. He had the athletic frame for it. "I am going to check the fridge and see what we can do for dinner."

She headed back down the hall to the kitchen and checked the fridge. Not surprised, since *Zio* had not expected to be gone, that it was stocked with fresh vegetables and meats, she pulled out spinach, kale, tomatoes, and sausage. Grabbing the ready-made dough, she scooped up the rest and started for the sliding doors.

Dillon returned, hurrying to slide them open for her. "Where are you going with all that?"

She strode over to the outdoor kitchen. "Here." She set down the ingredients on the concrete counter.

"Everything is spotless," Dillon noted.

"Tuesdays are cleaning days," she said with a shrug, popping a black olive in her mouth. "At least, they used to be, and I know he has not hired a new cleaning lady. She is like seventy and he adores her." She went to work setting the wood in the outdoor oven and started the fire. When she turned back, she faltered at how beautiful he looked standing there, arms resting on the island between them. No . . . no, she should not think about that.

Dillon jutted his jaw toward the ingredients. "What're you making?"

"Fire-roasted pizza," she said with a grin. "Zio Santi taught me how to make it." As she laid out the dough, she eyed him. "Any intolerances?"

"Only to hunger."

Laughing, she liked this. Liked him. Liked how he always made her laugh. "Once I get this made, we can take it down to the office and you can show me the picture, and I can get my phone."

"Sounds like a plan."

It was borderline therapeutic to make the pizza from scratch, watch it cook, and hang out with Dillon. Once it was done, he picked it up while she picked out Perrier bottles, and they headed inside. She retrieved the Faraday bag with her phone and headed down a level to the office. Punched in a code and accessed the secure room. With a *shink*, the door closed behind them. Then a steel panel slammed over that one.

"Now, we should be good," she said as he set the pizza on the large oval table in the middle of the private office. "Use any system you want."

Dillon moved to a computer and jiggled the mouse, bringing the screen to life as he sat down. "Password?"

After tucking the phone under her arm, Cove indicated for him to shift aside and typed the password. "Sorry—he swore me to secrecy."

"No worries." Once it unlocked, he opened a browser and navigated to a website. When it loaded, he logged into the portal. "Here's the photo."

Cove drew a chair closer and joined him. She leaned in and studied the image, her heart skipping a beat. "That is definitely Papà." Shaking her head, she noticed the other three men in the photo. Two were about the same distance from Papà, the third a good bit farther with his back to them. "That is Enzo in the foreground, and I assume the man whose face we can see is your papà."

Dillon nodded. "Recognize anything?"

"No . . ." She frowned, trying to . . . Her gaze settled on his dad. Some spark ignited in her brain, a memory flickering. "Wait . . . I . . . I've seen him before . . ."

Dillon snapped a look at her, their noses mere inches apart. "My dad? You've seen my dad before? Were you there? I didn't think you were because you aren't in the photo."

She grunted. "I recognize him, but not because I was there. I think . . ." She squinted as if that might clear up the image better. "I can't—" Sudden clarity shot through her. She gasped. "Wait!" Her heart crashed into her ribs, and she slapped a hand on his arm, gaping. "*Santo cielo!*"

"What?"

Cove leapt up and grabbed her phone from the center table near the pizza. She unlocked it and went to the photos. "I . . ."

"Gelato. What—"

"Wait-wait-wait." She flicked through the images. "Remember the story about Yemen, when I followed Enzo . . . ?"

He rose and came to her side.

She found the photo, her heart jarring in her chest as she zoomed in. She gasped. Thrust the phone at him. "Look!"

His dark eyes took forever to shift from her to the phone. Then he frowned. "Your dad . . . I don't—"

Realizing the phone had zoomed back out, she stretched two fingers away from each other on the screen. "The background, near the dock. The boat—"

"Holy fire! That's my dad!"

SEVENTEEN

Mykonos, Greece

FEELING THAT DANGEROUS, DEADLY THREAD of hope dangling before him again, Dillon ignored it as Cove sent the images to the monitor he'd been working on, so they could see the image on a twenty-seven-inch screen.

"I'm sending them to the printer too," she said as she worked her phone. "I can't believe this . . ."

It doesn't change anything, he repeated to himself over and over as he studied the images she'd sent. "Same day he disappeared," he muttered. These images were just more proof that Dad *had* been in Yemen. Which Dillon knew and had already visited.

And it did no good.

Like a balloon popped, Dillon felt that tendril of hope evaporate again. "This is amazing—great to see my dad. But . . . it's not really new intel. Or helpful."

"Look," Cove said, reaching across him, then hesitating. "Can I?"

Feeling defeated—angry at himself for getting his hopes up again—he dropped back against the seat. "Have at it."

Cove brought up two photos. "These are hours apart." She used the cursor to point to the one on the left. "This was the first image I took. The street was so busy. See the cars?"

"Yeah . . . ?" The point?

"And this one," she said, moving the mouse to highlight the one on the right, "is much later in the day—dusk."

That was clear from the shadowed lights, the street lamps that had a hint of a glow. But again, what was her point? He flicked his hands in question.

"*Look*, Dillon," she said, tapping the screen. "In the first one when he's near the warehouse? No backpack. But when he's near this boat at the dock . . ."

Breath snatched, Dillon sat straight, his gaze homing in on the later image. On the bulky shape strapped to his dad's spine. "Backpack."

"And it looks *hefty*," she said. "See how it sags?"

Hand over his mouth, Dillon stared at his father's likeness and ached to find him. Find him *alive*. "What're you doing, Dad . . . ?" he wondered aloud.

"Too bad we don't have a video to answer—" Cove gasped.

"What?"

Her wide eyes came to him. "There *is* a video—oh." She deflated. "No, I deleted it."

Curse the toxin of hope.

"Waaaait," she said, slowing deliberately. "I did delete it, but I also sent it to Zio Santi, asking if he recognized anyone in it. So it should be in the text thread still." She accessed her texts and scrolled through them. "Here." She opened and let it play. Drew in a sharp breath, hand flying to his arm again as she strangled a cry. "Look-look-look!" She thrust the phone at him. "Look behind Enzo."

He took it and watched. His heart skipped a beat when Dad stalked into view, completely unaware of the recording, angled around the warehouse, then drew back a panel door and ducked inside. "He went in the warehouse."

"*That*," Cove said with sharp emphasis and a big smile, "is a GIS warehouse. That means there's surveillance footage, because all our warehouses have cameras."

He looked at her, pulse accelerating. "I have to go back to Yemen."

"*We* have to go," she said, nodding and smiling. Then she wrinkled her nose. "Let's work out a plan and finish the pizza." They swiveled to the table and each picked up a slice. "Going by boat is out of the question—it would take us weeks to get down there."

Though Dillon nodded, his mind was locked on the video of his dad. It was profound, seeing him moving, in action after years of being told he was dead. Yet, this video was over two years old. Still . . .

"Hold up." He edged in closer. "No backpack when he goes in . . ." When she handed him another slice, he took it, gaze locked on the video. He folded a bite into his mouth as he let it play again. Zeroed in on the loud noise toward the end of the footage that sounded like a clap of thunder and sent the half dozen people in the frame scattering. Dust or smoke plumed, blurring the video. "What happened here, the loud noise?"

"Oh, yeah—that was so strange," she said, toying with her unsecured braid again. "I was in the alley, watching from the corner, when this SUV careened around the corner and rammed straight into Enzo's car. Barely avoided hitting several people."

Voices could be heard, some shouting at the careless driver. Then a man offered apologies. In English.

But it was the dark blur that stopped Dillon as he folded the last bite into his mouth. He backed up the video. Drew his finger over the screen, backing it up . . . back . . . back, each frame jacking with his pulse. "Cove!" He swallowed, thumping his chest for hurrying that last big bite. "Look."

She leaned in, shoulder pressing against his arm.

He froze the screen, zoomed in a bit more, and angled it to her. "Past the dust, past the accident . . . my dad. Coming out. *With* a backpack."

Gaping, she looked at the screen, then back to him. "He must have gotten it in there. But . . . what did he take?"

Dillon shook his head, trying to process what he'd found. Dad went inside, took something out . . . then vanished . . . and turned up in Tanzania. "Whatever he had in the backpack could be why he's missing." He eyed her. "Do you know what was in the warehouse?"

"Technology paraphernalia," she said with a slight shrug. "It is all technology related to heavy machinery for large agriculture and industrial controls systems. That is all GIS handles." She screwed up her face. "Why would he take something from the warehouse?"

Technology . . . control systems.

"Don't know, but it has to be important. Dad's not a thief." Studying the images, Dillon zoomed in on the picture of his dad at dusk. He squinted and craned his neck forward. "Hey, this . . . It looks like my dad is about to climb on that trawler."

Chewing pizza, Cove considered the image. "His body *is* angled toward it . . ."

"Even though the dock heads in the other direction." Bouncing his leg as his pulse raced, he stared at it, thinking. He met her gold gaze that trekked over his face. "Which could explain how he got to Tanzania, maybe. If I can find out who owns that boat . . . where it went . . ."

Dillon zoomed in on the boat's hull, but it was no good—angle was all wrong and the letters blurred, so he zoomed back out, took a screenshot of the trawler, and sent it to the printer. Nerves buzzing, he felt so close. Yet . . . entirely too far away. "We have to get to Yemen. Talk to the dockmaster. Check customs logs—that is, if we can convince them to let us see them. I'm going to send Helios a message and see if he can get on top of anything. Check camera footage, maybe verify my dad actually got on that boat."

"If it was over two years ago, do you think they still have any of that?"

"It's an international dock, so I am going to hope that they keep those records for years for legal reasons." Once again, it felt like him against the world. This time, though . . . he wasn't alone. Keenly aware of Cove next to him, of her arm touching his, he liked that they were in this together.

Cove set down her half-eaten pizza slice and cleared her throat. "So," she began quietly, rubbing the back of her neck, "this . . . this feels like maybe my papà is not involved in what happened to yours. He was not at the warehouse that night. He . . ."

Dillon felt her desperation to prove her dad innocent deep in his bones. It was the prime driver that had him crossing borders and laws to find his dad. "I wish I could tell you what you want to hear, but I won't say something just to make you feel better, no matter how much I want to." He flicked a hand toward the screens. "This new trail doesn't prove anything, for either of our dads. But it's a solid start. I hope it leads to the answers we both want. Our big problem right now is figuring out how to get to Yemen."

"Zio Santi might help us."

He eyed her and spoke around a wad of food. "How?"

She shrugged. "He has planes at his disposal. I will ask him to call a pilot to get us there."

"You really think he'd do that?"

"He is at the villa—so he will see all that, and if you share your story, I am sure he can be convinced to work with us."

"It'd have to be off the books. My name can't be out there. And neither can yours, since the thugs were looking specifically for you."

"I know." She eyed the computer, then picked up her phone. "It is only nine, so I should be able to reach him."

Dillon almost reached out to stop her, to tell her to wait. Why? No idea.

Nix that. He did. He wanted more downtime—with her. Just the two of them, safe, able to talk and just . . . exist. But that didn't track with logic. Having time with her, believing there was any safety until this was over, was an illusion.

"Hi, *Zio*." Cove sat forward, elbows on the counter as she cradled her head in one hand and the phone in another. "How are things there?" She eased back and put the phone on speaker.

"A mess," he spat. "First, I want to know why you have this man in my home when he broke into your home."

"He saved me from the gunmen who took Papà," Cove said, looking at Dillon as she shared the story of their escape through the tunnels. "I know if it were not for him, I would either be dead or kidnapped like Papà."

"Sì, sì, I saw them on the footage taking Massimo. Now, I am working with authorities to identify the men involved to see if we can find him. There has been no ransom or other demand. Does this have something to do with you—what is your name, young man?"

"Achilles," Dillon said quickly, afraid Cove might give his real name. "I am not connected to his kidnapping. I went to the villa to find a connection between Mr. Galtieri and my dad, who went missing roughly three years ago."

"Who is your dad?"

Dillon faltered. "With respect, sir, I would prefer not to say right now. Not yet. Not after what happened there. Those gunmen chased us for nearly a full day. They're determined, and that makes me think I'm onto something. Or maybe Cove knows something that could be dangerous."

"How so? Lay it out for me, everything you know."

So they did. Telling her uncle about the men, escaping through the tunnels, returning to get money and the vehicle. Dillon provided the barest of details on his search, identity, his dad's, but made sure it was solid enough information that her uncle would believe them. They explained their belief that the Yemeni warehouse might be key.

"That is a . . . almost too much to believe."

Cove flickered her gaze to Dillon. "It is all true, Zio Santi. Like I said, I have been trying to prove Papà's innocence all this time. And Flavio kept insisting I wear the pink dress, but I refused—and we heard men say they were looking for the woman in the pink dress. So, it is clear they are complicit in the attack and kidnapping Papà, I am sure of it. Ever since I saw him meet with that man in Yemen . . ."

"And now you both want to go to Yemen."

It wasn't a question. "Yes, sir," Dillon stated.

"Achilles . . . the hero of legend was notorious for being weak in the areas of rage and pride. Is that a problem for you, Achilles?"

Only when I'm being treated like a criminal. Stretching his jaw, Dillon told himself the question made sense, considering the fact he was sitting in a safe room in the man's house with the man's niece. Though he considered some sharp retort, he opted for straightforward. "No, sir." But to be fair, he had inherited his dad's short fuse. Santi didn't need to know that, though. "I am focused and determined."

"You have tactical skills."

Not really liking that the guy was probing his history, he also knew Santi could simply be looking out for his niece. "I do."

"*Zio*, I know you are concerned—"

"Of course I am concerned. My brother-in-law is missing, taken at gunpoint, and my niece has been on the run with a man I do not know who broke into the villa where her father was taken, and now you want me to help you get to Yemen, one of the most volatile regions in this world right now!"

"Fair," Dillon said, understanding the man's outrage, yet growing irked because he could not give the man what he wanted. "I hear you, sir. Get it. But I cannot provide you more proof or specific intel without compromising my father's life or what I'm trying to accomplish. And you're right—Cove shouldn't go down there with me. It is too dangerous."

"What?" she balked. "I am not being left behind! I have been investigating that warehouse and Enzo longer than any of you *balordo* men! This is as much my mission as it is yours!"

"Think, Ilaria," Santi said in a plaintive voice, "it is too dangerous. You are a beautiful young woman, and if anything happened to Achilles—*Dio* forbid—you would be on your own."

"If you make him leave me, I *am* on my own."

Dillon couldn't hide the smile—that logic didn't work.

"I will be there in two days, *Lupina*. Please, hear me."

Cove shoved to her feet. "I am not staying behind."

"If you defy my wishes, there will be no plane. I will not have that stain on my conscience. You stay, and a plane will get this man to Yemen. That is it. My only offer."

Aware of alienating her, Dillon had to seize the opportunity. "Agreed, sir."

"*What*?!" Cove's eyes blazed with hurt and shock. "How could you do this?"

"Achilles, be at the airport at seven a.m."

"Thank you, sir," Dillon said, holding her gaze, knowing she likely hated him. But this . . . this meant she would be safe.

Cove unsealed the room and stormed out. Her angry steps thudded down the hall.

Dillon didn't like the turn this had taken, but this shift in direction erred on the side of logic, not emotion. The thought of her getting hurt made his gut roil. No, this was for the best.

Though he considered rushing after her, he thought she might need time to calm down.

Who was he kidding? He just didn't want to see the hurt and hatred in those gold eyes again. So, instead, he sent an update to Helios and let him know what was happening.

SRY 4 DELAY. SAFE. VINE ATTACKED. ESCAPED WITH HEIR. SWIMMING WITH GODS. HEADED TO ORIGIN TMRW.

Next he looked up the directions to the island airport and ingrained them in his mind, then closed out and erased the history. Grabbing the last slice of pizza, he stood, glad to see her phone still here. At least in her outrage, she hadn't lost situational awareness or compromised operational security.

Braced for impact, he left the secure room, pulled the door closed, and climbed the stairs to the main level. He expected a lecture from the formidable woman. Fierce in her own right, she was also intelligent. Surely he could get her to understand the logic.

He hit the travertine stone floor and paused. Listened up and down the hall in both directions, but heard nothing from either way. Where had she gone? At the end of the hall, he spied light escaping past an open door. She'd said her room was on the opposite side of the house from his room, so was that hers? He moved quietly toward it, listening, but didn't hear anything. He peeked inside. Scanned the bed and chairs, then the wall of windows that looked onto a private terrace with stone arches. Another door with light spilling over the sleek floors turned out to be a bathroom, also empty.

"Cove?" He returned to the main living area, where he spotted a door ajar. He crossed the room and went outside, scanning the outdoor living area and kitchen where she'd earlier made the killer pizza. "Cove?"

He heard a quick intake of breath . . . below.

On the lower terrace.

Dillon shifted to the rail running the perimeter of the upper terrace and spotted her on one of the loungers that lined the pool. Hugging her knees to her chest, she stared toward the Aegean.

For a second, he considered just heading to his room because he did not want to have this conversation. Did not want those gold eyes eviscerating his conviction that leaving her was for her protection. She was safe here. Upset, yeah, but safe.

But he wouldn't be a coward. Not with her. So, he took the stairs down and joined her poolside.

EIGHTEEN

Mykonos, Greece

HER HEART FELT LIKE A BATTERING RAM AS he sat next to her. Jaw clenched tight, she dared him to tell her this was for her own benefit, for her "safety." But the minutes ticked by with him just sitting there, perched on the side, forearms on his knees. Head down.

Good. He should be ashamed of himself.

"It's better—"

"*Do not* try to justify this!" she snapped, rage radiating through her with a thrumming chill. "You *promised* you would not abandon me."

"This is *not* me abandoning you," he said in a low, dangerous tone. "Going to Yemen is about *me* finding my dad. It doesn't help your cause or dad. Endangering your life doesn't—"

"Stop making this about me!" She swung her legs over the side to face him. "This is about you being selfish. About you finding a way to get what you want—a flight to Yemen at no cost. You do not care about me or what I need to do. All you care about is yourself!" She stomped to her feet and started away, unwilling to listen to his excuses.

"Cove, that's not fair!"

"*D'accordo!*" She whirled around and found him immediately behind her, forcing her to draw back. "It *is not* fair. *Mio papà* is missing. That is *his* warehouse you want to go look at. Those photos show *our* fathers there. Together. Yet you treat me like a dog, telling me to stay."

"It's not that," Dillon countered. "I go into these places without thought for myself, but I know I could die trying to find my dad. I can deal with that. What I can't accept is putting your life in danger!"

"Oh, so it is okay for *you* to risk everything for your father and be heroic. But me? I cannot do the same for mine?"

He tightened his mouth and a fist, letting out a growl. "That is not what I said."

"But it is what you meant!"

"No. Cove—c'mon."

She backed up, shaking her head. "My mistake for believing it when you said your character and integrity were important to you. That we had a deal!"

Fire sparking in his eyes, he lifted his hands as if he wanted to box something—her, apparently. "If to you 'keeping you safe' means I don't have character and integrity, then so be it." He shifted in, all but snarling, "You called it."

Furious he would not listen, that he was so stinking arrogant, she let her own growl escape. "You are a monster! I hate you!"

"Yeah? Well, *this monster* is keeping you safe!"

She shoved him even as her mind registered how close he was to the edge of the pool.

He stepped back to catch his balance, and his foot hit the ledge, slipped down. He flung out his arms to avoid falling. They windmilled.

Cove gasped and caught his hand. But his momentum proved too powerful. Yanked her forward. For a fraction of a second, he steadied himself, but his pull upended her balance. She tipped forward. Thumped into him, sending them both into the pool.

His arms clamped onto her as they splashed, and she snapped her mouth shut. Water rushed over her, hollowing her hearing. She broke away. Felt the bottom of the pool—the shallow end, thank heaven!—and vaulted upward. Breaking the surface, she gasped, then shielded herself as he erupted. Fury coiled through her, and she just dared him to rage at her.

Instead, he whipped his head to the side to clear the water. It splatted her face even as he used a hand to jiggle the water from his ears.

"*Mostro*!" she spat.

Dillon met her gaze beneath the warm glow of the terrace and pool lights and the moonlight. He looked like a drowned rat, even with the crooked smile that split his intense features.

A laugh bubbled up through her, but she fought it—she was furious! Should not be laughing. Yet one glimpse into those dark eyes and the choked laugh erupted. But seeing his smile just made her angry all over again. She hated this—his relegating her to the wings of the runway when he was about to take flight. Literally. Hurt pushed her gaze away. She did not want to look at him or let him see her crying! Aware of her shirt sticking to her, she tried to pry it free as she turned to leave the pool. She could not deal with—

"Cove."

She kept moving, having to slog her sodden self toward the steps out of the pool.

Hustling, Dillon sloshed past her. "Hey, listen . . ." He moved into her path, forcing her to straighten and stop. "I don't want to leave you."

That stalled her heart, but she refused to believe him. "Then don't." She braved his dark, beautiful eyes lurking beneath that strong brow.

"I've been alone for thirty-two months," he said, his voice heavy, low. "In a dozen countries, sleeping beneath stars in alleys and rooftops. Scared, on the run, evading attention and authorities. I've dealt with it, gotten used to it. But being with you the last few days has been . . . perfect." He smiled, eyes hooded as he shifted a step closer. "Having someone to talk to, help me work things through, fight with—your help in the tunnel . . . I would still be there, likely stuck in that compression point, if it weren't for you." His hand slipped to her face, cupping her cheek, awakening a swarm of nervous jellies in her belly. "I never fathomed . . . *you*. Amazing, intelligent . . . beautiful you."

The words were glorious and warm, tugging hard on her heartstrings.

"I could never live with myself if something happened to you," he said, his thumb tracing her cheek. "It's dangerous."

"*You* are dangerous," she said quietly, only then realizing the distance between them had shrunk again. His proximity and dark eyes sent her pulse racing. Was he going to kiss her?

Kiss me goodbye *is more likely.*

"I . . . our time has been incredible—a gift. A blazing star in one of the darkest times of my life." His arm encircled her waist as he angled in, gaze homing in on her lips. His mouth captured hers.

Pulling in a breath, Cove considered pushing him away again but . . . it was a good kiss. A gentle one. As if asking permission. She found herself melting into it, surprised when he crushed her to himself and deepened the kiss.

There was a shift beyond her closed eyes. A . . . flickering. Was that the heavens rejoicing like her heart?

Dillon pulled back, gaze hooded as he considered her, then around her. "What . . . ?"

It took a second for her to realize the so-called heavens rejoicing was actually the exterior lights turning on and off. She frowned, seeing *only* the pool lights blinking . . . She looked up at the house.

"What's going on?" Dillon asked, hand on her waist still.

And then she knew. "*Santo cielo*," she muttered. "I think my *zio* can see us."

His brows lifted. "*He's* doing that with the lights?"

Cove let out a nervous laugh. "He is . . . protective," she said, leaving his touch and hating the chill that came with its absence.

"Try *creepy*."

Still a little stunned he'd just kissed her, she made herself keep moving. "I, uh . . ." She slogged up out of the pool. "I'm going to change."

"Cove."

She paused and robotically turned to look over her shoulder, un-suctioning her clothes from her body.

"I meant"—palming the edge of the pool, he cocked his head back to where they'd kissed—"all of that."

With the passion he had shown, she had no doubt. Even though that comment was about not wanting to leave her, the fact remained that he still planned to.

The heavy weight of his abandonment pushed her up to the house, each step thick with grief. After a quick shower to wash the pool chemicals from her hair, she changed into lounge pants and an oversized hoodie. For a second, she considered filling a backpack and trailing Dillon in secrecy tomorrow. Forcing her way onto the plane. Would it work? Did she have anything to lose?

Heart and mind confused—that had been a *perfect* kiss—she slumped onto the corner of the bed, staring out the window at the glittering black sea in the distance. Though she wanted to be mad at him, she knew he did not owe her a single thing. They had made a deal, but he clearly found a better one. Why in heaven was she being so ridiculous? She barely knew this man! They had been together through insurmountable odds over three full days. But that was it—three days. She scoffed at herself. Three days and she expected them to be . . . *appiccicati*?

No, not stuck together but . . . It felt like her heart had always known him. All that time in the tunnels, fleeing the gunmen . . . hiding in the stable . . . she had never felt safer. Never once felt unsafe. On top of that, their time together had filled her with a strong hope that she could finally prove Papà's innocence.

Papà . . .

She recalled the men dragging him to the chopper. Him collapsing, then being hauled into the helicopter. Closing her eyes, she sagged. *Santo cielo*, it was too much. So much. Mamma's death, Papà's scandal and kidnapping, being chased . . . Now losing Dillon and hope.

Warmth settled on her knee, startling her out of the chaos, yanking her from the morose to the strong, tanned, callused hand resting there. Her chest tightened.

Dillon sat on the leather ottoman at the foot of the bed, peering up at her as he set the backpack to the side. "I'm sorry, Cove."

Rolling her eyes, she chewed her lower lip to ward off more tears. Was he apologizing for abandoning her or the kiss? Perhaps both. "You are not." On her feet, she moved into the bathroom and grabbed a hair tie. "You are getting what you want, and that is what matters to you." Returning to her bedroom, she tied her hair up into a messy bun atop her head.

Standing, Dillon seemed distraught, his brow knotted and deep brown eyes churning in desperation. "I want you safe."

Arms folded, she tried to plaster a façade of utter calm. "I understand. You have a mission, and my coming along would compromise that." But instead of actually saying that, the words came out completely different, wrong: "And what if 'safe' is only found with you?" Her heart rattled in her chest, the words echoing in her ears. Suddenly embarrassed, she flung a hand to him. "Forget I said that."

His chest rose and fell unevenly. "I will never forget you saying that."

Rubbing the back of her neck, she avoided his gaze and peered out the window. Ironically, she saw her own reflection there—and him moving in behind her, closer. "Don't," she warned. "I am fine. We do not even know each other." She sniffed, proud of herself for getting those words out. "It has only been three days." She nodded, trying to convince herself. "I will be fine tomorrow."

But she would not. Because when he left, she would never see him again. The realization made her throat constrict, ache.

"I don't deserve you," he said in a husky voice.

She laughed, pushing herself away from him, struggling against the powerful draw to be in his arms again. "That is pretty evident." Oh, she hated the cruel words as soon as they left her mouth. She winced and tried to flash him a smile that felt more like a grimace. "Sorry."

"It's truth I can own." He nodded, then looked down. Pinched his shirt. "I . . . uh, borrowed the jeans and shirt from your uncle, but just double-checking before I take a change of clothes or two . . ."

Blinking at him, she couldn't quite process what he was asking. Then her brain came out of the fugue, right into the hard wall of the obvious—he was moving on. Already. No regard for her trampled heart. But she had said she would be fine. "Help yourself. He will not care."

Dillon gave her a long look, then bobbed his head and headed down the hall.

While she was hurt that he would leave, that his promises were effectively null and void, she would not be bitter. Because as much as she hated it, hated admitting it, there was not much reason for her to chase Yemen. If Papà had been seen down there recently, the fires of Hades would not stop her.

Recalling what Dillon said about how he got money to pay

for food and supplies, she grabbed the cash from her backpack and went in search of him. She found him in Zio Santi's room, meticulously folding a couple of black T-shirts. Those dark eyes rose to her when she entered.

Afraid she might change her mind, she hurried forward and extended the euros. "Here."

Dillon took a long second to pry his gaze from her to the money and straighten. "Why?"

Wagging it, she sighed. "You will need it."

Tentatively, he reached for the money. "Does this mean you don't hate me?"

"Do not push your luck," she said with a smile that never quite made it to her lips.

Regretfully, he accepted the money, then set it in the pack before closing the gap between them. "I'd like to come back to you after I find my dad."

She widened her eyes, those words detonating the last vestiges of her anger. But he *was* still leaving her . . . "I bet you say that to all the girls you meet."

A storm moved through his dark eyes and brows. "I get that you feel there's just cause to question my integrity . . . but there have been *no* other girls since I left home."

Feeling that splash of warmth in her belly again, Cove grew acutely aware of the distance vanishing between them once more. "Why . . . ?"

He frowned. "Why haven't there been other girls?"

"No—I—" She rubbed her forehead, frustrated that she could not think clearly with him so close. "Why do you want to come back?"

"Thought I made that obvious in the pool," he said with a smirk, his fingers entwining hers. "Cove, I've never felt like this about anyone. You weren't on my radar or plans."

"Still not, apparently," she murmured, feeling petty and childish.

"I know you hate me—"

"No," she countered quickly. Maybe too quickly. "I could not hate you. But you have hurt me. We had a deal . . ." She twisted her mouth to the side, trying to avoid crying.

Dillon drew her into an embrace. Pressed a kiss to her ear. "I know . . . I'm sorry. I just want you safe."

Coiling her arms around his waist, she savored the hug, his strength, then whispered, "But I'm safe with you."

He shifted his head to look at her, then kissed her again.

A light flared near them.

Breaking the soft kiss, Dillon huffed. "Does he have cameras everywhere?"

But that's when her mind registered the truth and she gasped. "That's not him." She pointed to the wall-mounted TV that had sprung to life. A red banner across the bottom made her heart plummet. "A door opened on the lower level."

Dillon tensed. "Aren't we the only ones here?"

She nodded, snatching up the remote. On the screen, she accessed the security feeds. "Yes, and it's too late for staff . . ." Scanning the various camera feeds, she spotted a shadow moving and gasped. "The basement! Look—"

"*Gun*men!"

NINETEEN

Mykonos, Greece

WHAT DO WE DO?"

"What's the quickest way outside?"

"The living room, but"—she pointed at her feet—"I need shoes."

Dillon grabbed the backpack and lifted the AK-47 he'd taken off the thug at the villa. Slinging the backpack on, he sidled up to the door, caught her hand and coiled it around his belt loop. "Hold tight and stay close." He did a quick look-see of the hall and found both directions empty. He snaked out with her in tow and hustled toward the corner. Peeked around and found it clear. Hurried across the open space, head on a swivel as he stalked forward.

Sounds coming from the stairwell at least one level below told him time was short.

At her room, he checked it for safety, then hustled inside. "Hurry. Every second counts."

She sprinted past him to the closet.

While she got what she needed, he slunk to the windows, saw

nothing, then repositioned himself so he had a line of sight on both the terrace and the hall.

A definitive *shunk* rang through the house as darkness slammed across the entire structure. Just like the villa. Gut tight, he saw shadows gliding past the pool. Holy fire, how many were there?

"Gelato, now!" he rasped.

She darted to his side.

"They're everywhere—pool and hall. Out the window."

Her eyes widened, then she hurried to the nearby window. Shifted the handle from a vertical position to horizontal. A noticeable pop signaled the catch release. She eased it open and climbed out, vegetation rustling beneath her intrusion.

Dillon followed, lowering himself to the huge bush, then closing the window behind him so they didn't immediately give away their escape route. Moving along the bush, they came to the corner of the house. He reached past her, pointing across the pebbled drive to a half wall that marked off another property behind the house.

Cove sprinted to the other side and climbed over the wall. Right behind her, Dillon hopped it and dropped to a crouch. They worked their way up the sloping hill, then down a narrow alley between two much smaller properties.

"Just keep moving," he said to her.

Cove did just that until they found themselves on a stone path with stark-white lines between the giant gray stones. The narrow passage stayed wide open for a good fifty, sixty meters. Soon, they were descending and curving around. Shops lined the path, and they were slowing down when plaster spat at them.

"Run!" Dillon hissed, and they both bolted away from the shooter. He spied a side street. "Right!"

Cove tried to slow to avoid a collision with a wall, but she had too much momentum. She stumbled and went down. To avoid crashing into her, Dillon tic-tacked the wall and flipped over her. Skidded to a stop. Caught her hand and hauled her back upright.

While he wasn't a fan of the claustrophobic cluster of buildings crammed onto the island, he was glad for it. Made it harder for a shooter to have a clear line of sight or get off a clean shot. More places to hide.

He had no idea how far they'd gone or how long, but when he realized they hadn't taken cover or heard a pursuer, he slowed, pulling to the side.

Cove joined him, holding on to his arm, her breaths coming in ragged gulps.

"I think we're okay . . ."

She swallowed and wet her lips, shaking her head. "How did they find us?"

He shrugged as they walked the darkened streets with the warm glow of lights throughout. "That's what I'd like to know." People were still awake, enjoying the nightlife.

"Nobody knew we were here! Zio Santi is the only person."

"The boat," Dillon thought aloud. "If they tracked or spotted it . . ."

"Oh." Chagrined, she inspected her elbow, scraped from her collision with the wall.

"Should have docked it elsewhere. I just didn't expect them to track us that fast." He eyed her injury. "You okay?"

"Stings like—"

A blur came out of the shadow.

Adrenaline-fueled, Dillon surged forward, right arm thrusting her back as he slid in front of her. Nailed the gunman's hand. Heard the gun clatter to the ground even as the shooter swung a left hook at his jaw. Dillon shifted but not soon enough. The punch connected, sending him staggering against Cove.

The attacker came in with another punch, but Dillon planted his foot against the wall behind Cove and used it to drive himself into the man. Bent, he grabbed the guy's waist. Dove backwards. He felt the guy's head crack against the wall along the narrow path.

That gave him the slight edge needed. Scrambled to get the guy in a headlock. Anchored his arms, using the walls to brace and prevent the attacker from getting free. The guy slapped and tried to claw and punch at Dillon. Each impact was slower, weaker. Finally, the guy stopped fighting . . .

Dillon held on to be sure the guy wasn't trying to flip the tables on him. Finally confident the attacker wasn't going to fight back, Dillon got his legs up under him, hooked the guy's shoulders, and hauled the unconscious form into a small alley. He retrieved the gun, used the ambient light from a nearby house and did a press check to verify a round was in the chamber, then tucked it at the small of his back.

"Is he dead?" she asked.

"Unconscious." He wasn't sure but knew she didn't need it in her head that he'd just killed someone. He caught Cove's hand and broke into a jog. "C'mon. Which way to the airport?"

"I . . . uh . . ." She stopped, glancing around, no doubt to get her bearings.

He tugged her onward. "Don't stop. Just get your bearings as we move. Aim us in that general direction." As they negotiated the tight passages of the city, he noticed her breath was ragged. It seemed she was limping. "You hurt?"

"I think I turned it wrong," she panted but did not stop. "So what is the plan?"

"Stay out of sight until we meet the plane."

"That's not for *hours*."

"I know." He also had to ensure she was safe. "Is there someone on the island you can stay with?"

In the darkened passage, her glower felt like a beacon. "You already tried that once." Ire flashed in her gold eyes as she stepped toward him, pressing her lips tight. "Stop trying to get rid of me!" she snapped, chest heaving—and this wasn't from being out of breath. She was furious. "I have lost my mom, my dad, and I am not going to lose you!"

Those words were like an RPG to his chest. They couldn't mean how that sounded.

Cove startled at her own words. She shoved her hair back and pressed the heel to her forehead. "I-I mean . . ."

"We just got shot at and run down—isn't that enough proof it's not safe?"

"*You* kept me safe. *That* is how I am safe—*with* you!"

What a sucker punch. "Don't do that."

"If you had left me back there, who knows what would happen. I am not putting my life in anyone else's hands!" Plaintive, hurt eyes settled on him. "We had a deal, Dillon. Remember?" Her lower lip quivered, and holy fire, that snuffed the fight out of him. "A plan to save our dads. You and me. Together. For the first time, I had hope that I could do this, prove Papà was innocent."

Duly chastised, he understood, but . . . "I don't want you to get hurt!"

"You pushing me away hurts. You not willing to help me hurts." She threw up her hands. "I have *nowhere* to go, no friends."

"Okay, okay." Man, she had hooked his heart and bludgeoned his ability to keep her at arm's length. He drew her into his arms as proof of that. "You're killing me, Gelato."

First, she thumped his chest with a hand. "*Stop* trying to leave me." She angled into his shoulder and rested her cheek there. "I have no options besides you."

Dagger to his heart. "I get it. I hear you, G." Exhaling heavily, he held her close, cupping the back of her head, thumb tracing her hair, still damp from their tumble into the pool. Remembered the night on the roof in Paris when he'd felt so alone, desperate, aching. How he'd cried out to God. And now . . . now he was with her.

She clung to him for a long minute, shuddering a breath.

Then lifted her head and looked up at him, uncertainty churning through her expression. "So . . . does that mean . . ."

"It means this monster," he said, recalling how angry she'd been when she called him one earlier, "is an idiot. We need to keep moving . . ."

Cove straightened. "So . . . for keeps." She blinked. "Well, not *keep* keeps, but . . ."

Amused at how she kept second-guessing everything she said, he cocked his head to the side. "Let's get going. And hope this isn't a mistake."

Cove hustled to stay in step with him. "At least we will make it together."

"What, do you think that's like some romantic trope or something?"

"No, but would that be so bad if it were?"

Dillon grunted as they moved onto a stretch of road that didn't incite him to violence with walls that closed in. They'd barely had a day's reprieve before being set upon again at the swanky ocean-front house. "I really hate how they keep finding us. Makes me wonder how . . ." They'd been so careful . . .

"The boat—you knew it had GPS."

"Yes, but it should've taken them hours to figure out that we were on it. No way they should've shown up already."

The buildings on this street had space between them, unlike the previous ones, and he could be glad for that. Felt like he could breathe again as the sea and tight-packed city grew distant behind them.

"What are you saying?" she asked as they rounded another corner.

He didn't like the thought taking root in his head. Before he vomited it out and made her angry again, he should let it marinate. "Talk later. Let's find a place to hole up near the airport."

"That could be tricky," Cove said as they slowed to a normal pace. Another ten minutes brought them up into a more open area with larger structures. "This area is not heavily populated like the shoreline. Not as many places to hide."

"We'll figure it out." Even as he said it, he felt her hand slide into his. He glanced down, then to her.

"You keep saying that and . . . we do." Uncertainty dashed through her expression. Instinct said to let her hand go, let *her* go. But he didn't. Couldn't. Because . . . he liked this. Liked not being alone. Liked not being alone *with her*. Though, he shouldn't because there was no way they could have a future together. They were from entirely different worlds. Sometimes, the wealth she existed in felt like another planet.

"This your way of making sure I don't escape?"

"Whatever it takes," she said with a rueful grin as they reached the airport. "Do we go inside the terminal? I know—"

"Negative. Too many eyes, both technological and human. We'll just find the plane on the tarmac. Assuming you know either the pilot or plane by sight."

"Papà and Zio use two different pilots," Cove said with a crisp nod. "I know them both. The airstrip is on the east side, but that whole airstrip is surrounded by a fence with barbed wire. There is a gate on the far side that does not have it."

"How on earth do you remember a detail like that?"

Cove shrugged. "That gate sits on a curve. One time there was an accident between a box truck and sports car with the top down. I remember thinking how lucky the sports car was that they hit the gate and not the barbed wire."

"Fair." Finally, buildings fell away and the land opened up to a flat plain. Dillon had never been more grateful for a clear line of sight. "Lead us to the gate, and we'll find a place to hunker down until seven."

Another half hour had them climbing the stone wall on the east side of the airport, where sheep were sleeping, most laid out but a few remained standing. He and Cove ducked behind what appeared to be a transformer, from the metal box and thrum of electricity through it. From this vantage, they could see the terminal, airstrip, and planes. Homes, a working farm, and other walled plats with cows and more sheep surrounded the area.

"We should be out of sight here." Sitting in the grass, back to the box and legs bent, he rested his forearms on his knees. For the first time in the hour-plus escape from the house, he let himself relax.

Cove shrugged out of her backpack and put it between her spine and the transformer, then stretched out her legs and checked the scrape on her arm.

"That okay?"

"I have had worse," she muttered and leaned her head back.

"Somehow," Dillon said, "I cannot imagine that."

She lifted her head and gave him a frown. "Why not?"

"Because you're . . . Cove Galtieri, fashion model and—"

"*Former* fashion model." She wrinkled her nose. "How do you know about that?"

Tipped his hand there, hadn't he? "Overheard some convos in Paris and saw a photo of you modeling in your dad's office." He shrugged. "So, you did the strut—the walk."

"Catwalk."

"That."

Wrinkling her nose, she tilted her head. "I was not *born* on the runway, even though my mamma modeled too."

"See? That's the same thing as being born with a silver spoon in your mouth."

"Oh, *santo cielo*! Tell me you are not one of *those*."

"One of what?"

"People who have a grudge against the rich, against my family."

"The only grudge I have is related to my dad's disappearance."

A sheep and her lamb moved across the yard toward the wall, drawing their attention. Far from the pulsing pop music that drowned the crashing of waves, they sat in the relative quiet. With little activity on the airstrip other than airport vehicles moving from one building to another, they could hear the rustle of sheep moving through the grass.

"I know it seems like we have it easy because of the villa," Cove said, watching the ewe and sheep, "but it has not always been good. When Nonno died, Papà inherited a crumbling estate that was in complete disarray. Papà had a degree in business and Mamma in corporate finance."

Dillon plucked a long blade of grass and stripped it, playing with it as he listened, understanding he'd made her defensive. "Translates well to saving an estate."

"Very well," she agreed. "They worked hard and a lot. They taught me to do the same. So, while I walked the runway and had some fame, they taught me to save, invest."

It did surprise that her parents had degrees and put them to work, but it also—more importantly—impressed him. Told him where Cove got her drive and determination. "Hey, sorry for making you defensive about your family. That wasn't my intent."

"Then what was?" She squinted at him. "The words that come from our mouths mirror what is in our hearts."

"*Out of the abundance of the heart the mouth speaketh*," he whispered, smirking as he twisted the grass around his finger. "No idea what verse that is, but my mom must have said that a million times."

"She sounds like a very smart woman."

Dillon nodded solemnly. "I know this"—he motioned in a circle—"me going off to find Dad, upset her. Stressed her." Woof, that was a bucket of raw ache there. "I hate that."

"So, why did you do it?"

"Had to," he said, tossing away the grass, irritated she'd even ask. Wondering if she blamed him, saw him in a bad light for that. "Nobody else was doing it, and I know he's alive. If you don't believe me or blame me—"

"No." Her hand landed on his. "That was not an accusation. Really, I simply want to understand more about you. Why you thought it was the right thing."

Dillon let himself look at her, finding affirmation of what she said, liking the warmth of her touch. "Because it *was* the right thing to do. I hate hurting her—Mom's tough. So smart. But . . . I just couldn't sit there anymore, watching her cry all day. Killed me to see what it was doing to her—she didn't think I saw. But . . ." He gave a cockeyed nod. "I saw. The red eyes. Heard her sniffles in the bathroom. Something had to be done." When only the lowing of sheep answered his raw words, he stretched.

"Does she know where you are?"

He shook his head. "If she knew, any of the three-letter agencies would know. If they knew . . ." He bobbed his head. "I'd get picked up and Dad would die."

"That is an enormous, unrealistic amount of pressure you have put on yourself."

Dillon met her gaze, loving how the moonlight struck her gold irises. "You would know something about that, what with trying to prove your dad's innocence."

"I think there is a subtle difference between our situations."

"Yeah?"

"I have been very open with Papà about what I have been doing, all the research and calls."

Ah, he got her point—the insinuation that he was doing things in the dark. In other words—he was on the lam. She was in the open. Didn't know why that stung, but it did. Doubt her dad was excited about her efforts. "Bet he did not like that."

"No," she said with a rueful smile. "There is a reason they call me *Lupina*, 'little wolf.'"

"What reason is that?"

"I nearly jeopardized my whole future when I punched Arabella Abarough during A-levels for calling my mother a name and insinuating very ugly things about her."

Dillon coughed a laugh. "Legit?" He angled to see her better, this information putting a new spin on the woman next to him. Had to admit, he'd pay to see her punch someone. No . . . no, he wouldn't. Because Cove . . . she had this gentleness, this refinement about her. Like Mom. And her going all Lara Croft on someone would dismantle that.

"I am very fierce about defending those I love. Zio Santi calls me cunning," she said with a shrug.

"You're a lot like my mom—and that's actually a compliment." What would Mom think of Cove?

"I hope I get to meet her."

Heart stuttering at those words, Dillon considered her. Understood that inference. What she was saying. Hadn't he just decided they didn't have a future together? They'd known each other three days and he was considering bringing her home to Mom?

You have lost your freakin' mind.

"Get some rest, *Gelato*." He'd considered using her family nickname, but one—that felt like it belonged to them; and two— he didn't like to think of her as a wolf, though well aware of her courage and cunningness. To him, she was sweet . . . "We've got a long day ahead of us."

TWENTY

Port of Aden, Yemen

GETTING OVER THE FENCE AND ON THE PLANE had been a lot simpler than Cove imagined. Much simpler than it probably should have been since it was supposed to be a secure area. Cristos, Zio Santi's pilot, taxied the plane over from the hangar at quarter till. They were aboard and lifting off twenty minutes later.

After laying out a general plan of what to do once they got to Yemen—the Arab Palace first, then the warehouse—they agreed to get some sleep aboard the plane while they could. Four hours of uninterrupted sleep. Half what she was used to, but she would take it.

"Beginning our descent," Cristos announced over the intercom.

When Cove rose to wake Dillon, she found him already awake and alert, looking out a portal window. "Did you sleep?"

"Sure."

That sounded a lot like he had not, but the plane's descent pushed her back into her seat.

Once they'd landed and taxied to the small terminal where Cristos powered down, he emerged from the cockpit, opened the door, then turned to them. "Ilaria, your *zio* said to give you these." He produced rial banknotes, the currency used here in Yemen, and a phone. "And of course . . ." He handed a laundered vacuum-sealed plastic packet.

She opened it, finding an abaya to cover herself. She slid it on over her body, then drew the niqab over her head, wondering about the phone that Cristos offered, since Dillon did not like devices. But this one was still in the package.

Dillon eyed the head-to-toe cover she had donned. "Don't like it, but that works, not only from a cultural standpoint but for our security." As he took the phone and local money, he nodded to Cristos. "Thanks."

"There is a car coming to pick you up," the pilot explained. "It is good idea here, yes?" His pocked face darkened as he looked at Dillon. "You protect her." Then he poked a finger at Dillon's temple. "Be smart. Or Cristos find and hurt *you*. Eh, big guy?"

When she saw Dillon's jaw and fist tighten, Cove caught his bicep and drew him toward the door. "*Sas efcharistó*, Cristos," she said, thanking the pilot. "*Sas efcharistó!*" She all but pushed Dillon out before he made quick work of the pilot as he had with the men last night.

"What—"

"Just keep moving," she insisted.

Crossing toward the tarmac, she again noted how much better this place looked than the first time she'd come. The cream, coral, and gray terminal with blue designs seemed like something straight out of the late seventies/early eighties, even with a new coat of paint. But the general state of disrepair with cracked, crumbling curbs, grass and weeds flourishing, always made her feel a little sad for an area with so much potential.

"This place looks like there's been an apocalypse," Dillon muttered.

"You can thank terrorism. The Houthis are a menace here,"

Cove said quietly, eyeing the Yemeni military guard near the terminal. "But this . . . this is actually an improvement. There was a betterment project to rehabilitate the airport and bring in traffic."

He headed toward the terminal, away from the tarmac, and past the security barriers with peeling paint.

Keeping pace, she noticed men coming toward her. Not military. Grubbily dressed. "Dillon . . ."

"I see," he muttered. "Stay close. How do we find the car?"

She resisted the urge to take his hand—a public display of affection here could get them both in trouble—and walked faster. "I am not sure. I always come with Papà."

They moved past the two buildings with Arabic script on the upper ledges—likely shops at one time. Now, they were shut up tight and lent credence to the apocalypse feeling. Once through the pointed arches of the terminal, they angled toward the exit. Past that, they scanned right and left.

"Miss Galtieri!" A man held up a hand, motioning to them.

She noted Dillon reaching toward the small of his back, where she had seen him tuck the gun he'd taken from the thug last night. Alarmed, she swung toward him and exuded as much calm as she could to deescalate his tension. "His name is Yasser Gadasi," she explained, anxious for him to *not* kill the man. "He has been a GIS driver for years."

Dillon's tension visibly lowered, and he inclined his head in understanding.

She waved to the driver. "*As-salamu alaykum*, Yasser."

"*Wa alaikum as-salam*, Miss Galtieri." He opened the Land Cruiser door for her.

They climbed into the armored black SUV. At the soft thump that sealed them, Dillon was looking around, watching their surroundings. "I don't like this."

The stuffy warmth of the interior felt heavy. "I do not recall you liking *anything* so far . . ."

"I liked last night."

Buckling in, she stilled at his words.

"Not the thugs," he clarified, peering back over his shoulder to look out the rear and side windows to check the entire perimeter around the SUV. "The pool . . ."

"It is not the best pool I have ever seen."

Dillon gave her a long look for deliberately misunderstanding his meaning. They both knew the real inference was the kiss. Funny that neither of them could say it.

Yasser opened the door and climbed in behind the wheel. Hit the locks, the definitive *thunk* sounding through the big vehicle.

Dillon leaned forward, catching the front passenger seat, and waved the wad of money Cristos had given them. "A favor, Yasser. Leave the keys. Take a day off. Let us use the SUV."

Yasser's wide brown eyes rose to the rearview mirror, where he met Cove's gaze in question.

She smiled. "It is okay."

"No trouble?" Yasser asked, his expression concerned.

"No trouble," Cove reassured, though she hoped she was not lying. "Go enjoy the beach with your wife and kids."

That made the driver grin and take the money. "Thank you." And Yasser was gone.

Dillon climbed into the driver's seat and tore open the phone package.

While he did that, Cove unceremoniously hiked—rather, *struggled* to make the transition to the front amid the endless length of black fabric shrouding her body. "I do not know how they tolerate these things," she complained. Now that she was up in the seat, the fabric was tangled. With a few grunts, she partially stood to get the fabric untangled. "*Santo cielo*," she hissed. Finally, she dropped back down and adjusted the eye slit and huffed. Looked at Dillon, who was sitting, watching her, a smile wavering on his lips. "So help me, if you laugh . . ."

"Duly warned," he said, pocketing the phone before he pulled into traffic. "For the record, I prefer the dress from Paris."

Surprised he remembered that, Cove wondered at how much he was flirting with her now. "Give me my lounge pants and oversized hoodie all day, every day."

"Like what you had on in the pool," he said, as if making his point about liking what happened there.

Cove gaped, turning to look at him—a feat beneath the niqab—her face heating.

"By the way, if you're gaping or blushing, I can't tell." He eyed her. "Not entirely fair."

"Says the *man* in normal clothes."

"Fair." He turned onto 90 and headed toward the Arab Palace Hall.

"*Mostro.*"

Those dark eyes found her and gave a long look. "That's amazing—even with the niqab, I can tell you're glowering at me."

She smacked his arm for taunting her.

Dillon laughed. "And now, I do not need a visual to know you're angry."

"You are a beast. Real women have to *live* in these things, you know."

He sobered, his smile not quite leaving that handsome face as he dragged a hand over his mouth and shook his head. "Okay, so . . . First things first—the spot you followed Enzo to a couple years ago and subsequently saw my dad . . ."

"Right, yes. That was at the Arab Palace Hall." Cove peered through the windshield to gauge their surroundings. "The hall is on the way to the GIS warehouses."

"And you're sure there won't be a problem getting into the warehouse?"

"I am certain," she said. "I simply tell them I am there to do some work and check records. Papà made me communications director last year so I would have access to what I needed in order to prove his innocence."

"So, hall first, then warehouse. It'll be darker—less people."

"True."

Ten minutes later, he turned left off Main and navigated to a spot across from the Arab Palace Hall. Cars and vans littered the road.

Dillon glanced up and down the cramped street, then homed in on a person exiting the building. "Looks like we can get inside. Any security cameras?"

"Not that I recall. While it is one of the prettier event halls, it is not high-end."

He gave a curt nod. "To walk me through, do we need to go inside?"

Cove eyed the building, thinking through that night. "I . . . I don't think so." She looked at him, still feeling that giddy squirt of excitement in her belly at having his gaze so wholly focused on her. "Nothing happened here, except that I overheard Enzo talking. The hall where the guests were eating got so loud, I ended up with a headache. So I stepped into the outer foyer for peace and quiet. That is when I heard him say 'Massimo is distracted with the dinner. We can meet at the docks . . .'" She hunched her shoulders. "I am unsure what it was that unsettled me, because that did not exactly spell out anything nefarious, but I had this knot in my stomach . . . so I followed him and overheard the conversation about weapons."

"It's called instinct," Dillon said with an affirming nod. "Clearly, it's a good thing you followed him, or we wouldn't have this trail."

Appreciating that he gave her credit for that, she managed a soft nod. "Thank you. I am glad too." Because otherwise, he would already be out of her life. "When Enzo left the hall and got in his car, I scrambled to follow. I had to dart back inside and ask Yasser, our driver, to let me have the keys. I lied"—she gave a sheepish shrug—"and told him I left something in the vehicle. But I hurried out and spotted them back on Main, turning left onto a street to the dockyards. Trailing them, I parked near a three-story building across from big round silos. I do not know what the building was. From there, I went on foot."

"That's what we'll do too." Dillon shifted the SUV into gear and nodded. "So, right at the end of the street?"

"Yes, then the first left—not the turnaround, though."

— • —

"No turnaround. Got it," Dillon murmured as he pulled out after a dinged-up silver sedan puttered past, looking like it was literally on its last wheel.

Strange buzzing vibrated through him as he pulled into the left lane and visually targeted the turn. There, he slowed into the cross area and waited again for traffic to clear. But to be here—to be at the same dock where Dad had been . . .

Tapping his thumb on the steering wheel, he felt the zing of excitement ripping through his veins. Maybe a hint of nerves too. They'd gotten away from the shooters in Mykonos, but that problem wasn't going away. Someone wanted Cove. And he wasn't really sure why. Did they want to leverage her against Massimo? Or maybe she knew something . . .

"Right there," she said, pointing to a white-and-blue building. "I parked there."

Where she indicated was on the left. To have parked, she would've had to cross the street. He guessed the lot of the plat that had the silos would be too open, visible. Smart girl.

Detouring to the spot, he pulled between two vehicles, the SUV notably higher-end than either, and killed the engine. Even with antitheft advancements, the SUV had a very real chance of being rehomed before they got back. He hoped not, but he was realistic.

Grabbing the fob, he looked at Cove, who was peering out the side window, toward the docks. "You good?"

She glanced at him, seemingly weighted by the world, then nodded.

They climbed out and he swiftly gained her side, moving down the road. Humidity exacerbated the high temperatures here in Yemen, pushing into the "excessive heat" category. In the hazy distance, he spotted rugged mountains that were not the lush green of the Catoctin mountains in Northern Virginia. These were formidable but def not inviting. Through the buildings he could see cargo ships gliding through the sea, navigating around trawlers.

"From here," Cove said as she reached the half wall lining the road, "I could see his car and two others glide in the direction of the main GIS warehouse, which is that gray building along the dock."

"Got it."

She pointed more westerly. "We have three other warehouses across the dock on that side—the explosion happened over there, but the offices are in that building. That is why I got concerned that night, because nobody should be in there after dark. And when I got closer, I did not recognize the men."

"Did you tell your dad about his right-hand guy seeing unknown individuals in his warehouse?"

"No," she said around a thick breath. "I had not been working long with Papà, and the week before, I made a foolish error in judgment. I thought I had found a mistake and suspected Enzo, but then it was proven false. Papà was not happy."

"No doubt that ticked off Enzo too. Let me guess—he's the one who proved your mistake was wrong."

She nodded and groaned. "He was very angry, but he . . . let it go."

Dillon sniffed. "Smart move on his part—let you eat crow so he could look better to your dad and maybe play his hand later."

"I kept this to myself since I could not make sense of what happened. There did not seem anything terribly wrong. It was just here"—she tapped just below her ribs—"that doubts have bred. It hurt my heart to see how upset he and Flavio were . . . and to have my papà's anger aimed at me taught me to be very careful before accusing again."

"And I bet over the following weeks, months, and years, Enzo made sure you stayed uncertain of yourself and your capabilities."

Cove had to shift her entire upper body to look at him. "What do you mean?"

"Gaslighting," he said with a shrug. "Making you doubt yourself, question if you're recalling things correctly. Saying you misremembered. Maybe even using your mom's death to suggest you're tired and not thinking clearly."

Only when he'd gone a few more steps did Dillon realize Cove had stopped. He shifted back to her. "You okay?"

Her eyes were a molten gold beneath welling tears. One slipped free. "That is *exactly* what he has done. When I returned to the office after that fiasco with the error, nothing was as it had been. The printed-out sheet did not match, and he said I was misremembering. When I questioned him about what I saw here that night, he said I was simply tired from grieving Mamma, that I could not understand. He insisted the man he met with was a Georgian I already know. That it had been dark, I was too far away . . ."

"He convinced you not to believe what your own eyes saw." Dillon nodded. "Classic gaslighting and a legit form of evil, in my opinion."

She lifted a hand to her mouth, the niqab flattening beneath her touch, giving him the faintest impression of her face. "*Balorda!* I cannot believe . . ."

"No idea what that means, but . . ." Dillon drew her away from the road and pedestrian path that served as a sidewalk, so they were no longer in the open. "Losers like that aren't worth the air they breathe. You're an intelligent, capable, knowledgeable young woman. And your devotion to your dad is off the charts, paired with a deadly chunk of courage."

"You will make me cry again."

"That's the last thing I want to do, but knowing how this guy got in your head . . ." Dillon hated they were on the street, that she was in ridiculous garb that made it next to impossible to see her expressions. "Just let me get my hands around his neck and you won't have to worry about him breathing another lie to or about you."

Her fingers caught his in a subtle-but-lightning-rod gesture that struck straight to his heart. "Thank you. I needed someone to tell me I was not crazy."

Some great weight settled on his chest that made it hard to breathe as he stood, fingers linked, staring at her gold eyes, notably bright against the void of material consuming her. Fighting the urge to pull her into his arms, protect her from this piece of work who had her doubting herself and her intelligence . . .

A horn blasted, startling them both.

Heart jarred into a normal rhythm, he regretted having to release her hand, but it was considered haram here to hold hands in public. "Come on. Let's find a way to prove that guy wrong." And even though he couldn't see her mouth, he could tell there was a smile by the twinkle in her eyes.

She led them down one street, traversed a small alley, and darted across another road to stand in the alley between two buildings. "See there?" She indicated diagonally, beyond the street to a crossroad that ran parallel to the dock itself and the GIS warehouse. "That first building is the smaller GIS warehouse and offices. Behind it, another warehouse. And beyond that, the dock with dinghies and fishing boats, where your dad—"

"Yeah, yeah." His heart skipped a beat, imagining Dad being

here. "I see it." He shook a finger toward across the road. "That two-story gray building was in the photo with our dads. I used it to lead me here. Spent a couple of days looking around but couldn't put anything together." This location, at night? Visibility would be reduced. Not impossible, but enough that it probably gave that *mostro* Enzo the ammo to make Cove doubt herself. His gaze hopped from light to light across the dockyard. Enough light to make identifying an individual credible.

"Looks like there aren't many people at the office," she said.

Dillon noted the two compact vehicles haphazardly parked. Driving rules here seemed more like general guidelines than hard-and-fast laws. "Hey . . . You mentioned a car accident when you were here . . ."

She indicated to her right. "It happened at that corner. That car was going way too fast for this congested area."

Dillon nodded, taking in the location, the warehouse, the docks. Another nod. "Okay, you ready?" When she didn't answer, he glanced at her.

Leaning back against the building, she had her eyes closed.

Concern speared him. "G? You good?"

"I don't know if I can do this . . ."

Surprised at her sudden doubt, he edged in. "What happened to that courage I just saw?"

Her eyes snapped open and locked onto him. "I do not like lying to people."

"Then . . . don't lie."

She blinked, irises dancing with questions that vied for attention and explanation.

"Remember," Dillon said, "the likeability rule: Be likeable—and I know you ace that. Everyone who has met you likes you."

"You haven't met Enzo yet."

"And that is the only reason he's still alive."

She laughed softly. "You are so very heroic."

His thoughts threatened to jump into the sea at her praise. "Not really, but I like that you think so." *Head in the game, HotShot.* "In the office," he said, nodding to the warehouse, "just tell them you have work to do."

"What if they know Papà was taken?"

"Use it." He inched nearer and tucked his chin in meaning. "You belong in there, and they shouldn't question that. Everything they say should be measured with that in mind. Use them knowing about your father's kidnapping to your advantage. People distracted by grief will overlook a lot."

"That seems wrong."

"It's effective," he said, not giving her doubts room to fester. "This is not the time for uncertainty. Walk in there like you own the place, which you kind of do. Authority is another rule—acting like you're in charge lets others *not* be in charge, and most people don't want to be in charge. They simply want order. If someone will lead, they'll follow, so . . . lead."

She groaned as she used the niqab to fan herself. "I am not cut out for spy stuff."

Dillon smirked. "Just say less, not more. Explaining and being chatty gets you in trouble."

"It is like you know me."

He bit back a laugh. "I know people." He indicated toward the GIS building. "You lead, I'll follow."

"Reverse that, and I would feel much better."

"I've got your back, G."

She flashed that award-winning smile. "Deal."

They stepped from the alley and made their way down the street. Dillon's mind flashed back to the picture of Dad at the dock. Of course, the boat he'd boarded wasn't here now. But it was haunting to be here, knowing Dad had been before washing up in Tanzania. It was a crazy thought, but being here somehow made Dillon feel closer to finding him. Had a spark of hope again. And that had a lot to do with the Italian heiress at his side.

He caught the door handle, half expecting it to be locked. To be denied—a common theme these many months since he'd set out from Virginia. Instead, it came open freely. He held it for her.

Cove slipped inside and immediately removed the niqab, which she manipulated to wear like a hijab as they made their way along the southern wall. Pallets of boxes stacked thirty or forty meters high filled the cavernous space. The unmistakable reek of seawater drenched the air and would've likely seeped into the boxes had they not been wrapped in shrink-wrap. "Office is up on the second level," she whispered.

Trailing Cove, he kept his head on a swivel and hands free, ready to grab the handgun at his back. They climbed the metal stairs to the upper level. Clapboard walls barricaded the offices and had two windows and a door.

Cove strode in with all the confidence he knew her to possess.

A man sitting at a desk to the right lazily looked up. His eyes bulged when he saw who stood before him and shot to his feet. "Miss Galtieri. So sorry. I did not know you come."

"*As-salamu alaikum*, Mohammed," Cove said, offering the standard Arabic greeting with a smile—a nice sight after being hidden on the streets—that was both warm and welcoming.

"*Wa alaikum as-salam*, Miss Cove," Mohammed replied quickly, lowering his salt-and-peppered head in deference, his gaze then taking in Dillon. "Mr. Enzo did not say you were coming."

Another man emerged from the far left, where a door led to a room with several desks visible. "Miss Cove, we hear about Mr. Galtieri. I am so sorry."

Her gaze shifted to Dillon, then back to the man. "Thank you, Ali. We pray for his quick return, but that is part of why I am here. I need to do some work."

"Of course," Ali said, motioning her to the room with desks, then eyed Dillon curiously. "Your . . . security guard is welcome, of course."

Cove shot him a look. "Oh—"

Dillon gave a sharp nod to the man. "Guard" was a good assumption because he *would* guard Cove. Protect her with his last breath, if needed, and he liked that these men assumed that was his role. That they perceived a level of threat from him that implied security detail. "This way," he said, holding a hand to the room with workstations.

In the office, she strode to a desk in the back corner and sat in the chair, which faced the door. Good.

As Dillon trailed her to the back of the work area, he scanned the ceiling and walls for security cameras but found none. Once she sat down, he positioned himself behind her, back to the wall, feet shoulder-width apart as he palmed a fisted hand, standing as sentry.

Cove powered up the system, then logged in. She eyed him over her shoulder. "You look so . . . terrifying standing like that."

"Kinda the point," he said with a smirk, noting the locals remained in the reception area.

"I have no idea what to look for . . ." she whispered, looking at the monitor again.

Shadows skittered and slid toward them. "Incoming," Dillon subvocalized.

"Please, miss," Mohammed said as he hedged into the long room. "We go home now. Yes?"

"Of course," Cove said with all the ambivalence of a royal dismissing a servant. "I have my guard. Good night."

Dillon kept his expression blank.

"Yes, thank you. Thank you." He backed out, then both men exited the offices and headed down the stairs.

"That works," Dillon muttered, crossing the workstations and out into the reception area. At the window in the door, he watched the two men exit the main warehouse. He closed the blinds in the window, flipped the lock, then returned to Cove and motioned to the computer.

"What am I looking for?" she asked.

"Any bills of lading from the night you saw Mostro here with the unknown male."

Snickering, Cove went to work.

"In fact, maybe check the accounting books for that week too." Dillon planted himself at a terminal across from her, pulled up a browser, then accessed the site to connect with Helios. He typed in a message.

SECURE SITE. NEED HELP. AROUND?

"I already looked at that," Cove murmured absently.

"Can you access security feeds? Maybe get an image of that guy he was with?"

"I . . . have no idea how to access that."

"Okay, give me a sec." He sent the message to Helios.
Bling.

GA.

Relieved at the shorthand for *go ahead*, which meant Helios was on the other end and able to help, he sent another message.

NEED INFO FROM THESE SYSTEMS. CAN YOU ROOT IN?

STILL HAVE USB? PLUG IT IN.

Uh . . . Dillon grabbed the backpack and found the USB, which he stuck into the drive, then typed the response.

DONE.

"What are you doing?" Cove asked, ditching the niqab altogether.

"Giving my friend access so he can help us." Dillon rotated toward her. "Did you find the records?"

"Yes, but . . ." She scanned and scrolled, clicked . . . all while frowning. Covering her mouth, she leaned an elbow on the desk as she stared at the monitor, that divot between her eyes deepening.

"Something wrong?"

TWENTY-ONE

Port of Aden, Yemen

THESE ARE . . . DIFFERENT. WRONG." FINGERS flying over the keyboard, Cove opened another browser. "I am going to remote-access my system at home because . . ."

Dark eyes considered her for a long second. "Enzo getting you to doubt yourself again?"

It infuriated Cove that she had all but handed Enzo the means to rip the confidence from beneath her feet as if it were an old, tattered rug. "Perhaps," she conceded, "but as I said—I want to be very careful before accusing someone again."

"Trust yourself, Gelato."

Wisdom said double-checking facts should be done before she again took a strident position. But she appreciated Dillon's belief in her. It was . . . rare. A gift. As juvenile as it sounded, he made her swoon. "I need to be sure I'm remembering correctly." Once she'd remote-accessed her files at home, she pulled up the very documents Enzo had said she misremembered. They were in a batch that had been scanned in, along with some digital receiving files.

"The only reason I remember this file"—she looked over to the other doc browser she had open—"is because I studied this, *memorized* it, after that nightmare. I kept staring at it, confounded that Enzo told me it wasn't what I thought. That I was misremem—"

Words left her as she stared at the file retrieved from her home system. Her heart jostled in her chest, pulse rapid as she flicked her gaze between the two. "I was right." The breath whooshed from her tight chest. "I cannot believe it."

On a wheeled chair, Dillon rolled over to her station. "What'd you find that proved what I already knew?"

"It has been falsified or altered or something." She pointed to the lading numbers. "Look—same numerical sequence . . ."

Dillon shifted toward the screen, taking in the information, the two different documents. "Idiot altered it and forgot to adjust the bottom line."

"I believed that *mostro*."

Dillon looked up at her with a smirk. "Glad you're using that word on someone else now." A *ding* from the other terminal made him roll back to that computer. "My friend's in the system." Typing, he said, "I'm having him find the security feeds from that night."

He fell silent as he reviewed files, and Cove kept working, more determined than ever to not only prove Enzo wrong but that he was complicit in whatever was happening with Papà. She pored over the data, digging through countless customs forms, manifests, and accounting documents. A solid hour or more into it, something pinged in her mind. "Wait . . ." Her heart drummed.

"You good?" Dillon asked from her left.

"This name . . ." Why did she know this name? "It is familiar, but I cannot recall how or why. I think . . . Rasulov. Where . . ." In her mind's eyes flashed a face.

"My friend Yusif Rasulov."

"That's right . . ." she breathed, her mind racing to connect the dots.

"Cove?"

She flinched and looked at him. "What?"

"It seemed like you found or figured out something."

"I . . ." She shifted her gaze back to the logo on some documents, the initials on a few others. "On several ladings, there's an RHB . . . *Rasulov Holdinqlər Birləşdirilmişdir*—"

"*Gesundheit.*"

She frowned at him.

He waved her on. "Lame joke. Go on."

"At the Paris event—"

"I remember Paris," he said with a wink, no doubt insinuating the near-kiss into the conversation.

"Would you stop flirting with me!"

"Never."

"Dillon—"

Understanding her mood, he snapped an unrepentant salute.

"At that event in Paris, the Georgian minister my father has done business with for years introduced me to a man I had not invited, a man GIS certainly had *not* done business with—at least to my knowledge . . ." Again she considered the evidence trail. "One Yusif Rasulov, an Azerbaijani National Assembly chairman."

Dillon jerked straight, his amusement gone, dark eyes intense and focused—finally. "Hold up. Georgia . . . Azerbaijani . . . this port . . ." Brightness flashed on his screen along with another ding, drawing both of their gazes. It was an image of a well-lit warehouse with two men standing mere feet from the camera angle. One was Enzo and the other—

Cove sucked in a hard breath. "That's him! That's Rasulov with Enzo!"

Dillon's complexion went near-white. "This?" he asked, pointing to the Azerbaijani. "Unibrow is Rus-o-lot? You sure you saw this guy?"

Anger sprouted through her chest that he would question her, doubt her. "I did not just see him," she bit out. "I talked to him and shook his hand—made my skin crawl."

"Holy fire, Cove."

"What? Don't you believe me?"

His dark eyes widened. "No, I do—but I don't want to."

She scowled. "Why?"

"Because this man you called Rasulov?"

"Yes? What?" she spat, growing angrier.

"This guy has been dubbed *Qanlı Qılınc,* the 'bloody sword.' He's the mastermind behind *Yanan Günəş,* the Blazing Sun Project. He's the one pulling together all necessary resources, experts, materials—you name it—to insure the viability of Iran's nuclear program. After that war between Israel and Iran in 2025, he's been in high gear. There are more people under this man's toxic thumb than any in the course of history."

She let the information sink in, more than a little dumbfounded. And sick to the stomach too. "Did *you* see him in Paris?" she asked, heart pounding. "He was there—he was there with *mio papà* just before I spotted you. Did you—"

"No, thank God," he said, looking pale. Then recognition wavered in his eyes. "Wait—I . . . I saw some men heading to the bar with your dad that night. Didn't see faces . . . It's a good thing he didn't see me either." His expression darkened. "I barely escaped his henchmen in Armenia."

Cove started. "Why would he be chasing *you*? How do you even know of him?"

"Besides that fact he's Satan's spawn?" Dillon gave a grave shake of his head. "He wants me dead because for a while there, I was convinced he'd taken my dad."

Heartsick, Cove realized something that, in a twisted sense, gave her hope. "This means our paths are more aligned than we believed. That me coming here with you was—*is*—important."

"I think you mispronounced *dangerous*."

A couple of dings made them both glance at his computer.

Dillon shifted closer, then grunted.

Nerves aflame at the discoveries they were making, Cove struggled to stay calm. "What? Something wrong?"

"More than both of us being on a collision course with *Qanlı Qılınc*?" He furrowed his brow, then clicked the image of Rasulov. He zoomed in.

"What is it?"

"My friend," he murmured, "said to look in the background."

"It's the interior of the warehouse…" Uncertain what this friend noted, she kept looking because she only saw stacks of—

Dillon shot to his feet with a strangled shout. Bent closer to the monitor. "My dad!"

Heart in her throat, she leaned closer, searching the grainy image. "Where?"

He tapped the screen's upper right corner. "Here."

Sure enough. Looking beyond Rasulov's shoulder, far down into the warehouse and ensconced in darkness, lurked the ghosted image of a man. "This is so good! Actual footage of what he was doing here!"

"He sent the feed." Dillon double-clicked the icon of an MP4 file and played the footage. This was from a different angle. "Strange that Dad didn't worry about the cameras . . ." he murmured, watching.

"It's dark in the bay on this one," Cove noted. "Must've been after everyone left."

"Still, he would know cameras are there . . ."

"Maybe he was hurrying?" An idea struck Cove. "Remember, you had mentioned the photo of our fathers was taken during the day." She indicated to the computer. "Is this proof he was still alive after your government says he died?"

Tightening his jaw, Dillon frowned. Bobbed and shook his head. "Maybe. But I already knew he wasn't killed in that car explosion because he showed up in Tanzania after they said he'd died."

"Right."

Dillon watched his dad stalk up and down the rows of pallets. "It's like he's looking for something specific," he noted.

Finally, his dad stopped at one in the corner that was in perfect view of a camera and glanced around. Vanished into a darkened spot out of shot of the camera, but returned a moment later with a metal bar and a—

"Backpack," Cove murmured, her heart skipping a beat.

"Explains how he got it."

Next, his dad used the steel bar to break into the enormous crate, then he pried open an inner container.

"Son of a flaming-hot biscuit," Dillon breathed. "Weapons cache."

"GIS does *not* ship weapons! That cannot be . . ." Cove balked.

"Say what you want, but they're right there." He frowned, squinting as he angled closer again as his dad started loading up the backpack. "What the . . . ?" Palming the desk, he strained to see. "Those aren't weapons he's grabbing . . ."

Cove felt out of her depth. "What is it?"

Dillon shook his head, scowling. "No idea." He grabbed the keyboard and typed in a chat box at a site that had pizza slices all over it.

SAVE ALL THIS.

A reply appeared:

ALREADY DID.

GOOD.

WHO'S THE WOMAN?

Cove started. "How does he know I'm here?"
Fingers freezing over the keyboard, Dillon drew back. "Good question."

YOU SEE US?

PSYCHIC.

But then an image came through of them both staring down at the terminal.
"Where . . . ?" Dillon's gaze raked over the room, angling this way and that, clearly trying to locate that camera. His gaze hit on something. "Freak!"
That's when Cove saw the open laptop on the desk near the front, angled straight toward them, the green light glowing. "Oh no . . ."
"Your friend is watching us?"
"If he can, anyone can," Dillon muttered even as new letters tracked along the bottom of the screen.

INCOMING. GO!

After a few keystrokes that killed the pizza page and then a few more, Dillon rushed to the front area and peered through the slats. "We've got company, G."

"This way!"
Dillon pivoted and spotted Cove heading for the back of the main office area. She flung open a door to another stretch of the warehouse. He caught up with her and hustled down the steel steps

behind her, trying to keep their movements as quiet as possible. "Did you log out?" he asked once they hit the main floor.

"Yes. Cleared the history too," she said, slipping on the abaya. Smart girl, remembering to grab it.

They rushed to the far wall, still ensconced in shadow despite the lights popping on in the warehouse in response to the movement of the incomers.

"Besides the bay doors, the only door is at the front," Cove whispered.

Figured. Dillon nodded his understanding and started working toward the front, sticking to the wall to keep the lights from betraying their position.

Which did not work.

"Run," Dillon rasped, and they broke into a sprint. Rounded a corner and aimed for the brown metal door. Shouts came from somewhere in the warehouse, and served to propel him faster. He punched the door and felt the heat of Yemen rush him.

A yelp ripped his heart from his chest—Cove. He pivoted just outside the door and found her in the grip of that slick dandy from Paris. Dillon skidded to a stop, weighing whether or not to coldcock the guy.

"Ilaria, what are you doing here?" the guy asked her, giving Dillon a dismissive glance as he held her in a firm grip. "My papà said you were here, but I told him he was out of his head because your papà had just been kidnapped. 'She would not be that foolish,' I told him."

"Release me, Flavio!" she insisted, trying to writhe free.

"I do not think so."

"Let her go," Dillon demanded.

"Oh, I most certainly do not answer to you, Rogue. You are far beneath our lovely princess here."

There was a dark menace in the guy's gaze that told Dillon he might have to use the weapon at the small of his back. "I won't say it again," he warned. "Let her go."

Flavio curled his lip. "I don't think—"

"Noticed." In a lightning-fast strike, Dillon glided in and coldcocked the guy, who dropped like a bag of rocks. He caught Cove's hand. "C'mon." They spun toward the corner.

A dark shape bled from the shadows, forcing them back. "It would seem," came a menacing voice that a moment later manifested into none other than *Qanlı Qılınc* himself, "my men failed me in Armenia." Beady eyes considered them from beneath that bushy unibrow that looked as if the man's mustache was in the wrong place. He toed the dandy on the ground, unconscious. "I will not make that mistake again, Mr. Jacobs."

Dillon had guessed the guy remembered him. Backing up, he gauged his options, scanning the area. Recalling what he'd seen when they came in. Knew if they could get across the street, the darkness and tightly packed road would aid their escape.

"Miss Galtieri."

Hardness edged into Cove's gaze as she stiffened. "Mr. Rasulov."

"Ah, you remember," he said with a low laugh. "You are not like most women, with that sharp mind in a pretty head. It seems you have a knack for recollection and intelligence. It gets you in trouble, I think."

Threatening Dillon was one thing, but threatening her—a game changer that *really* ticked him off. Easing back, he angled slightly toward Cove to shield his retrieval of the gun at the small of his back. "Alleys," he whispered to her, but even as he did, he felt something jab into his back. The unmistakable imprint of a weapon. Jaw tight, he lifted his palms, abandoning his attempt for the gun.

"You did not think I came alone, did you?" Rasulov said, his unibrow wagging.

No doubt the thug behind Dillon would try to take the concealed weapon.

"Now, Miss Galtieri, where are the triggers?" Rasulov demanded. "And I will warn you, I am not known for patience. Violence?" He lifted a shoulder in a shrug and pursed his lips. "Most definitely."

"I don't know what you mean." She took a step forward. "Where is *mio papà*?"

"Not here," *Qanlı Qılınc* said calmly, *too* calmly. "And I would say 'safe,' but it is not good to lie. Now—the triggers!"

Triggers . . . triggers . . .

Dillon's mind ricocheted around the word and put it together with this demon-spawn. The truth slammed into him and tightened his gut—the triggers were nuclear! He tensed, understanding that Dad had found the nuclear triggers in that cache.

Yes. Dad had stolen nuclear triggers from the man responsible for ensuring Iran became fully nuclear. *That's* what this was about. That—*that* was something Dad would give up his cushy life in Virginia to thwart. Any modicum of anger he felt toward his dad at abandoning their family to pursue some mission evaporated as he understood that by doing so, Dad had ensured the world stayed safe.

Only then did he realize the guard hadn't seized the gun. Had he not seen it?

Dillon stole a look behind him. Spied a guy about his age. But unlike Dillon, the guy seemed inexperienced. Scared, especially with the way he waved that AK-47. A scared gunman was unpredictable and dangerous because fingers got twitchy.

Another guard stood behind *Qanlı Qılınc*.

That was it? Two guards? Were there more Dillon hadn't seen? Surely Rasulov hadn't counted on Flavio for protection. Hands still up, Dillon angled a little closer to Cove. Felt the fabric of the abaya and tapped her shoulder blade. Felt her tense.

Dillon stepped back and aside. Saw Scaredy's weapon. Grabbed the stock and yanked hard, even as he drew the gun from the small of his back. Felt the rear guard stumble, weapon coming free, as Dillon fired the Ruger at the second guard. Whipped the rifle at Rasulov, connecting solidly with the temple of the man who barely saw it coming and went flying backward. Rounding on Scaredy, Dillon aimed the Ruger at him. Seeing the kid's terrified expression—yes, he saw the irony of thinking of this guy as a kid despite being the same age—he cracked the AK-47 over his head. The guy went down.

"Go, run!" he huffed to Cove, noticing *Qanlı Qılınc* moving on the ground, groaning around the banger of a headache he no doubt had now.

They sprinted across the road. "Alley," he rasped to her. The report of a gun cracked through the night.

Plaster spat at them as they dove into the alley.

Cove cried out, stumbled.

Heart in his throat, he caught her shoulders. Pulled her back up and urged her to keep moving. "You hit?" Though he tried to search her, the shadows were too deep and the light too distant.

"No." She caught her balance and was up and running again.

Only as they reached the road where they'd parked the SUV did he understand where she was headed. But halfway down the street, he realized the shiny black vehicle wasn't there.

Cove must've noticed too, because she slowed.

"Don't slow," he huffed, aiming her toward the line of vehicles along the road. At least they'd have cover.

"It's gone!" she balked. "Someone stole the Land Cruiser."

"Focus on what we can control. We need to get out of here," he said as they jogged onward. "Just keep moving in and out of alleys and roads."

Ahead, lights flared against the blanket of black.

"Wait." Dillon caught her shirt and drew her aside.

She complied, clumsily, but shifted course. They ducked into the narrow road that squeezed between two multistoried buildings and glanced back as two vehicles slid by, windows down, and that unmistakable white hair and black unibrow evident in the passenger seat.

Although they were fully entrenched in darkness, Dillon still would not slow or stop. The longer they stayed in the area, the more likely *Qanlı Qılınc* would find them. They streaked down the road to another. No sooner had they stepped out than shots erupted.

Cove took off, sprinting to the right, then zigzagging between buildings, but she wasn't fast. She was flagging, yet she did not stop. And her direction seemed focused and intentional.

While he didn't like not being in control or familiar with the area, he could trust her, especially since she really seemed to know where she was going. That pushed him on.

Where a building met a half wall, Cove paused, gasping for breath.

"You okay?" he asked, stepping around her and considering their situation and location.

Despite heavy breaths and swallowing to keep her mouth and throat wet, Cove nodded. "I cannot believe Flavio was working with that *mostro*."

"Don't think that word is strong enough to describe *Qanlı Qılınc*."

"Agreed."

———— • ————

Oh, how her lungs burned. Cove pushed on, taking them on a parallel route to 90, away from the docks. Away from anything that Rasulov might think was familiar. That made sense, right, to head toward things that might be unfamiliar? Though, she had been here enough times that she had a very solid overall sense of direction and idea of what lay ahead.

They came to a park that was well-lit and, despite the hour, alive with music and people. Cove slid the niqab back on, but it was too difficult to breathe with it covering her mouth. She let it drape around her neck. With Dillon at her side, she was pretty confident they could conquer anything. Maybe even survive this night.

"You were impressive back there," she said around thick breaths, feeling sweat slip down her spine. Thank heavens she had remembered the abaya, or she might have been mobbed and beaten for being indecent in public. "When I saw Rasulov, I was sure we were going to die."

"Nah," Dillon said, gaze steadily roving as he navigated them toward shadows and out of the light. "He wanted something, so that would've kept us alive."

"Yes," she said, glancing at him. A wave of dizziness crashed over her and she stumbled. "He said *triggers*."

He swung those beautiful eyes, laced with concern, in her direction. "You okay?"

"Fine." She gulped a breath, more sweat making her clothes stick to her. "What are the triggers—wait! I remember now—I heard him talking in Paris about triggers." She looked to him. "Is that triggers like on guns?"

"I think it's worse," Dillon said as they walked along the paved area with the sea on their left and park on the right.

"How so?" Perspiration dotted her brow and upper lip.

"Remember the video we saw of my dad in the warehouse and we wondered what he took?"

The ominous note in his words worried Cove. She eyed him, dread stirring nausea through her belly. "Yes . . . ?"

"I knew whatever Dad was looking for had to be important. He didn't care about the cameras and was very focused. Determined."

Her legs were so weak from all the running, a tremor ran through them, but she tensed them and forced herself to keep going.

"Let's cross." Dillon indicated to the other side of the street. "We're too open and there's too many innocents here. I don't want anyone getting hurt because of us. Once we get into the congestion of buildings, we can find a place to hole up and get our bearings."

"Sssounds amazing."

He frowned at her, his beautiful gaze staring at her.

Cove swallowed, hating the stickiness of wearing the abaya that was plastered against her body. "I'm fine—just hot and sweaty. And tired. Now"—she wagged a hand—"what did your dad find in the warehouse?"

"Nuclear triggers."

She widened her eyes, mind spinning. "That's what Rasulov meant by triggers? Are you joking?"

"Wish I were."

They climbed the tiered terraces of the park, moving past people enjoying a late night and not caring about the darkness or hour, and then headed to the street.

"I think that's why my dad went missing," he said. "It all really tracks now. For the longest time, even though I knew there was a reason, I couldn't figure out what my dad found so important that he'd give up his life and family . . . me. I knew him, *knew* it had to be big. I just couldn't have fathomed *this*. Now knowing about Rasulov being *Qanlı Qılınc* of *Yanan Günəş*, the Iranian nuclear proliferation project, it only makes sense that's what sent my dad back into covert ops. That's what convinced him to sacrifice his life and family. I get it. Iran having nuclear capability is not a good thing for our world. We staved it off once . . . I can't believe we're staring this down again, and so soon."

Dizziness washed over Cove as she approached the road. She must be dehydrated. When had she last had water? Or something to eat? They had been going, going, going for days. It was exhausting!

"I hear people say that, but I do not really understand politics or nuclear armament," she said once they got to the other side and made it onto a side street. "Personally, I wish nobody had ever created the things."

"You're not alone in that."

Cove did not want to seem naïve or dumb, but she really wanted to understand this thing that had so viciously embroiled her life and family. "So, why is it so bad for Iran to have them? If the US can have it, if other countries can, why not them?"

Dillon nodded, not bothered by her question, and more importantly, did not seem to think her ignorant or dumb. He was more sexy with each moment she knew him. "First and biggest reason is that the stated goal of the Islamic Republic of Iran is to wipe Israel off the map. They probably wouldn't nuke Jerusalem, but Tel Aviv would end up one big glass disc," he explained as lights swam and spun around them. "Second is it would destabilize the entire Middle East. Iranians hate the Saudis, so the Kingdom would be next in line to attain their own nukes."

Cove really wasn't sure she understood what he was saying . . . and why did he sound so far away? She stopped and glanced back at him, wondering why he was several paces behind. "Why—" Her hand thudded against his chest. Confusion rolled through her, mind blurring.

No—vision! Her *vision* was blurry.

Alarm erupted through Dillon's face. "Cove!" Then he blurred out.

A strange echo sounded in her head. And she realized . . . it matched the movement of Dillon's mouth, his words garbled. The edges of her vision grayed.

Hands clamped onto her arms. Jerked her upright. "Hey, you with me?"

The hard shake snapped her back to the present. She groaned

and looked at him, overwhelmed by a very sick, numb sensation crawling over her body. "I . . . I . . . do not . . . feel right."

"Cove! Cove, stay with me!" His strong, capable hands framed her shoulders. "Cove!"

The world tilted and Dillon's face loomed over her as the sky moved behind him. What . . . ? She felt a thud against her head.

"Cove!" Dillon cursed.

Everything felt thick and sludgy as she had a peripheral awareness of Dillon hovering over her, alarm carved into his handsome face.

Crack! Thud!

A blur of white careened in front of them.

Alarm shot through her—danger!—and adrenaline stabbed through her weakened, dehydrated body, telling her a van had pulled up behind him. Trouble. Danger.

Dillon shouted, and even as the world ghosted into oblivion, she saw armed men rush out, stuff a black hood over his head, and haul him away.

Nooooo!

TWENTY-TWO

Aden, Yemen

HEAD HEAVY AS IF HE WERE UNDERWATER, Dillon tried to extract himself from the thickening goo that filled his brain. What…happened?

In a rush, it all came back—froze him. Warned him not to make big movements. To silence the groan climbing his throat. A hood had been snapped over his head seconds before hands had hauled him backward. He'd been taken. Kidnapped. He hadn't gone down without a fight. Fists slamming into guts and jaws. Head cracking against someone else's.

"*Hit him*," a tenor voice gruffed right before a prick stung his thigh. Seconds before the world vanished in a haze.

Now, he had to get his bearings. Figure out where he was. What he faced. All before letting the enemy know he was conscious. Around him, he heard activity. Shoes scratching against a hard floor. A chair squawked distantly—the force of someone shoving it back.

The soft thud of steps drew near.

"Anything?"

"Nah," came a male voice. "Out cold."

"Would've thought he'd be more resistant, considering all he's put us through."

Something clattered behind Dillon, near his head. Maybe a table?

"Boss wants him up," the male said. "Can we get that going?"

Dillon dared a peek. Found a burly guy standing with his back to him, weapon in a thigh holster, tapping a machine. Awareness flared. The others were more distant.

Now or never. Dillon shot up, his rubbery legs almost uncooperative. But he managed to hook the guy's neck. Hauled him backward. They tumbled, but Dillon negotiated a good grip, even as he slid the man's Glock free and put it to the guy's head.

Shouts erupted in the large, dilapidated space, which came alive with men in tactical gear, weapons out, shouting for him to let him go.

Dillon counted four. Not undoable, but it'd mean he'd end up with a few extra holes in his body. That plan didn't excite him. "Where is she? What'd you do with her?"

"Let him go." A well-muscled black man moved toward him, palms out in a placating gesture. "This is unnecessary."

"*Where. Is. She?*" Dillon roared, feeling the strain of those words, his own heart thundering that nobody was answering him. He recalled too clearly seeing her collapse. Only then seeing the shininess on her black abaya indicating she'd been shot. It was his fault. "I don't let him go until—"

"Jacobs!"

Hearing his surname volley from the right yanked Dillon's gaze there. He found a six-one operator striding forward.

Hair cropped in a high-and-tight, temples edged in white, the newcomer glanced to a man who looked Native American. "I told you to check him for weapons."

"I did, Chief."

Only at the name and the gray eyes boring into him did Dillon register who this was. What this was.

"It's mine, boss," rumbled the big guy still under Dillon's control.

Frustration roiled through the older guy's face. "Jacobs, you made your point."

He didn't care who they were. "I thought I made that point years ago, but here you are. All up in my business again, Pike." He locked onto the chief. "Where is she?"

Chief Auberon planted his hands on his tactical belt and tightened his jaw. Then indicated to the door he'd just come through. "Surgery." He jutted his jaw. "Brick isn't as limber as he used to be. Want to let him go?"

"Not particularly." But Dillon shoved the guy forward. "Why'd you interfere with us?"

"Don't know, Chief," the muscular black man said. "He seem a touch ungrateful to you?"

Pike didn't answer, just held Dillon's gaze with a ferocity that belied the placid expression plastered on his face.

Brick turned and extended his hand to Dillon, motioning to the Glock. "Mind?"

Without looking at the guy, Dillon did a press check, ejecting the lone bullet in the chamber, dropped the magazine, racked the slide, and removed and set the pieces in the guy's hand. "Not at all."

"Let's talk." Pike pivoted and strode out the door he'd indicated to a second ago.

Furious that Omen Tactical had interfered, that they were here, had taken them off the street, Dillon gave the remaining team a long look, especially landing on the one who hadn't spoken or stood. "Dante."

His Scion brother gave a slow nod, then quirked an eyebrow in the direction of Pike.

Pulling in a ragged breath, telling himself to power down the fight-or-flight mode, he left the room. Found himself in a long, empty corridor with brick walls and cracked tiles. Two doors to his right looked shut tight. In the other direction, Pike was disappearing through another door.

Dude was going to make him work for it.

Hauling his irritation into check, Dillon headed after him. Rounded the corner. Hands yanked him upright and slammed him into the wall. His head thudded against the industrial concrete as his gaze blurred, then filled with blazing gray eyes. A forearm thrust into his throat, cutting off his air. Startled, panicked, he grabbed the elbow and wrist, but delayed the instinct to twist them in opposite directions. Because he had a steep self-preservation instinct that told him he'd never get one over on the former master chief.

"You *ever* put a gun to the head of one of my guys again, I will *end* you," Pike snarled, his voice low, preternaturally calm despite the very real threat. "Clear?"

Dillon stared at him, wanting to throw every bit of fight into defying him. But instead of fighting him, snapping at him, he just . . . waited.

"You got a dangerous attitude, Jacobs." The chief shoved him, then stepped back.

"I was doing fine—"

"Fine? You call getting an innocent girl killed 'fine'?"

Killed? Shock punched the air from Dillon's lungs. "What— she—you said she was in surgery!" Only when Pike drew up did Dillon realize he'd stepped into the chief's personal space.

Pike pivoted and stalked to the end of the wall, then stopped and looked back at him. Waited for him to cover the twenty paces where a window waited.

Knees going weak, Dillon clutched the window sill to steady himself as his brain registered that he was looking into a surgical bay. Two doctors were working—operating—on someone. Not just someone—Cove. A small curtain provided a modicum of modesty.

Pike stared at him. "The bullet entered just to the left of her spine. Hit her spleen."

Dillon hung his head. Closed his eyes. "She . . . she was fine . . ."

"She *wasn't*, and if she doesn't make it out of this, her death is on you."

"How could I have known?" Dillon demanded, anger sprouting violent tendrils through his chest and gut. "We were running. She said—"

"*You* put her life in danger! *You* brought her down here without resources, without backup against a notorious, powerful terrorist!"

Defeated, broken at what he'd put Cove through, Dillon turned his gaze to the window again. He would hate himself—scratch that. He already hated himself. She didn't deserve this. Why hadn't he listened to himself in Greece? Now . . . now she might not make it. "I didn't mean to . . . they hit the villa . . . came after us in Italy."

"And in Greece. When were you planning to take the hint that you couldn't do it alone?"

Rage colored his vision as he pivoted to the guy. "Do not turn this into a 'this is punishment for not working with Omen' lesson! You wouldn't do anything to save my dad. He's been missing for three years and what have *you* been doing?"

"Who do you think sent you that photo of Max and Massimo?"

Being struck with a baseball bat would not have rung his bell as much as those words. Dillon stared, his pulse hammering. "What . . . That came from Helios!"

Pike, confidence never wavering, gave a cockeyed nod. "Try again. And that chat last night showing the security feed in the warehouse?"

Dillon faltered, taking in this man who had been his nemesis, a thorn in his side. "No way. I contact him—"

"Pizza site?" Pike sniffed. "Talk about amateur hour."

"Helios—"

"Has been locked down since Paris."

Shock pushed Dillon back a step, squeezed the oxygen from his lungs as he wrestled the words and vehemence in Pike's tone. "No . . ." He shook his head, felt like he was about to toss what little was in his stomach.

The chief angled aside, flicked open a door to an office with a desk and chair. "Before you pass out, sit your sorry backside down and listen."

Fight hammered out of him, Dillon staggered over to the chair. Everything . . . all those communications . . . "That . . . was all you?"

Pike leaned back in the swiveling chair. Ran a hand through his hair. "Not me personally, but Omen, yes. Dade Tycho is our comms specialist. He easily spoofed the site."

Def going to be sick. Dillon sat on the edge of the chair, elbows on his knees, and swallowed the bile rising in his throat. "I should've known . . ."

"Yeah, you should have. No nineteen-year-old kid can do all that and hack a secure system." The derision in the chief's tone was duly warranted. "But I'll hand it to you, Jacobs. You did well. A lot better than expected."

Dillon peered across the hall, watching the doctors working in the medical theater to save Cove's life.

"Your connection with Galtieri was unexpected," the chief noted quietly.

"Tell me about it," Dillon muttered, pulling his gaze back to the floor, to himself. To all the danger they'd been in since they met.

"She matters to you."

Dillon met the steely gaze, wondering what that meant. Why he said that. Was it to use her as leverage? Was Auberon that sick?

"I've been monitoring your every move long enough to notice a shift in your behavior patterns since she entered the picture."

Irritation pushed Dillon straight. "Why? Why are you doing this—tailing me?"

Pike exhaled heavily and considered him. "Frankly, because you can do what I can't."

That statement had nothing to do with skill level, because Dillon knew Pike Auberon had Dad's respect, and that was hard to earn. "Dad said you were a man who got things done . . . but you didn't."

After a long, icy second, Pike nodded. "Hands were tied."

"Bullspit." Dillon didn't buy that for a second. "You're Pike Auberon. Omen has a reputation."

"We have that reputation because while we get things done, we do them through the front door."

Dillon frowned.

"We don't come in the back door, break laws. We respect the countries we operate in and with. If we have US government backing, we have a little more freedom and flexibility, but when that vanishes, so does our ability to operate. I don't want Omen to end up on the headlines of a scandal tabloid, so we play by the rules."

More of the shock that pushed him back a mental step hit Dillon. "That's why you've been helping me . . ." Which still messed with his head that it hadn't been Helios all this time. "Because I haven't been playing by the rules . . ."

"Taking matters into your own hands is not something I condone, but you have been able to get done what I couldn't touch. I sent you leads because you were too skilled, had too much potential for me to just walk away from. So this was part me protecting Max's son, part me wanting to find your dad. And I had this gut feeling you were like him. Driven. Intense. Focused."

That definitely described Dad. Not so sure it applied to him.

"And thick-skulled."

"Now you sound like my mom."

"She's who I heard it from first."

Wariness parked at the corner of Hesitant and Eager in his mind. "You talked to her?"

"Don't worry," Pike said. "She doesn't know where you are."

Relief made Dillon breathe a little easier. "She doesn't need to worry."

"Not knowing doesn't stop the worry, son. She's your mother," Pike said, "but she's also been married to an operator for nearly three decades. This is old hat for her."

Dillon nodded. "Fair." In his periphery he noted movement in the surgical bay and stood as a female doctor came toward the window removing a scrub, which she stuffed in a bin, then stepped into the hall. "How is she?"

The late-twenties woman glanced hesitantly to Pike.

"What? Tell me!" Dillon demanded, panic drenching his actions. He told himself to get a grip, to stop reacting, but Cove . . .

The chief joined him in the hall and indicated for the woman to go ahead.

"She's critical but will survive," the woman said, her expression and words tight. "The bullet nicked her spleen, so she had a lot of internal bleeding, but we got it under control. Had it been five, ten minutes later before we got to her, we'd be having a very different conversation." She gave Pike another nod, then excused herself, retreating down the hall.

"She blames me," Dillon said, moving to the window. As she should. "I had no idea . . . When we fled the warehouse, she stumbled, but said she was fine. We ran . . ." Holy fire, she'd been bleeding that whole time . . . "I nearly got her killed." Angry at himself, he felt his breathing go shallow. Knew if Pike— He turned to the chief. Met his gaze, mustering all the contrition he had left. "Thank you. If you hadn't been tailing us . . ."

"But I was. And she's going to make it. That's what matters." Pike shifted toward the window where the other doctor was applying a bandage.

"She just wanted to prove her dad's innocence against rumors that he was taking bribes."

"He was."

Dillon faltered. "*What*?"

"That's a whole different convo." Pike angled his head toward the corridor. "Tariq will let us know when you can see her. For now, let's get back to the team. I can fill you in there."

Not really wanting to leave Cove, Dillon hesitated for a second. "She'll be okay."

He'd failed to protect her, and he had the unrealistic thought that staying at her side would keep her safe. Truth was, she was probably safer *without* him. He returned to the large open area with Pike and found the team gathered around the long table.

"You met Brick," Pike said, indicating the burly guy Dillon had put into a chokehold.

Dillon nodded but the big guy didn't return it.

"Luther is my right hand." Pike pointed to the black man, who was athletic and amused. "Crow Rawlins is our sniper." The Native American. "And Dade Tycho is your pizza place hacker."

Something in Dillon tightened, grateful he'd been sparing with details while communicating with Helios.

"Casey is our analyst," Pike continued with the introductions, pointing out a woman at a bank of computers. "Okay, why don't you run us through what you know and found in the warehouse."

Dillon sat in a chair and looked up just as Brick pitched something at him. He caught it and found a paper-wrapped hoagie from a local place. "Peace offering?"

"Or poison," Brick said with a lazy shrug as he sat down.

Right. "Guess I deserve that." He set the sandwich on the table and tried to gather his thoughts. "So y'all know about Paris and Italy?"

"We know the basics," Luther said.

"Any intel come out of those?" Pike asked.

"No, I—wait. Yeah, maybe," Dillon said, remembering unibrow. "At the event, Cove said one of her dad's business partners had brought a man she didn't know. That man turned out to be Yusif Rasulov, also known as *Qanlı Qılınc*." He gave the chief a blank stare. "But you listened in on all that, so you already know."

Brick clapped. "A mite slow, but he's getting there."

"Not slow with your weapon," Dillon bit back.

"Okay," Pike said, knowing that was heading south fast. "Dial it down. Jacobs, we only had visual on you tonight. Audio wouldn't sync. Lay it out for us."

"*Qanlı Qılınc* showed up at the warehouse. He's the one who shot Cove when we escaped. That footage you sent tonight proved he was here more than two years ago when my dad went missing, so he's in deep. He demanded the triggers."

"Which your pop stole?" Luther asked.

There was an intimacy of knowledge there in his words. "Yeah." Anger tightened Dillon's chest. "Hold up—so you knew all this and you—"

"We knew he was in Yemen, but we lost contact with him," Pike said. "Keep talking."

Dillon hesitated at first. "Well, you saw the footage—he searched the warehouse. Seemed to know exactly what he was looking for. Found a crate, broke into it. Stuffed the contents in a backpack and left. Cove was there that night, unwittingly videoed Dad boarding a trawler. I had no idea what he took until we ran into Rasulov. Dude demanded to know where the triggers were. That's when I put it together, the one thing that would convince my dad to leave us, to do whatever it took . . . nuclear triggers."

Pike stretched his jaw.

Surprised there hadn't been more of a reaction from the chief, Dillon studied him. "You knew."

"Suspected," Pike confirmed. "Had zero proof. No idea where to look. Your dad was brought onboard to help rout the truth about GIS when we started seeing ties to Rasulov." He shifted to a dark-haired man. "Dade, you got her phone?"

"Yep."

"Find that video and find that boat."

"On it, Chief."

"Why are you looking for the boat? My dad ended up in Tanzania."

"Washed ashore."

Dillon stilled. Shouldn't be surprised at this point that the chief knew so much. "You sent me the images."

Another demeaning applause from Brick. "Not sure he's up to Max's level with that slow brain."

Dillon glowered, but focused on the chief again. "What do you care about the boat?"

"Think about it. Your dad shows up in Tanzania. What's he missing?"

Nearly cursing himself, Dillon should do the applause for the slow brain himself. "The backpack."

"Dude," Brick said. "That's record time. See? Being around OTG is good for him."

Why hadn't he thought about that? "So, the triggers . . . If *Qanlı Qılınc* didn't have them, then maybe we can prove her dad's innocence too. That's what Cove wanted."

"Got that backwards, son," Pike said. "We were out to prove his guilt."

"What . . . ?"

"Galtieri's company is a big-tech company with access and authority to get sensitive materials into and out of ports around the world. They're reputable and powerful—primed to be manipulated. And that's exactly what we believed RHB did by killing Galtieri's wife and threatening his daughter."

"Killing his wife?" Dillon balked, knowing it'd devastate Cove to know her father's business partners had murdered her mom.

"It makes sense—why else would a man appoint his daughter, who has no training or experience in leadership, as comms director?"

"Because she's intelligent and astute."

"Don't doubt it," Pike stated blandly, "but she wasn't qualified. Your dad believed RHB forced Galtieri to let them ship through GIS. Max was meeting with Galtieri, hoping to convince him to let your dad insert and dig around to find out the names involved."

"Good news, bad news, Chief," Dade called from the computer. "Found the boat—it's based out of Tanzania. Ship was attacked by Houthi pirates and sank."

Biting back a groan, Dillon realized . . . "That's why my dad washed up on the shore of that resort, looking like a vagrant."

Pike's gaze sharpened on Dillon with a quiet nod. "That tracks."

"So, the nuclear triggers . . ."

"Could be at the bottom of the Indian Ocean."

"Chief." A Middle Eastern man appeared in the far corner and thumbed over his shoulder. "She's coming to."

The words punched Dillon out of his chair. He hustled over to the doctor. "Where . . . ?" But even as he asked, he spotted her laid out on a bed in an adjoining room. The female doc who didn't like Dillon was adjusting an IV taped to Cove's hand, which rested on the light blanket. He all but threw himself into the chair next to the bed and caught Cove's free hand. Couldn't believe how pale she was, the color leeched from her pink lips and cheeks.

He cursed himself for not realizing what had happened. "I'm sorry." He kissed her hand.

Lashes fluttering, Cove gave a soft moan, her gaze drifting to him.

"Hey," he said quietly as he bent toward her.

A smile quavered on her lips. Sound hummed in her throat as if she was trying to talk.

"Your throat will be raw for a while," the female doc said as she touched Cove's shoulder. Her blue eyes glittered at Dillon with no little amount of anger.

Yeah, message received and duplicated. I hate me too.

"What . . . ?" Cove's brow furrowed and she wet her lips. "What happened . . . ?"

"You wanted a souvenir." He wanted to take back the words as soon as they left his mouth. "You got shot when we were fleeing Rasulov." When her eyes widened, Dillon cursed himself. Worked his jaw, remembering her collapsing in the alley. The way her eyes had rolled and she went down . . . "You nearly checked out on me, Gelato." Man, his throat felt thick.

Worry shaded her gold eyes as she peered at him.

"Bullet hit your spleen. You were bleeding internally."

"I thought I was too sweaty," she noted wryly, then she looked around. "Where are we?"

"Safe, Miss Galtieri," Pike intruded, coming to stand at the foot of her bed. "I'm Pike Auberon with Omen Tactical Group."

Cove's gaze found Dillon's again, and it did something strange to him that she sought reassurance and understanding from him. It shouldn't affect him—the simple fact was that she did not know anyone else here.

"We pulled you and Achilles from the street last night."

Last night? Wait—what time was it?

"If you don't mind, I think time is against us, so I need to borrow Mr. Jacobs."

"No," Dillon said, standing. "I'm not leaving her. She just had surgery—"

"Both your fathers and six nuclear triggers are missing."

A buzzing started at the back of Dillon's head. "How do you know how many there were?"

"Because I'm informed," Pike stated frankly.

"You've known this whole time," Dillon snarled, anger rising through him. "You let us chase leads that made me tell you what you already knew?"

"My job demands I stay abreast of situations and escalations. I would call anything related to the nuclear proliferation of Iran an escalation. Every piece of intel is critical. I had to hear it from your mouth to know if I was missing anything."

"You have been playing me—"

"Dillon," Cove whispered, squeezing his hand. "It is okay."

"No," he countered, glaring at the chief. Every time he thought this guy could be trusted . . .

"I'm tired," she whispered, her eyes fluttering closed.

"Your attitude is not going to serve you well in this, Jacobs."

"My attitude is what has gotten me this far."

"On the contrary—that instinct you inherited from Max is what did that. The training he gave you over the years instilled in you a deep suspicion and need to find the truth—*that* is what got you here. It also is why you neglected this young lady and nearly cost Galtieri her life."

"How dare—"

"I do. Because you've jumped with both feet into a race against Iran's nuclear capability." Fire lit through Pike's face. "Now, are you done throwing your tantrums over the illusion of control and ready to get this thing resolved, or do you need more time alone with your attitude?"

Outrage charged through Dillon. His jaw felt like it'd crack as he stared down the chief.

"I have a proposal for you, *if* you can get rid of that and hear me out."

Hand fisted, Dillon struggled to keep himself in check. "I wouldn't work with you if you were the last person—"

"I am. I am the last person, the last chance you have to save your dad." Pike stepped back. "When you're ready to act instead of whinge, come find me."

TWENTY-THREE

OVER THE COURSE OF A DAY, COVE FELT HER strength return rapidly. It surprised her how quickly a body could recover from surgery, and even more—that she had run for miles with a bullet in her back.

"The running is probably what aggravated your injury," said the woman who had been tending her. "Your spleen was pretty bruised and chewed up, but we did what we could."

Cove eyed her. "You helped . . . did my surgery."

"I assisted Mr. Wadi," the woman confirmed. "Tariq has his doctoral degree and I'm a combat medic working on my doctoral as well." She extended a slender hand. "Nora Glace."

Cove shook her hand. "Cove Galtieri."

"Oh, I know you. I followed your modeling career," she said, wrinkling her nose. "One has to make up for being in tactical boots and kit somehow."

Surprised yet again by this attractive woman, Cove could only gape. "You could give any model I know a run for her money. To be a medic on top of it . . ." Beyond the small room where more cots were set up, she saw several men in black pants and shirts moving around. Dillon was in there too. "So, you are a part of this . . . Omen?"

"Oh, not them," Nora said softly as she switched out an empty IV fluid bag. She looked into the room. "The man in the tan-and-black tactical shirt is Tyson Chapel, and I'm on his team. We were in a nearby country for training, so Pike asked for our help."

Unable to miss that Dillon sat, arms folded and positioned so he had a line of sight on her, Cove felt the fear of losing him stealing over her. He belonged with these people, these military types. She did not. This was not her world.

What is *my world?*

"Have you known him long?"

She eyed Nora. "I'm sorry?"

"Jacobs."

"Who?"

"Dillon Jacobs—have you known him long?"

I did not even know his last name. The daunting realization made her sad, wonder if their different worlds were *too* different. Only when Nora glanced down at her did Cove understand she had not yet answered. "N–no, we . . . uh, we met"—somehow, saying she met him when he broke into her papà's office felt like a betrayal because she could sense that tinge of annoyance in Nora regarding Dillon—"about a week ago."

Had it really only been a week? It felt like months!

"Then you don't know much about him," Nora said, as if she had just proven a point.

It might be true that her knowledge of him was little, but she wanted to know more. Wanted to know everything. And it scared her to think that their paths might part. That he would leave her.

"I know what I need to know," Cove said quietly, letting that still the brewing storm in her heart.

It sounded like Nora harrumphed.

"You do not like him."

"I don't like that he had no awareness of your injury, that you almost died because he drove you on and on . . ."

"I am pretty sure the shooters did that," Cove said. "And how could he know?"

"He should know the signs—he's an operator."

"But he's not an operator, not officially. And should I not know the signs? It is my body." Her heart pounded, anger stirring at this woman's accusations. "You may think I do not know him much, but you do not know him at all. He wanted me to stay behind so I would be safe. I refused."

Nora crouched at her bedside and set her hand over Cove's. "I am sorry. Clearly there are strong feelings involved. I have . . . seen many bad things done to women by ruthless men."

"He may be ruthless toward the enemy, but he has never been ruthless to me."

A flicker of relief seemed to wash the apprehension from Nora's pale features. "I am glad to hear that. I really wanted to hurt him when we got you in and saw how close you were to death."

Cove started. "I was?"

"Any longer and it might have been too late. That's why I was so upset with him." She managed a smile. "You ready for another walk around the room?"

With a nod, Cove drew her legs to the side of the bed, feeling the pinch of the bandage taped to her side. As Nora hovered before her, she came to her feet. Waited as dizziness washed in, then out.

"You good?"

"Yes." Cove slowly made her circuit around the room, glad that her body was managing this time much better than last.

From the front room came heated, angry words. She stilled, breath backing into her throat. "That is Dillon . . ."

A second later, he entered the room, his dark eyes roiling with some heavy storm that seemed to vanish when he saw her. "You're walking again."

Unsure what that dark look had been about, she smiled. Loved how his expression so noticeably changed because of her. "I am, though I would probably classify this as staggering."

"You're vertical and trying—that's what counts."

Nora waved him over. "Stay with her. I need to do something."

Eyebrows lifting in surprise, Dillon did not wait long. He joined her, and once Nora was gone, he muttered, "I didn't think she liked me."

"She said I was near death."

He winced. "Yeah . . ."

She eyed him, noting the stress lines around his eyes and lips. "I am okay, Dillon."

"No thanks to me," he muttered, tilting his head to indicate for her to keep moving.

"Hey." She turned and caught his arm. "I see in those beautiful, dark eyes the blame you put on yourself, but please—do not. Even I did not know what happened. I thought my back ached from Greece, when I crashed into the wall. And that abaya was so hot while I was running, I thought I was sweating. I had no idea it was blood."

"I should've seen the signs. It's—"

"Stop." Cove pressed a finger to his lips. "Please." Aware of the audience they had, she lowered her hand. "I am going to be okay."

"I nearly lost you . . ."

Touched at the very real, visceral pain in his words, she smiled. "They do not call me *Lupina* for nothing."

Torment wrung his brows and gaze. "What can I do? How can I make this up to you?"

She sagged beneath his self-condemnation. "This is *not* your fault. I have never and will never hold this against you. We had a deal, Dillon—to find our fathers. That is all I want."

Something flickered in his gaze. "Me too." He turned and slid a hand to her cheek. "I'm so sorry, Cove. I hate that you got hurt. That you—"

"New deal." She shrugged to trap his hand between her jaw and shoulder. "You cannot mention this anymore as we finish this search for our papàs. Yes?"

"I'm not sure I could ever tell you 'no' again."

"Mm, I think I like the sound of that." Giddy at his words, at his weighted expression, Cove felt her belly squirming beneath his prowling gaze that took her in. The intensity of it proved powerful, drawing her in like some forceful vortex. She gave him a coy smile, not sure what the roiling potency of his gaze meant. Why he seemed so . . . attentive. Was he still feeling guilty for her getting shot? That had been all over his handsome face earlier, but this seemed . . . different.

Her legs trembled. Or was that her heart? "I think I need to sit."

He guided her to a chair and helped her ease into it, mindful of the bandages.

Dillon perched on the edge of her medical bed. Held her hands. "I . . . I'm not sure I can forgive myself—"

"Nope." She touched his face, feeling the prickle of his stubble beneath her palm. "You can't talk about that, remember?"

Looking miserable, he peered up at her. "I . . . I don't know what . . ." He hung his head.

She wanted to hug him. Go into his arms, but they had many witnesses and she was too weak to move again. So she set her hands on his shorn head. This time, it was her turn to cup his face. "You saved me, Dillon." When he started to object, she gave him a warning look. "I have never felt as alive or as . . . right as I have since you stormed into my life."

His dark brown eyes flicked over her face. Uncertainty wreaked havoc on his expression and the words she desperately wanted to speak.

She had nothing to lose—she had, after all, nearly died. She couldn't risk that happening without saying this. "I cannot imagine my life without you."

His brows knotted and he seemed tormented. "Cove . . ."

With an airy laugh, she set her forehead to his. "I know . . ." It was crazy, wonderful, magical, being this near to him. "We've only known each other a week."

"Six days, thirteen hours, forty-five minutes." Amusement glinted in his eyes. "Give or take five."

Surprised that he knew the exact count, she started to say something, but then closed her mouth.

"And if you count Paris, add five months, twenty-eight days to that."

Her eyebrows lifted on their own. Heady realization swam through her chest, thickening her arteries, making it harder for her heart to pump. *He counted the days . . .* Knew them. Then had . . . he felt the same?

"I don't know what comes after this . . ."

Still dumbstruck, Cove couldn't think, thrilled that he knew the number of days. That could only be possible because he liked her. She recalled him telling her in Mykonos that he wanted to come back for her. What did—

He shifted closer, their faces mere inches apart. "I'm falling for you, Gelato."

Breath snatched, she glanced at his lips. No, no, this wasn't the time for a kiss.

"Correction," he said, angling to catch her mouth. "Already fell." He teased her lips with a kiss. "Just . . ." Another light, taunting kiss. "Don't hate me. Remember this. Okay?" He let the next kiss linger. "My promise."

A throat cleared behind them.

Having trouble shifting her brain back to reality, Cove felt this weird twinge. A . . . warning. "I would never hate you," she breathed.

"Good." Dillon smirked at her, drawing back. He tilted his head toward the intruder, but didn't look there. "Dante, meet Cove. Cove, Dante."

The tall, athletic man shifted closer. "Pike wants you."

Dillon eased up and stole another kiss. "Keep her company. Anyone hurts her, I'll hold you personally responsible."

"That include you?"

"Not cool, Dante." Dillon strode past him.

Thrilled at his "promise," but feeling awkward that he'd done that in front of the others, that he'd made sure someone remained with her, she tried to shield the awkwardness as Dante joined her. "He knows you," she said.

Dante nodded. "Our dads worked together."

Wait—she knew this. What had Dillon said the children were called? "Scions."

Surprise widened the man's eyes. "He told you?"

Glancing after Dillon, who strode into the main room, she nodded. "A little. He keeps things very close."

Dante eased onto the chair where Dillon had sat a moment ago. "Including you, it seems."

That heat returned to her cheeks. "We have been through a lot."

"Apparently."

Where she expected to find condemnation or reprisal, she only found curiosity. "How long have you known him?"

"Since he was born."

Now it was her turn to be surprised, and curiosity got the better of her. "What is he like?"

Dante stabbed a finger toward the voices that were quickly rising between Dillon and the older man. "That." He chuckled. "Dillon has a very particular idea of how things should be handled, and he does not tolerate anything to the contrary. Girls always wanted his attention, but he never had time for them. He was too focused on getting where he wanted to go."

"Are you saying he did not date?"

Dante lifted a shoulder in a shrug. "He tried once or twice, but it annoyed him. Girls in high school, he said, were more concerned about popularity or the next fashion trend."

She had been that girl ten years ago. "And he wasn't?"

Pursing his lips, Dante shook his head. "I think Dillon was born with a battle plan in his tightly balled fist—how to conquer the world."

Cove laughed, instantly regretting it when her stitches pinched. "Oh," she said, lightly pressing her hand to the spot. "When we met in Paris, he seemed so . . . in control. So determined, intense, focused. I could not help but be drawn to him."

"That's his superpower." Dante smirked. "I was years older and jealous of that."

This time, she made sure to keep her laugh light. "I think I would follow him to the ends of the earth."

Dante studied her for a long moment. "And for the first time in his entire life, I think he wants the girl to do that."

Surprised and in awe of what he spoke, she considered him, then Dillon.

"There's catered food in there. You up to eating with the team?"

If it meant being closer to Dillon and being out of the bed— "Yes."

He extended his arm and she climbed back to her feet. For such a tall, athletic man, he was surprisingly gentle.

"Do you have a girlfriend?"

"Fiancée," Dante said with a grin. "She's another Scion—McKenna. Wedding's four months out."

"And is she okay with you doing this, being here?"

He inclined his head as he helped her into the main room. "She works at an embassy in Armenia."

"There is political unrest there. Are you okay with her being there?" Cove asked, curious. "I apologize—that is not for me to ask."

"All good," Dante said. "The situation that brought us together gave her a lot to consider. That's why she's stepping down after the wedding and is trying to get a job at the White House or Capitol Hill."

He led her to a table with three large disposable trays of food and big plastic utensils. The first tray offered rice and the second had peppered meat. The third, vegetables.

As he filled a plate for her, she considered his story. "Will you keep doing"—she motioned around the room—"*this* after you marry?"

"For now," he said with a nod. "If Mick can't find a job, then this is our only income."

"Ah, that makes sense." Chagrined that she had not even considered finances, she kept that to herself. It was not because she was Massimo Galtieri's daughter, but because she had wisely invested all her modeling money.

Dante guided her to the table and set the plate before her along with plastic utensils, then snagged a bottled water.

Cove did not miss how five sets of eyes swung to her. She managed a smile, wondering if coming in here had been a mistake. She eyed Dillon in a stiff conversation with the older man who seemed to be the leader. The dynamics in this room reminded her of flint against flint, sparking with tension.

"That's Pike," Dante noted quietly. "The chief."

"I don't think they like each other."

"Pike doesn't *like* much." Dante ducked even as Pike drew closer with Dillon.

But suddenly an argument erupted and Dillon stormed off.

Lowering her fork, Cove looked after him. Should she go after him? Her gaze shifted back to the team leader, who was looking straight at her.

He strode toward her with a grim expression. "Dante, when she's done, get her to Dade so he can get her credentials sorted."

"Understood, Chief."

"Credentials?"

"ID, passport," Pike said, then nodded. "So we can get you back home."

"What about Dillon?"

"His are already in order."

"Oh." Gaze on the door where he'd vanished, Cove wondered what had set Dillon off. "But . . ." Something wasn't right. She recalled how he had been so adamant about not using legal documents that could be traced. "Is it not dangerous to use real documents when my papà is still missing? And his dad too?"

Dante touched her back. "We got you, Cove. Nothing will happen to you."

For some reason, that did not provide the reassurance that it should have. Something . . . something was off. It tingled along her nape. Made the hairs on her arms stand on end. Even as she gave them the information, she kept looking toward the door, waiting for Dillon to return. To set her world to right again.

The men of the team were funny, snarky, and raucous. It was . . . exhausting. But once her documents were done—again, which made no sense to her—she needed to lie down. Her legs were trembling and her arms felt like anchors.

Dante helped her back to the bed, and she sat on the edge of the mattress, anxious to know where Dillon had gone. When the others were distracted, she pushed off the mattress and went to the door. Found a hall. The right was a dead end, so she wandered to the left, which led to a juncture. Another passage spread to both sides.

"Dillon?" she called quietly, fighting a strange tremor of panic.

The right had two doors that seemed locked tight. She started in the other direction and stopped short when a man rounded the corner.

It was him, the leader. The man who had a personality like a slab of granite. Pike moved with determination until he saw her. Something in his visage shot dread through her stomach.

"Dillon," she murmured, refusing to believe what every nerve ending in her body told her. She braced against the wall. Made herself ask. "Where is Dillon?"

Pike walked toward her. The answer was written all over his terse, determined face.

"He's gone," she whispered, a wave of dizziness crashing over her. "No no no. He wouldn't do this to me. He *promised*." Tears exacerbated the blurriness. "We had a deal!"

TWENTY-FOUR

CAN YOU PLEASE JUST BUY ME A TICKET?" Dillon brandished the cash at the man as an airplane screeched across the tarmac beyond the barrier wall. "I don't care—"

"No, no!" The man waved frantically. "Go away or I will call the police."

"Please, I am not a bad person. I just need to get out of the country, and my passport was stolen." He again wagged the money at the thirtysomething Yemeni, who shoved him then stalked down the street. Straight toward a police car.

Dillon took the hint and hustled around the corner. Negotiated his way to another corner and tried again, this time with an older man. "Excuse me, I am in trouble."

"Go away, American!" the gray-haired man shuffled off, going so far as to cross the street.

Wandering back toward the front of the airport, Dillon dragged a hand over his mouth, telling himself not to think about Cove or her reaction when she realized he was gone. It had to be done. Hated that things would end this way but—

"You the American looking for a ticket?"

Dillon pivoted and all his Spidey senses went off. Man, he did not need trouble already, though he knew he was practically begging for it. He tucked his hand in his pocket, shedding some of the paper money. "I am, but"—he produced two bills—"I don't have much. I just—"

With a mutter that sounded a lot like a curse, the hard-edged man turned around and left.

Dillon did the same, heading to the far side. When a car slid around the corner, he felt his breath back into his throat—a police car. Lights *wrrp*'d.

Shoot.

He launched himself down an alley and was halfway through before he realized it was a dead end. At least, for a normal person. He tic-tacked up the wall and hiked onto the roof. Bolted across it to the higher vantage. Scaled a pipe up to that tar-riddled surface. As he sprinted, he got his bearings. Knew he was on top of the main airport terminal. Crouch-running, he headed in the direction of the main street. Took a knee as he scanned the area. Eyed the plane taxiing. A queue of people climbing stairs into a jet with Arabic script on the side. Then the street again.

Three vehicles wove erratically through traffic, tires screeching in front of the terminal.

Time to move. He pushed to his feet, checking their direction as the people deployed from the trio of vehicles.

One spotted him. Shouted.

He took off running.

* * *

Port of Aden, Yemen

Sitting alone in what Omen called the bunkroom, Cove hated Dillon for leaving without a word, but more importantly—without her. In the first few hours after his departure, she had tortured herself, wondering why she had been so easy to abandon.

Did I mean so little to him, that at the first opportunity to bail, he did?

It was not the first opportunity, she argued with herself. Regardless, he had known he was breaking their deal by walking out of this building. She doubted he felt bad about it—he had, after all, done it in secret so she could not stop him.

Santo cielo, she hated that Pike had been so callous about it. She had completely fallen apart when he gave her the news, and all he had done was step around her, call Dante over, and tell him to get her back to the bunkroom. Stiff and silent, he then strode toward the bank of computers where several of the team were now busy.

And here she sat, hours later. This team would want her gone, eventually. She supposed they might help her get back home— even if that was not their plan, she would make sure they did. Otherwise, she had no way to get anywhere. But without Papà, what life waited for her back in Italy?

Over the last few days, she had begun to construct a different life, a . . . full life. With Dillon. Now that she had been abandoned, she realized the futility of that idea. He was American, with a life and home . . . Where had he said he lived? Virginia.

"Uh-oh," one of the guys said. "Looks like it's getting real."

"Think he'll be okay?"

The question pulled Cove off the bed and into the room, though she hovered back far enough so as to not draw their attention. But they all stood with their backs to her, huddling around a monitor that hung on a rack.

"Dude's a freakin' monkey with those parkour moves."

Parkour? That . . . that sounded like they were talking about Dillon.

She drifted closer, catching sight of what they were watching.

It took a moment for her mind to figure out what she was seeing. A white oval moved across a light gray . . .

Wait. Not an oval—a shape. A person—*Dillon*—running across a . . . roof? From the high vantage of the camera, she could also see cars swarming the street.

Frowning, she slipped nearer, hugging herself. When she saw Dillon crouch at the corner of the building, she tried to figure out what was going on. "How can we see him, this?"

Heads swiveled toward her, but she kept her gaze trained on the monitor.

Then Dillon straightened, turned toward the swarming cars, pivoted, and bolted toward the end of the building.

"No!" someone shouted.

"No . . . no . . ." the burly red-bearded guy muttered as he watched. "Won't make it."

"It's Achilles," Dante countered. "Twenty says he'll make it."

Cove drew in a breath as Dillon went airborne. She covered her mouth with both hands, terrified he would fall and kill himself. But just as his Scion friend said, he caught the light post and slung around it.

"You owe me twenty," Dante said with a smirk.

"I wasn't dumb enough to take that bet," the burly guy said.

Mortified that these men were betting on Dillon's life, Cove shifted to rail at them, her heart racing. "How—"

"Wait . . . wait . . ."

"Here we go." Pike nodded, hands on his belt as he stared at the screen.

His words had the effect of clapping silence through the room. Tension tightened. Drove Cove's gaze back to the feed. Her breathing slowed to a painful rhythm as she watched a pursuer gain on Dillon. *No. No no no . . .*

They caught him. Jerked him backward. Pounced on him.

Groans echoed in the room.

"How can you just watch this? Why are you not doing something? They will kill him!"

Pike met her gaze. "He made a choice."

At first, her mind would not quite comprehend what he had just said. But when it finally hit, she threw herself at him. "*Mostro*! You beast!"

To intercept her, Dante caught her around the waist. "Wait, no—"

Pain exploded through her midsection. She screamed, even as her vision ghosted and the world fell away.

Undisclosed Location

Hood over his head, hands bound behind his back, Dillon struggled to remain calm. This wasn't unlike being in the tunnels, having his sight blocked and the air still. Only difference was that here, he didn't have Cove to talk him through it.

Hands clamped his arms and he was yanked out of the vehicle, the diesel engine rattling. Unable to see and guide his foot placement, he missed a step. Crashed down, scoring his shin. He grunted the pain away, trying to maintain focus on location and direction. But he was at a disadvantage, since he'd been in a vehicle. Before that . . . he had no idea because—if the sluggishness in his head was any indication—he'd been drugged.

The men around him cursed in Arabic and dragged him on.

Unwilling to have his knees shredded, he struggled back to his feet. Let them pull him, but he would do this under his own strength.

A distant *adhan* sang through the air, haunting as it called people to prayer. Paired with the Arabic epithets . . . and the unique, woody, spicy smell mingled with the reek of waste and garbage, he was somewhere with a Muslim population.

They negotiated stairs—that was fun, since he was all but blind. He earned a few more bruises and cuts on his shins when he wasn't able to predict the turns and varying heights. Soon, stone gave way to uneven terrain. Hardpacked earth, he'd guess.

Wood creaked.

"Get back!"

Me? How was he suppo—

"On your knees, face down in the dirt."

Guessing they were shouting at someone else, Dillon waited, noting the rattle of a vehicle passing on the left. So a street was nearby . . . ?

A definitive *shink* sounded, then wood creaked, groaned. Someone grabbed at the hood over Dillon's head. Anticipating they were about to remove it, he braced. Closed his eyes, readying himself to take in his surroundings as quickly as possible. Doubted they would give him much time.

The hood ripped free. He blinked rapidly. Saw a building to his left and straight ahead. Felt the metal cuffs fall free just as he registered the gaping void at his feet. Which a violent shove sent him spiraling into.

Instinct made him tuck his head to roll, but the ground was closer than he'd anticipated. His shoulder cracked into the ground. Pain ricocheted down his neck and arm. "Augh!" Arching his spine against the pain, he caught his arm to keep it immobilized even as he saw a wood pallet drop. He flinched, expecting it to land on him, but when it didn't, he understood it was a door. The *shink* sounded again, locking him in. That's when the rancid smell overpowered him.

"*What* is that smell?" he groaned, squinting into the smothering darkness, stretching his shoulder, which had taken the brunt of the fall. Not dislocated but it hurt like crazy.

"Me," rasped a hollow voice.

He froze, shifting aside. Even with the hollowness, the emptiness in that lone word, it sounded a lot like—

"*Dillon?*"

Pain could not hold him down. He shot upward, grimacing. Angled toward the voice. "*Dad?*" He groped in the darkness, searching. Desperate for the unmistakable voice to take form. Solidify. "Dad!" His fingers found a cold bony hand.

"Here," came a choked-out word along with a sharp cough.

"Dad," he whispered, stunned by the miracle of this moment.

"He heard me," Dad sobbed, a wracking cough painful to hear. "He . . . heard . . . me. God heard me."

Not letting go, and ignoring the fire in his shoulder, Dillon scrambled toward his dad. "I'm here."

"I have prayed every day that I would be found." Dad fell into another coughing fit that had the rattle of pneumonia to it.

Swallowing around a thick throat, Dillon wrapped his arms around his dad's rail-thin shoulders. Frail. Anger and distress coiled around his heart and mind, made it impossible to say anything more than "I'm here."

Dad collapsed against him, sobs wracking his body as he clung to Dillon.

It broke him, hearing his dad—the strongest, most capable man he had ever known—sobbing like a baby. All his questions, all his plans took a back seat as his own tears coursed down his cheeks and a rising fury promised violence of action against those responsible for what they had done to this onetime Navy SEAL. To his dad. Max Jacobs.

No idea how long they sat like that, and he didn't care. This formidable, fierce man never cried in front of him, so whatever he'd been through . . . he needed time to haul himself out of it.

"Sorry," Dad muttered, pushing himself free and upright, coughing more.

Even in that simple motion, Dillon felt the tremor of weakness in Dad's arms. "What have they done to you?" he growled before he could think better of it.

Dad scoffed. "Don't worry about it. The real question is how you're here."

"I've been looking for you." Dillon thought that would've been obvious.

"With Omen?"

In the blackness, Dillon could tell his dad was looking at him. "No, though not for want of Pike trying. After they"—before the words left his mouth this time, he reconsidered mentioning the funeral or how Mom had fallen apart and changed course—"declared you dead."

"Not surprised," Dad said, his voice hoarse from the seizing coughs. "What I was working to prove and stop could get the government in a lot of trouble."

"But you found them," Dillon said. "The—"

"Don't say it."

Faltering, he wondered at the adamancy. That sounded like Dad, the ever-confident one who never missed a step, was afraid. "Understood."

Dad sniffed. "You really found me. On your own . . . ?"

"Don't sound so surprised. You taught me well." Dillon huffed a laugh. "I've spent more than two years running around the globe looking for clues. And while I want to take credit, I've recently learned it was a group effort."

"Usually is. There are no one-man shows."

"You used to tell me that all the time."

Dad patted his hand in the darkness. "How's your mom?"

Looking down, he knew to be careful with that intel. "Your death hit her hard, but . . . she's Mom."

There was a long pause in the darkness. "I miss her . . . The thought of her and you kids kept me going."

"We're going to get you out of here."

Silence gaped back at him for a long second. "I would love nothing more, but . . . I'm in bad shape."

"Leave it to me."

More silence settled between them. "No matter what happens . . . I am proud of you, Dillon."

"No, don't do that. No sappy talk. You're not dying. Not while I'm around."

Dad huffed a laugh, and by the sound of it, narrowly staved off another cough. "So . . . we have the time. Tell me the whole story. And don't filter to spare my feelings. I survived BUD/S and your childhood."

"Fair," Dillon said with his own laugh that felt hollow in his throat.

"Where'd you start looking for me?"

"Where you were last seen."

"How'd you find that?"

"I thought Helios and I unearthed that, but turns out Pike sent me the image. Took me an insane amount of time to figure out you were with Massimo Galtieri."

Dad grunted.

"Followed him to Armenia, where I got to see Mickey—oh, speaking of, she's engaged to Dante."

Dad barked a laugh and coughed through it. "Did not see that coming."

"Well, hang tight because it gets better. I was tracking Galtieri"— he needed to ask Dad about the billionaire, but it just seemed owed to Dad to give him good news first—"and ended up in Paris for an event he was hosting, when my paths crossed with Apollo."

"But he's like fifteen."

"Twenty-two now, and engaged to a secret Saudi princess."

"Go big or go home," Dad teased with a rattle of a cough barking through him.

Dillon waited for it to subside before continuing. Avoiding mention of Cove, he shared about Paris and Italy.

"What are you leaving out?"

Should've figured . . . "Always could read me."

"Because you're so much like your old man. So—for lack of better words—cough it up."

Dillon groaned at the bad joke. "I . . . Galtieri's daughter . . ."

"Cove."

He looked at his dad, though he could not see him, surprised to her hear name on his lips. "You met her?"

"No," Dad conceded, "but dads talk . . . So you and her . . . ?"

Feeling like he was twelve years old, he shared about Galtieri's kidnapping, the tunnels, Greece. Naturally left out the kiss. "We ended up in Yemen, so she could try to prove her dad was innocent of corruption charges, and so I could find you."

"Impressive." Exhaustion dripped from Dad's reply. "You in love with her?"

"I've only known her—"

"Not what I asked."

Still staring at the dark void where Dad sat, Dillon tightened his jaw. "I . . . don't know."

Dad huffed, coughing a few times.

"Pretty sure she hates me now—I left her with Omen to come find you."

"Bad move."

"No," Dillon said firmly. "She got shot, and I . . . watching her nearly die in my arms . . . no way I could do that again."

"Because you love her."

He could argue till his last breath, but it wouldn't change the truth. "Maybe." He scratched his head, really needing to change the topic. "Do you know where Galtieri is?"

"Here," Dad breathed, the sound labored.

Habit had Dillon looking around the darkness. This hole wasn't big enough to hide a man. "They have more cages?"

"He's not in one."

Gaze drifting back in Dad's direction, Dillon felt his gut tighten. "Where is he then?"

"With them, with Rasulov."

No. Oh man. This could not . . . "You mean he really is corrupt?"

TWENTY-FIVE

Undisclosed Location

DAWN STREAKED THROUGH THE SLIVER OF spaces left by wood boards that had shrunk and warped from water wear. Nearby, Dad slept, wheezing each breath. Only as the darkness surrendered to the soft awakening of dawn did Dillon understand the terrible condition that had his dad at death's door. Lips and fingertips tinged blue indicated his body's struggle for oxygen. Deep, dark circles around his eyes added to the gaunt frame. Emaciation was a clear sign of the starvation he had endured. His beard and longish hair were splotchy because of malnutrition.

If he did not get Dad out of here immediately, there would be another funeral for Max Jacobs, this time, *with* the body. Mom would have to bury the man she loved a second time.

The approach of voices drew his gaze to the wooden door. Shadows fell over it.

Soon the *shink* registered and he looked to his dad, who still had not roused.

The wood lifted back and three men stood aboveground: a dark-haired man he did not know, Yusif Rasulov, and Massimo Galtieri.

Dillon straightened to his full height, head just below the door. "My dad needs medical attention immediately."

"You do not give us orders," Rasulov snarled. "You should be thankful you are still alive."

"I'm alive," Dillon growled back, "because I know the location of something you're looking for."

"Dillon," Dad rasped. "No!"

Rasulov stared at him hard. "You learned the location?" His gaze shifted to Dad. "From him?"

"No," Dillon bit out, glowering at Massimo. "Your daughter mistakenly thinks you're a good man."

The broad-shouldered man who stood in a stylish suit tried to bury his reaction but couldn't. "What do you know of my daughter?"

"That's she's a better human being than her father. That she believed in you so much that she risked her life to prove your innocence."

Regret flashed through the same hazel-gold eyes that Cove had inherited.

"Enough!" the third man snapped. "If you want your father to live, tell us where the triggers are."

"Not happening," Dillon ground out, laser focused on Galtieri. "But I'll take you to them on two conditions."

It was ludicrous—they'd never follow through even if they agreed, but he had to try.

"You are in no position to give orders," Rasulov barked, aiming a Glock at him. "We shoot you and take your father."

"You've had him years and couldn't get him to give up the location. That's not changing now that he's near death and knows I alone hold that secret." Okay, maybe not *alone*, but they did not need to know that. No way he'd tell Galtieri his own daughter knew. Anger coiled through Dillon that he'd have to tell Cove her father was not only guilty but a monster.

A preternatural calm possessed him as he stared beyond the muzzle of that Glock to the evil eyes behind it. "You have no triggers, therefore the nuclear proliferation that you've already announced—prematurely, it seems—to the world is ineffective. Don't think for a second the US won't come in and obliterate it once the timed email I sent is delivered to key government assets."

Yeah, so that hadn't happened either, but he needed more leverage.

"Is he lying?" Rasulov asked Galtieri, who studied Dillon intensely.

No doubt mentioning Cove had already unseated the billionaire's confidence. "So, tell me, Mr. Galtieri," Dillon plowed on, wanting to feed more doubt, test the Italian's loyalty to his family, "did you know they tried to kill Cove in Greece? Or that the man next to you shot her in Yemen? A bullet struck her and she nearly died in my arms. Is that the type of man you are, that you'd sacrifice your own daughter?"

Though Galtieri said nothing, did not move, his eyes widened and his lips parted.

Good to know.

Rasulov fired a shot at Dad's head. "Tell us or he dies now!"

Dillon lifted his hands in surrender. "Tanzania."

TWENTY-SIX

Off Tanzania's Coast, Indian Ocean

KNOWLEDGE WAS POWER. AND POWER KEPT his dad alive. Dillon had deliberately not told Rasulov the triggers were at the bottom of the Indian Ocean until they had hit Tanzania.

"Just leave my dad here. He doesn't have to come."

"Do you think I am stupid?" Rasulov demanded.

Def. "*I* have to dive. He can't help—make him dive and we both die, because he's not strong enough to dive, and I won't leave him to die alone."

Rasulov shoved the weapon at Dad's head. "He is your motivation."

Dillon clenched his jaw.

"We understand each other." Rasulov motioned with his weapon, indicating his men to carry Dillon's feverish, perspiring dad aboard the dive boat they'd hired. He'd been too incoherent since last night to tell Dillon where on the trawler he'd hidden the triggers and just kept saying "all."

The ship's captain, Chiku, had been distressed at having his son and ship commandeered by Rasulov and his men. Not for the first time did Dillon thank God he'd left Cove behind. She didn't need to see the coward her father was, nor did he want her used for leverage the way they were his dad. If she hated him, it meant she was alive to do it. He'd take that any day over the other option.

"Tell us where."

"No," Dillon refused, assisting his dad into the covered, sheltered wheelhouse. "I'm not giving you the coordinates so you can have more thugs out there. You'll shoot us and make the dive on your own."

Logic wasn't a hundred percent, but it'd do for now. Helping Dad onto a stool bolted to the deck, Dillon stayed in the wheelhouse with Chiku and his son, Faraji, until they were at the designated spot. That's when he moved to the stern, where Faraji helped him suit up with scuba gear.

"You really know my Cove?"

Dillon didn't look past the man's slick slacks. He wanted this piece of work to suffer for what he'd put his daughter through. "You call her *Lupina*."

The man drew in a breath and shuffled closer. "This is not what you think," he whispered.

Straightening to shrug into the tanks, Dillon squinted at the billionaire. "Talk is cheap." He fastened the straps over his chest. "She believed in you." In his mind's eye, he saw her on that bed, pale, lips cracked from dehydration, and would never forgive this man for what he'd invited into her life, the violence. Again, he breathed in relief that she was with Omen.

"Where is she?"

"You don't think I'll really answer that, do you?"

"She is my daughter!"

"Should've thought of that before you risked her life." He

clenched his teeth. "She's safe. That's more than you deserve to know."

"Swear it."

"I said it. Unlike you, I'm a man of my word and don't lie." He stepped backward off the boat and dropped into the water. Bobbed there for a second to test his rebreather.

"If you don't come back, I will kill your father," Rasulov snapped.

Dillon would not justify that with a response. He gave a thumbs-up to Faraji, then slid goggles over his head. He submerged and swiveled around, glanced at the depth meter on his forearm, tapped on the shoulder lamp, and kicked to descend. The trip down gave him plenty of time to worry about Dad, whether Rasulov would kill him, and how much Cove hated him for leaving her. That'd pale next to learning her dad was working with Rasulov.

There was that seed of hope that she'd forgive him, and he chastised himself for focusing on their feelings for each other, but it was what kept him going. After all, part of what he loved about her was that uncanny knack for being reasonable. Seeing past her own preferences and conceding when things were right, even if she didn't like them. The woman was perfection. Everything he didn't know he needed or wanted.

But how . . . how could they make it work? She was Italian and lived in a villa. He was from Virginia and had moved back home to live with his mom and siblings after Dad went MIA.

Hold on, Mom. I'm close. Dad will be home soon. Please, God.

His pulse skipped a beat when the haunting hull of the trawler came into view. Glad he'd worn gloves, Dillon used the rail to pull himself toward the front.

He had to think like his dad or he'd never locate them. Couldn't imagine Dad had been below—that didn't track. The lower levels were largely tanks for the fish. Then again, Dad would want to make sure this wasn't easily found.

With precision and care, he searched the main deck, avoiding the broken, rusted swing arm that was still anchored by a thread and floated above the deck. He swam under it. Spotted a couple of wood lockers with barnacles that were anchored down. A rusted lock prevented him from checking inside, but he scoured around and found a metal rod tangled in netting. He extracted it and returned to the locker. Smashed it against the lock, which was a muted effort because the water fought his momentum. The lock jangled and barnacles broke free. A third blow finally met with success. The lid floated up, along with something black.

He tensed—*backpack*! He snatched and caught it, only to realize it wasn't a backpack but a black slicker. Tossing it aside, he resumed his search.

C'mon, Dad . . . where would you hide nuclear triggers?

A squid floated out of a door at the wheelhouse. Okay . . . that would make sense. At least they would be protected against impact or being dislodged, right? But would Dad have gotten into the wheelhouse?

Def. Dillon had come by his skills and instinct honestly, and if Dad wanted to get into something, he did. Yeah, like a fight against Iranian nuclear proliferation.

Catching the jamb of the missing door, Dillon let the shoulder lamp clear the way inside first. When he didn't see any sharks or stingrays, he pulled himself into the confined space. Holy fire, this was nearly as bad as the tunnels.

Nearly.

But he'd take the tunnels over this any day due to one factor: Gelato.

Light skimmed wooden steps and the wheel with seaweed coiled around it. He checked his air levels. Twenty minutes left. Where . . . where was the backpack?

What if someone had already gotten it?

No way. This had to be why Dad was still alive.

Maybe he had gone below, hidden it . . . Dillon angled around.

An eel slithered through the crack in the front deck windshield. Likely a bullet hole, but time had widened it, broken and splintered it more. Maybe from settling on the seafloor. Wheeling around to avoid the eel, he noticed his lamplight hit something below a work shelf with a chained, floating logbook. His heart tripped as he dove in for a better view. Couldn't believe it—on the gray panel wall, someone had drawn in black permanent ink a black flower.

The *nightshade* flower—Dad!

Dillon surged at the panel, hands frantically tracing the rectangular shape. Its corners. Found a missing screw. Dug his fingers into the sliver of space. Tugged. It came loose with a groan that startled him. But it was enough to shove his hand in. His heart skipped when he felt the rough treads of a nylon strap. He pulled it from the tight space, adrenaline coursing through him, jacking his excitement.

He unzipped the bag and saw a wad of plastic secured and protected with duct tape. Dad had thought of everything. Dillon had never felt so proud of his dad as he did right now. He zipped it back up and threaded his arms through the straps so the pack rested against his chest, tied the loose strap around his waist, surprised and grateful they were still strong despite having been down here, soaking in seawater, for years. Angling his wrist to see the depth, he twisted the round dial four clicks to the right, then three back, then pressed the side button. A dull blue light appeared around the 6, then disappeared.

To his right, a shadow bisected the light cast by his shoulder lamp, shoving his pulse into overdrive.

Dillon whipped in that direction, realizing his situational awareness was lousy. That something had cut through the beam of light meant it was *close*. And in a split-second he registered the shape. The distinctive back-and-forth swimming pattern jammed his heart in his throat even as he saw the fin slice around the half wall, turning back toward the wheelhouse. Shark!

Shoving himself backward, he felt the jarring impact of the tank against something metal clang down his spine. Backed into a corner, he had nowhere to go as the marine predator banked into the wheelhouse.

Holy fire, I am dead.

Her fury at the chief had not abated in the hours following his cruel words. But the team packed up and boarded a Saudi cutter provided by the Central Kingdom's royal family. When she'd asked why they were going after the triggers and not after Dillon, she'd just been told the triggers had to be secured. War thwarted. As much as she hated the answer, she understood. Mostly.

Sitting in a command room belowdecks with the team, Cove tried to avoid the root of bitterness digging through her mood and heart. She glowered at Dante and another guy when they left the room.

"Tracker died," someone said.

Pike nodded, a visible tension in his tanned face. "Deploy the drone." He pressed a button on something. "Squid 1 and 2, you are clear."

Luther disappeared for a few minutes, then returned.

"Halo1 online," Dade reported from his laptop.

"Put it on the wall," Pike instructed.

The screen came to life.

The other members of the team moved toward the screen, effectively blocking most of her view. But that was fine. She had been told to come because she did not have any other options.

"Rig sighted."

Tempted not to care about this effort, she noticed a strange energy thrum through the team as they watched. A stark-white ship came into view on the screen.

"Zoom in," Pike ordered.

For a second, she thought she saw someone on the surface. But when she blinked they were gone. Three men were on the back of the boat.

What . . . was going on? "Is someone else diving?"

"Back off," Pike said, patting Dade's shoulder. "If they spot Halo1, it's over. Luther, have the captain move within striking distance."

"Striking?" Cove balked. "Why are we striking them? Are they stealing the triggers?"

"Miss Galtieri, I'll have you removed if you can't remain quiet."

Anger dug in harder, but something told her—warned her—to be patient. To . . . trust. Which made zero sense. The chief had been so cold and callous. "You would not help Dillon, and now you just stand by while someone is getting nuclear triggers that could save my dad and his? Why are you not doing anything?"

Pike's gray eyes bored into her. "Get her out of here."

"No!" She stamped around him and went to the chief. "I know you did not like him, but I did not—"

The man straightened and faced her, and it was not unlike confronting a hurricane. "You do not know the first thing about me—"

"Except that you are evil, a *mostro*!"

"—or his plan."

"I understand now why he would not work with . . ." Her brain tripped over his last two words and finally caught up with her. "Plan?" A blazing beacon signaled the truth that rang her like a bell. What Pike had said. "*His* plan." A strangled cry worked up her throat as realization washed through her. "This was Dillon's plan." He hadn't just left her. It wasn't that simple. It was far more complicated and nuanced. "You knew . . ."

His gaze returned to hers. "An educated guess when he asked me to make sure you had credentials." A half smile appeared and vanished just as quick. "Our team doesn't need credentials to travel." He gave a small nod. "Gotta give the guy credit—he's got some serious chutzpah. Knew RHB would come after him."

"But why would he do that? They will kill him!"

"That's what I'm trying to prevent." He pointed to the screen and moved to check on something.

Again, it took her brain too long to catch up. "Wait—Dillon is here? In the water?"

"Yes," Luther said as he returned. "Jacobs baited Rasulov into finding him at the Aden airport. They took him to the one place we had never been able to discover—where they were holding his dad: Lebanon. He convinced them to bring him here. Just like he predicted."

"Wait—his dad? What about mine?"

Something flickered through Pike's expression.

And scared her. "Wh-what is that?"

"Beacon's back online!"

Pike jerked toward the screen and grabbed a handheld. "Squid 1 and 2, go go go!"

In the split-second as the shark barreled at him, Dillon recalled the hole in the windshield. The way the glass bowed. If he dove at it, would it give? He had no other way out. Toeing the opposite wall, he shoved up and away—but got jerked back. Only as he tried again did he realize the tank had caught on something.

The gray shark came unyielding. Jaws opened, revealing the teeth aimed straight at Dillon's chest.

God, help me!

Punch it!

With no time to spare, he drew back his fist. Knew this had to be hard and true. Used every ounce of his strength to drive down on the nose of the shark. The thing thrashed and swung up and away.

He would not get another chance to escape. If he had time, he'd shed the tank, but with the triggers strapped on, it'd take too long. He shoved off again and felt a modicum of give. With all his might, he shoved up. Tic-tacked up the wall, flipped, and felt the tanks give. Drove his feet at the window. It surrendered easily. *Thank You, God.*

He shot through the opening and kicked hard, aiming for the surface. Knew so many little things had to have worked for him to escape without—

He felt more than saw the incoming shark. Apparently, SharkTooth hadn't given up. Probably ticked after being punched. Dillon swung a right hook. SharkTooth angled aside—but that put Dillon's right leg right in its path. It chomped down. Searing fire seized his leg even as he pummeled the shark.

Somehow, it let go.

Blood plumed in the water around him. Dillon knew it would be aromatic to other predators and shot upward, kicking for all he was worth. *Please . . . God . . . if I die, Dad dies.* He couldn't let that happen, no matter the excruciating pain.

Spitting the rebreather out a meter from the surface, he fought the urge to scream at the agony. Focused on the faces looking down from the boat, not on the water churning around him. No doubt they'd seen the crimson stain. He surged free of the water. "Pull me up, pull me up!"

TWENTY-SEVEN

Indian Ocean

GROANING FROM THE BITE WOUND ABOVE and below his knee, Dillon fought to control the bleeding. It was a flat-out miracle Shark Tooth hadn't bitten off his leg completely!

Faraji rushed to the side and grabbed the medical kit.

"No!" Rasulov shouted, "He gets no help until I have the triggers."

Dillon ground his teeth. "The shark tore the pack. They're at the bottom of the sea."

"Then your father dies," he snarled and motioned to Galtieri. "Get the American."

Shutting out the blinding pain and the warmth of his own blood spilling over the deck, Dillon dragged himself to the side. "Don't." Thank goodness the billionaire didn't have a weapon, but if he brought Dad out here . . . "I can go back down. Just let me tie this off—"

"Why are you not moving?" Rasulov demanded of Galtieri. "You know we have your daughter—"

"They don't!" Dillon barked, levering himself up, feeling blood slick down his leg. "She's safe. With my team." Not exactly *his* team, but . . .

"You swear . . ."

The man had asked him that earlier. "I didn't want her in danger, so I left her with them. She'd had surgery to save her life from the bullet *he* put in her!"

Galtieri's gold eyes flashed but he looked down.

"Don't do this," Dillon growled.

But the man kept staring at the deck.

"She believed in you. She—" He faltered when the billionaire looked at him, then down again, deliberately.

Dillon glanced at the wet deck. Why . . . ? Holy fire—a weapon.

"Get Jacobs. He needs motivation."

Even as the guy spoke, Dillon threw himself forward. Dove into a roll, and came up, staggering, blinding pain putting him off-kilter, but he still managed to aim at Rasulov. Fired.

The Bloody Sword became . . . bloody.

More shots echoed through the air. Unibrow's body rattled beneath the spray of rifle fire by the two submersibles that had surfaced, bearing Dante and Crow.

Dillon careened into Galtieri as a firefight erupted between the team and Rasulov's remaining thugs. Staring over the long deck, he saw a large cutter bearing down on them. Knew that Cove was on that ship. He held her father in a death grip. "Tell me you were not helping them."

Galtieri shuddered beneath him. "They killed my Saveria," he said, plainly grieved. "Vowed to kill Cove, too, if I did not help them."

"And she almost died anyway." Head swimming, he felt his strength draining. "You watched them starve my father . . ."

"No, Dillon."

He glanced to the side, stunned to see his dad staggering toward him. "Dad!" He tried to get up, but the pain drove him back down.

Dad collapsed next to him. "Massimo"—he coughed hard—"kept me alive."

"You are nearly dead!" But Dillon still released the billionaire.

"I would have died had he not snuck me medicine."

"I tried . . ." Galtieri cried. "But then they moved him. I could not find him."

He couldn't reconcile the truth, his dad's horrible condition, nor the fact it could've been so much worse. Dad could have died. And Cove too . . . But . . .

"Rasulov's dead," Dad rasped, reaching for Dillon. "The triggers."

His gaze hit the dead butcher on the deck, then gritted, holding his leg. "Safe. Omen should have them by now." The pounding of feet on the deck told him Omen and Pike had boarded. "We're going home, Dad. We're going home."

"Sydney . . ." Slumped against the deck, Dad gave a wistful smile.

A bright, beautiful face hovered over Dillon even as his vision ghosted. "Cove . . ."

EPILOGUE

Four Months Later
Loudoun County, Virginia

HOW'D IT GO?" DILLON HUNCHED OVER HIS phone, smiling at Cove's face in the chat program. It had been too long since he had seen and held her. "Did they hand down a verdict?"

She smiled in tremulous relief. "Acquitted—all counts."

"*Fire,*" he said, feeling that tightness in his chest ease. Now that the trial was over, Dillon and Cove could figure out their future. "I'm so relieved for y'all. For us."

Cove bobbed her head. "Me too."

But that . . . that smile and her words . . . she didn't seem excited. His heart spasmed, wondering if absence had dulled her feelings for him. "Is—"

Shouts from the barn made him look over there, taking in the white chairs, streamers, and flowers for McKenna and Dante's wedding. He saw Owen and Spencer, two of his Scion brothers, adjusting blazers and ties, their boots and jeans a contrast to what most groomsmen wore for a wedding. But when the bride was a cowgirl and her father a cowboy, this was what happened.

Dillon adjusted his tie, feeling like he was being choked. Or maybe that was the fear that Cove might be having second thoughts about them. "Wish you were here." He shifted and tucked himself next to the trunk of the large white oak tree that blanketed the grass in red and gold leaves all fully in the glorious grip of fall.

Cove tilted her head as she leaned in. She must be in the courthouse still or something, because she was protecting herself and the environment. "Thank you for understanding."

Holy fire, she hadn't said she wished that too. Were things over? He glanced around to be sure he was still alone. "I miss you."

She gave another weak smile, then looked to someone out of sight and nodded before she refocused on the screen and him. "I need to go. Sorry."

Crestfallen, he pursed his lips. "Right. Of course. Tell your dad congrats for me."

"I will. Okay, bye."

Dagger to the chest that she seemed in such a hurry to bail on their call. That she had not said she loved him. Of course, he hadn't either before she disconnected. This long-distance dating was rough. Was their relationship already over?

"Was that Cove?"

Frowning, thoughts entrenched in what her reticence meant, Dillon turned toward the voice and found Dante joining him, wearing a blazer and boots too. "Yeah. Her dad was acquitted."

"Excellent. Man, that is fire."

Dillon smirked, still rattled. "That's what I said."

"Everything okay?"

"I . . ." He rubbed his jaw. "I don't know. She was acting strange. Distant. Like she didn't want to talk."

"You just said it was her dad's trial."

"Fair." But it didn't untangle his thoughts or the knot in his gut. "I . . . I don't want to lose her. Maybe I need to go over there . . ."

Dante clapped his shoulder. "Maybe do that *after* my wedding. Mick would kill us both if you left now." He cocked his head back toward the barn.

"Right." Dillon gave a nervous laugh. "Sorry—this is your day. And it's time!"

They strode across the lawn to the barn where guests were already taking their seats. As they made their way to the front to stand with the other Scion groomsmen, Dante glanced over his shoulder. "Favor."

"Anything."

"Don't steal our thunder."

Dillon frowned. "Wouldn't dream of it." Was that his way of telling him to get his head in the game? Even as the music changed to signal the start of the ceremony—with the arrival of the bridesmaids—he moved past Owen and Spencer to stand to Dante's left at the front of the altar.

The first bridesmaid down was McKenna's sister, Sophia, who wore a pretty dress with boots and a pink cowgirl hat adorned with a tiara and flowers. She glided to the other side of the floor and faced the back. Next came Tala, Owen's half sister, in the same cowgirl fare. Next was McKenna's best friend from college, Cat Something-or-other, in a coral dress and hat, her head tucked so the wide brim covered her face. Was she okay?

She looked up.

That is not Cat. Dillon forgot to breathe. In the split-second it took his brain to register the pink lips and gold eyes, he jolted forward.

"Thunder remember?" Dante muttered.

Dillon did not care. Four large strides carried him to Cove. He pulled her into his arms and crushed her to himself. "You're here."

She laughed, stabilizing the hat that nearly came off. "I could not stand it anymore."

Laughter and applause yanked him back to their surroundings. Cove blushed. "We should . . ."

"Yeah. Right." He bent and kissed her, afraid to let her go. Afraid she would get away. "Don't go far."

"Five feet," she said, indicating to her spot next to Sophia.

"Yo, move," Dante hissed. "My bride is coming!"

Dillon grinned like a fool at Cove as he let Dante haul him back to the side. He saw McKenna walk down the aisle in an amazing dress and white rhinestone tiara-hat with her burly dad, who pulled Dante into a tight hug before giving his daughter to him.

Heart still thundering—*Cove is here!*—Dillon swallowed. Met his dad's gaze, found that look Dillon had always sought—pride, joy. Dad nodded his approval, and Mom slipped her hand through Dad's arm and smiled at him, tears streaming down her cheeks.

Guess she approves too.

He felt bad—no idea what the pastor said, knew there were the standard vows and a killer kiss—along with *whoops* from the operators in the chairs—but his mind never got past Cove standing there. He stared at her. The whole freaking time. Knew . . . knew someday . . . they would be at this altar too.

All this . . . the families—the Riddells, Jacobs, Metcalfes, Neeleys—were all because of one man who sat on the second row next to Dad: General Olin Lambert. He'd handpicked the Nightshade team decades ago. Put Max Jacobs in charge. Out of that decision came all . . . this. Love, grit, patriotism, godliness, and commitment to the values that kept their families, country, and liberties safe. That was a lot to live up to, but more than that—it was an honor to have grown up beneath that powerful legacy. And with the beauty on the other side of the stage, maybe someday he could help perpetuate and sustain that legacy.

Thank You!

Thank you so much for reading *Achilles*. We hope you enjoyed the story. If you did, would you be willing to do us a favor and leave a review? It doesn't have to be long—just a few words to help other readers know what they're getting. (But no spoilers! We don't want to wreck the fun!) Thank you again for reading!

We'd love to hear from you—not only about this story, but about any characters or stories you'd like to read in the future. Contact us at www.sunrisepublishing.com/contact.

PROLOGUE

Two Years Ago
Outside the Wire, Bagram, Afghanistan

THE SLEEK, SEXY BODY SAILED THROUGH the air, effortless in its raw intensity to catapult itself across the sun-heated desert at the fleeing form. Muscles defined and rippling spoke of the relentless training and pace kept to maintain readiness. With a thud that knocked the breath from her intended target, Marvel K027 sank her teeth into the arm of her target. That thousand pounds of pressure locked in place, she landed. Skidded around without breaking her hold and snapped that powerful neck in a jerk that pitched the target down.

Sergeant Crew Gatlin sprinted toward the seventy-five-pound Belgian Malinois, noting Marine Corporal Ehretz, weapon tucked to his shoulder and sights trained on the target, skirting up around the front. They'd been on routine patrol when the unfriendlies started firing on them.

Crew reached Marvel, caught her collar and held firmly—though did not instruct her to release.

"Drop the weapon," Ehretz demanded of the combatant as

Mouse and Taco flanked him, weapons trained on the local fighter who'd tried to take potshots at the team that'd been patrolling the area.

Boots dug in, Crew clipped the lead on as he held onto Marvel's collar, proud the military working dog had done her job with fervor. The target tried to hit Marvel with a rifle, but the Malinois snapped her head, side to side. Dug her paws against the arm, trying to extract a chunk of flesh as punishment.

The man howled and went to his knees. Adrenaline and pain were likely interfering with his ability to make smart choices, but Crew willed him to let go of the weapon.

Blood slid along her jowls and down that powerful corded neck.

Finally, the rifle clattered to the hardpacked earth.

"Marvel, out!" In tandem with the command, Crew drew Marvel's collar straight up, a move that encouraged her to release the arm by restricting her airflow, a measure that invariably forced her to unlock her jaws.

The man broke free with a yelp and scrambled away, shielding his arm, and trying to put as much distance between himself and the fur-missile.

Crew drew Marvel away, though she resisted, eager for another chance to eliminate a threat. The girl was as hard-hitting as many of the elite operators they'd worked with.

Crack!

Thwat-thwat-thwat!

Pivoting, Crew was about to release Marvel when he registered the scene before him—the target was now deceased. Taco was cursing up a storm as he held his arm. The local must've had another weapon, and rather than die of humiliation in an American holding cell, he chose death by operator. A request granted by Taco and a short burst from his M4.

With no apparent threat present, Crew deployed the tethered Kong and let Marvel snag it from him. He gave a couple of good tugs to let her know she'd done a good job, then produced her black Kong. When he showed it to her, she immediately released the roped one, and he flicked the rubber chew toy into the air. Effortlessly, she launched upward, her muscular, well-toned body violence in motion, and snagged it from the air. She landed, chomped it twice, then trotted to the side and dropped to the ground where she crossed her forelegs, and squeaked her reward. Crew let her, knowing the team would need to call this in.

Ehretz muttered an oath. "Let's load up and head out."

Crew frowned. "You mean, let's call this in—"

"Hassle, man," Ehretz grumbled. "I just—"

Gaze locked with the corporal, Crew keyed his mic. "Base, this is Charlie Four on patrol with your recon team alpha. Situation now secure, but we came under fire. One enemy target neutralized. We'll need clean up. Sending location now."

"Good copy, Charlie Four," came the reply through comms.

"What was that?" Ehretz demanded, stalking toward Crew. "I said—"

Marvel swiveled into position, head down, lip curled around the snarl that told the Marine to back off.

Hand up in surrender, Ehretz shifted backward with a nervous grunt. "I said we'd leave it—"

"I'm not letting some Marine grunts derail my career because they don't want to be hassled with protocol." Crew felt the same curl to his lip that Marvel still held. No wonder the guy was still a corporal ponying his rank around newbs on their first deployment.

"You need to remember you're assigned to this team. You follow—"

"Don't." Crew flatlined his expression. "Don't go there, or you'll be eating your stripes for dinner."

The ruddy-faced kid faltered. Couldn't be more than twenty-five. Maybe a hundred pounds dripping wet, trying to engage in a manhood battle with an operator who had ten years, multiple deployments, and more kills than he wanted to admit. No way he was going to let a punk like this tank his career because he was too freakin' lazy to follow protocol.

"Whatever, man," Ehretz growled. "Load up. We're checking out the field two klicks north."

Two klicks . . . Crew glanced in that direction. A hill blocked his view. "That area's off limits." He started back to the mine-resistant ambush protected vehicle to let Marvel enjoy the A/C.

Ehretz rolled his eyes and stomped back to the MRAP with the others.

"Hey," Taco said as he hung back. "Don't let him get under your tac vest. He's just jealous—dude wanted to be a handler like you. Couldn't get in."

Jealousy? Seriously? What was this, middle school?

Minutes later, they were packed like sardines in the MRAP and he sat with his legs V'd and Marvel between them. Her fur radiated the heat of the Afghan summer as she panted heavily. He'd need to water her and make sure she got some A/C time. Maybe do that while Ehretz and the team broke protocol yet again by scouting the off-limits area.

What am I doing here, man?

He'd transitioned to handling a K-9 within Special Forces teams, but he'd been pulled in for yearly qualifications again. To keep Marvel fresh and vary her experience, he'd requested a couple of routine patrol opportunities. But it sucked being stuck with a corporal who had a thirst for power. He missed the teams, his buddies.

Missed Havoc. He grinned, patting Marvel. While the dog at his feet was pure violence and raw power, she'd been bred for that. Malinois were little more than psycho and all business. But Havoc on the other hand . . .

Years ago, rumor told of a stray hanging around the base that had been mated by an MWD. Breedings weren't allowed outside the strict military confines of the DOD breeding program, but the SEALs handling the sire thought it funny. Made lewd comments. The dam delivered six pups . . . Havoc being one of them.

At least, that was the story. Crew met the thick-chested, goober of a dog when the Malinois was about two years old. Assigned to Bagram, he saw the dog all the time. Even off base. Knew better than to befriend a stray, but the dog wouldn't leave him alone.

One day, Crew noticed possible blood and realized the dog had been shot. He'd put his field vet training to work and operated on the eighty-something pound dog. Took care of him. Fattened him up—well, really, just got him less-scrawny. And that dog turned into one of the most beautiful working dogs he'd ever encountered. On medical hold with a torn meniscus, Crew spent his downtime with Havoc. Fed him. Trained him. The dog was lethal-loyal. Military refused to let Crew run him through certifications, though. Told him to focus on the dog assigned to him—Marvel. Sexy girl that she was.

Crew smoothed a hand over her sleek skull, and she lifted her jaw straight up, to look at him . . . upside down. "Psycho."

At the affectionate misnomer, she thudded her tail hard against the steel deck.

The MRAP lumbered offroad and angled down. Through the narrow slats-for-windows, the terrain made itself known. Hard to tell for user in an armored personnel carrier, but it seemed this was a bowl, a valley. The thought made his gut churn. Not a great position for them since they were apparently on the floor of said valley.

Crew had a bad feeling about this. "Ehretz," he shouted toward the front where the leader sat right, front. "I need to get Marvel back. She's overheating." It was a partial truth. She was hot—most MWDs were in the Afghani heat.

"After this," Ehretz barked back. "Everyone out."

This guy was looking to get killed. "This isn't smart—"

"What's not smart is disobeying my orders."

"Despite your ego, Ehretz, I do not answer to you. I'm tasked to this patrol, but I will not do anything that puts my super"—he nodded to Marvel, who was one rank higher than him as rules stipulated—"in danger."

"Then stay here, you whining pansy."

Don't. Don't do it. Killing a corporal wasn't a good way to end your career.

Maybe, but it'd feel good.

"Do you need some crayons to find your way back?" Crew regretted saying it as soon as the words escaped his lips. He wouldn't get in trouble—much—but it wouldn't help the situation here.

In response, Ehretz cut the engine on the MRAP. Which meant Crew had to bail with Marvel or they'd get baked alive waiting for the team to return. "Your funeral," Crew muttered. "Marvel outranks everyone here, and you'll get dereliction of duty for letting a superior die when you could've prevented it."

"If you're so worried about how your career ends, then I suggest *you* not be found guilty."

I'm going to kill him.

Instead, Crew took a moment to let Marvel get some water, rustled the thick fur along her neck, and sighed. "You can rip out his throat any time you want. Okay, girl?"

Marvel stood, tail wagging her whole backend. If Havoc were here, he'd have gone for the kill.

"Guess you hate him as much as I do." He caught her ear, gave a firm squeeze, and drew his hand up, rubbing it in the way that nearly drew a groan from her that he took as her agreement. "Knew you were a clever girl."

They climbed out and he slung his weapon to the front, holding firmly to Marvel's lead. Climbing out the back, he found the team standing at the edge of a flattened area. Hills rose on three sides, and to his two o'clock a crevasse cut through the hillside, winding hard to the right and disappearing. But between here and there? Flat open 'kill me' space.

"Look." Taco pointed across toward the crevasse. "It's one of ours."

Frowning, Crew couldn't see what the guy referenced. He angled aside and that's when he saw the tail end of a military Jeep. What in the world was it doing out here?

Mouse drew out his nocs and peered across the distance. Cursed. "I think there's someone in it—I see blood. I think."

What? How did that . . . ? There weren't any reports of missing vehicles or men.

Guess they could've come out here after Crew and the Marines left base. But wouldn't they see tire tracks out to the truck?

Something wasn't right.

Only then did Crew realize Marvel was shifting, sniffing—in that deep-throated way of hers when she was really hauling in scents—and turning. Had she caught wind of something?

She turned several circles, then lowered her back-end and piled a deposit in the dirt.

Right behind—

"Okay, fan out," Ehretz said, sounding tough and official. "Eyes out. Gatlin, you're with me."

"Neg—"

Ehretz stepped back. Right into the smelly brown excrement. Cursed. Slipped.

Boom!

Boom!

Even as he secured Marvel and struggled to understand where the threat was coming from, Crew felt the soft thud of dirt and rocks hitting his shoulders. Dust and screams filled the air. That hadn't been weapons' fire but explosions. Was someone launching RPGs at them? Grenades?

Weapon up, Crew scanned the chaos. "Marvel, heel. On me."

He patted his leg. Saw a plume of dust that slowly settled into a mound of dirt. Then his mind began to assemble what he was really seeing. It wasn't rocks . . . it was chunks . . . arms . . . fingers.

Son of a . . .

Mouse. Mouse was gone.

Howling came from Crew's four—Taco was there, his face shredded and bloodied.

Crew took a step forward, and somehow, amid the tight panting of Marvel, the shouts of Ehretz demanding to know where the shooting was coming from—panicked idiot—heard the all-too-quiet *click* of a pressure plate. Freezing in place, he cursed.

Marvel started forward.

"Stay!" he shouted, which he knew better than to do. *Emotion travels down-lead.* "Marvel, stay. Down." He lifted his gaze to the others. "Nobody move—it's a minefield." His thoughts were catching up, racing his heartbeat. "This whole thing is a trap."

A private lay curled on the ground, holding his arm that was now handless. To Crew's five, Ehretz was simpering as he held his gut where a large piece of shrapnel stuck out. His face was peppered with small holes. Likely nails. It was a crude, cruel method that was all the same effective.

"Base, this is Charlie Four. We are in need of medevac and ordnance retrieval. Team is trapped in a minefield and have one fatality and multiple injuries." Crew swallowed and forced himself to think quick around the adrenaline. "I'm on a pressure plate." He flicked his gaze to Marvel. Had she taken any shrapnel? She'd been close to Ehretz. Even as he wondered, he saw the blood glistening on her coat. And neck. No! "MWD has taken shrapnel as well."

"Charlie Four, this is Command. Situation understood. We are deploying QRF and medevac. ETA in twenty mikes."

Twenty minutes? Were they freakin' kidding?

He eyed his girl. Recalled how she'd been acting weird, going in circles. She'd smelled the ordnance. All around her. No doubt it'd confused her.

She slumped onto the ground, her pink tongue dangling far out as she panted rapidly, making him worry that she had more wounds he couldn't see. Internal wounds.

"Guess you don't have to worry about your career ending . . ." Ehretz's lame attempt at a joke was sick.

His life ending wasn't in his plans for the day. "Not what I meant."

Ehretz shifted. "I'm . . . I think I'm clear. Going to get the medkit."

"*No!*"

The corporal took a step.

Boom!

The blast was close—too close.

Crew had a second to brace. To tell himself to keep his leg in place. Even as the concussive wave punched his chest. He felt himself falling back. Angled. Contorted to keep his boot on the plate.

He landed hard. Teeth jarring. Dirt and dust raining down as he waited for the blast that would take him off the map. Instead, he felt blood trickling down his temple and neck. His gaze landed on his boot . . . still on the pressure plate.

But he wasn't. He was a solid ten feet away. Separated from his boot . . . and the lower half of his leg. *Holy . . . !* Dropping back into the dirt, hearing hollowing out, Crew knew the countdown to Death's arrival had begun. Scrambling, he unbuckled his tac belt. Slid it out. Strapped it below his knee where blood was gushing out. Pulled it tight.

He growled, gritting his teeth. Feeling his gut heave.

Tighter. Tighter. Tighter.

It hurt like a mother, but if he didn't cut off the blood flow . . .

His vision blurred.

Strength fled his body.

Garbled noises reached him. He opened eyes he hadn't realized he'd closed. Saw a haze . . . blurs . . . a small black form blurring toward him. He cringed. When a slobbery tongue swiped his face, Crew tried to laugh. "Hav . . ." He felt violent, jerking tugs . . . backward . . . back . . . and surrendered himself to Death's embrace.

Ronie Kendig is a bestselling, award-winning author of over forty books. She grew up an Army brat, and now she and her Army-veteran husband have returned to their beloved Texas after a ten-year stint on the East Coast. They survive on Sonic runs, barbecue, and peach cobbler that they share—sometimes—with Benning the Stealth Golden and AAndromeda the MWD Washout. Ronie's degree in psychology has helped her pen novels of intense, raw characters.

To learn more about Ronie, visit her at roniekendig.com and follow her on social media.

When a woman running from the mob meets a ranger haunted by his past, the Grand Canyon's dangers might be the least of their troubles.

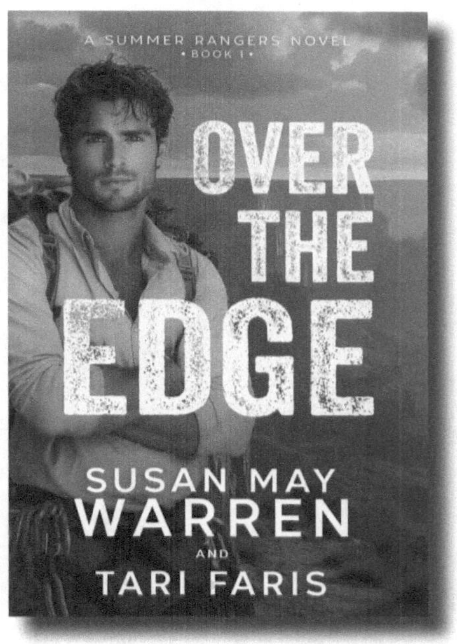

Dive into book one of

SUMMER RANGERS

We solve the problem of what to read next.

WE THINK YOU'LL ALSO LOVE...

Fire Department liaison Allen Frees may have put his life back together, but getting the truck crew and engine squad to succeed might be his toughest job yet. When a child is nearly kidnapped, Allen steps in to help Pepper Miller keep her niece safe. The one thing he couldn't fix was the love he lost, but he isn't going to let Pepper walk away this time.

***Expired Return* by Lisa Phillips**

Infiltrating a dangerous militia to save her troubled brother, Jamie Winters finds herself kidnapped. Only Logan Crawford, the man she once broke, can rescue her—but he demands a promise in return. As they navigate peril in the Alaskan wilderness, their unresolved feelings spark a chance for love and redemption.

***Burning Hearts* by Lisa Phillips**

When an attempt is made on Grey Parker's life and dead bodies begin piling up, suddenly bodyguard Christina Sherman is tasked with keeping both a soldier and his dog safe... and with them, the secrets that could stop a terrorist attack.

***Driving Force* by Lynette Eason and Kate Angelo**

We solve the problem of what to read next.

WHERE EVERY STORY IS A FRIEND,
AND EVERY CHAPTER IS A NEW JOURNEY...

Subscribe to our newsletter for a free book, the latest news, weekly giveaways, exclusive author interviews, and more!

---

follow us on social media!

Shop paperbacks, ebooks, audiobooks, and more at
SUNRISEPUBLISHING.MYSHOPIFY.COM